Series

Paranormal Stories

War on Darkness

Darkness Defined (MM)
Order of Light (MM)
Knights of Nyx (MM)

Moons of Mystery

Sara's Moon (MF)
Charline's Solstice (MF)
Diana's Eclipse (MF)

Kisin Novels

Courting Death (MM)
Death, Love, & Tacos (MM)

Fated Mates

Truth in Exile (MM)
The Inescapable Truth (MM)
Truth in Lies (MM)

<u>Contemporary Romances</u>

Ulwich Preparatory Academy

Our Last Fall (MM)
Our Secret Winter (MM)
Our Epic Spring (MM)

Oak Haven Romance

One Brave Thing (Enby/M)
All the Hype (MM)
The Bright Side (MM)
Any Which Way (MM)
A Thin Line (MM)

Truth in Exile

S Bolanos

Chaotic Neutral Press LLC

Contents

Chapter 1

Aidan

Some people lived their whole lives as outcasts. Those people had it fucking easy. Try doing that shit as a werewolf. The Stormfire pack built its ranks by rescuing *weres* from defeated packs. But they didn't take in every wolf, only the ones with potential. Whether you lived up to it or not was your own problem. After twenty years of lying, cheating, and stealing, it was *my* problem. It didn't matter how well or fast I did what I was told; I was still a disappointment, still struggling for the pack's approval. Could be worse, though. I could have been a lone wolf. Packless.

I shuddered just thinking about it as I shrugged on my cut and swung a leg over my Harley. The junker was no cruiser, but I'd get there one day. Until then, the ride was smooth enough.

"You good, Aidan?" Scott asked, righting his bike and knocking back the kickstand in a fluid motion. "Not cold, are you?" He let out a barrel laugh.

"Har har," I clapped back. Like werewolves actually got cold. Forget that we ran hotter than the average human. We were also in fucking Kentucky in the dead of summer. We probably wouldn't even be around when the weather turned cold. The Stormfire pack was unique like that. No settled territory, just wherever the wind took us. Sometimes we lingered for a few weeks, others, a few months. But we never *stayed*.

The afternoon sun glinted off the strands of red in Scott's brown hair as he turned to look at me with an expression that made his face look more like leather than it already did. "Don't be going soft on me now. We've got work to do."

"Not me." If there was one thing a Stormfire wolf couldn't afford to be, it was soft. Before Scott could say some other bullshit, I pulled the clutch and cranked the bike to life. I closed my eyes and relished how the steady rumble rolled through me. There was no better feeling in the world and now that we were in Kentucky, we didn't have to fuck around with helmets, either. "Let's ride!" I yelled, taking off like my ass was on fire.

Scott let out a whoop and burned rubber, his engine roaring as he sped to catch up. I joined him in shouting into the wind. It was a beautiful day for a ride. Unsurprisingly, we passed several other bikers that gave us sidelong looks. Some had colors, some didn't. Most bikers signaled, and some nodded as we were riding. We nodded back. For now.

Whether the bikers were a club or just weekend riders, it was safe to assume that none knew the significance of lightning striking fire emblazoned on the back of leather vests. They didn't know to show respect. However big a dog they thought they were, they'd never be bigger than a wolf. But they'd learn soon enough. They always did.

Too short of a drive later, we pulled up at our temporary headquarters. Assuming today's scouts brought something Alpha liked, we'd have a permanent place soon enough. Well, as permanent as we ever got.

Scott and I parked our bikes along the line and made our way to the front of the doublewide.

"Looks like a full house," Scott commented, glancing back at the long row of bikes. We weren't the biggest pack or even the biggest gang, but that's what came of being exclusive.

I untied the bandana around my forehead and ran a gloved hand through my hair. "Sure does." I knocked some of the mud from our last stop off my boots, then caught sight of my littermate at the door. A grin nearly split my face in two as we slapped hands. "Hey, Jace, we the last in?"

He shook his head, causing the sun to glint off his bald scalp. Why he shaved off all his hair was beyond me, but then we'd always been opposites, right down to me being one row up from the pack fuck-up and him being one rung down from perfection. Jace could do no wrong and I... I seemed to redefine it daily. Not today, though. Today, I was gonna win.

"Nah," Jace said, running a hand over his smooth head. "We're still waiting for Carver and Elliot to make their way back. Looking like we've got a lot of good options this go 'round. That's a nice change."

Scott laughed. "Fuck. Anything's better than that swamp we holed up in last month. I swear I can still hear them gators growling. You'd think they'd never seen a wolf before."

Jace and I shared a look. The sharpest tool in the shed, Scott was not. But he had one thing neither of us did—seniority. I angled my head at Jace to signal I'd take this one. With my thumbs looped through my belt loops, I turned to face Scott.

"What?" he asked, catching my look.

I did what I could to hold back a chuckle. "I hate to be the one to break this to you, but they probably haven't."

"Yeah, Scott. Ain't no wolves in Florida," Jace backed me up.

"Yeah?" Scott rubbed the side of his mouth as it slowly morphed into a grin. "They sure as fuck know what one looks like now."

The three of us were still howling with laughter over the trouble our pack had gotten into with the local reptiles at our previous camp. Poor Carver still had the bite mark from when a gator had a go at him. Apparently werewolf healing didn't cover pissed off dinosaurs. Course, Carver also had all the fucker's teeth now, too.

Right on cue, Elliot and Carver rumbled up to the trailer. The three of us stood back while they parked and cut their engines. I couldn't help the tide of envy that rose as the sun glinted off the cherry red of Elliot's brand new Harley. Every inch of the machine was custom chrome perfection, from the charcoal leather wrapped handles to the gorgeous pipes that would make a tiger jealous.

Naturally, Elliot caught me ogling his ride and snickered. Fucker. "You find us another cow-patty riddled field to camp in?" He asked me while he slapped hands with the others.

I bared my teeth at him in a poor imitation of a smile. It was no secret that we didn't like each other, never had. Elliot had worked his way up pack ranks by stepping on the backs of others, most notably *mine*. If I had to pick one wolf out of the pack responsible for my shit status, it'd be him. Asshole.

"Aw, El, every pup makes at least one scouting mistake," Scott said, slinging his hefty arm over my shoulders.

Elliot barked a laugh. "One, maybe. But our little Aidey has made a career out of it. Remind me again how you ended up on scout patrol?" He tilted his head to the side, causing his eyes to glint yellow in the afternoon sun. "That's right," he sneered, "you couldn't be trusted to do anything else. Not even the supply crew wanted you after you came back with expired food that gave the entire pack food poisoning. Fucking illit-erate piece of shit." He spat on the ground.

I lunged forward, my mouth already shifting to make room for larger, sharper teeth, only to be pulled up short by Scott tightening his arm. Elliot cackled like a goddamn hyena and sauntered past unscathed into the trailer.

"Easy, buddy. You know he only says that shit to rile your fur. Today'll be different. You found a great spot for the pack to shack up for a few months, or even a year, if we wanted," Scott said, giving my shoulders a good squeeze, though he didn't let go until my wolf canines retreated into average human ones.

"Hell yeah, I did. Gonna make that jerk eat his words this time."

Jace clapped me on the back. "There's the spirit. Now let's get on with it. I'm starved!"

I chuckled. Even by werewolf standards, Jace was always hungry. We moseyed inside behind Carver, and made our way to where the other scouting parties were standing, ready to give their reports. I glanced around the trailer, noticing how tight the fit was.

The Stormfire pack wasn't large by any means, but we'd picked up a few new members recently and now it was a wonder we all fit inside the cramped double-wide. Then again, I didn't expect our numbers to stay swollen. Once the pups hit their first change, we'd have a natural downsizing as many sought their own way.

Personally, I'd never understood that. Sure, the nomadic lifestyle we lived wasn't for everyone, but how could they stand to leave their pack? Not having a pack was a death sentence. I shuddered again.

Scott shot me a sharp look. "You sure you're not comin' down with something?" he asked quietly.

I curled my lip to reveal a fang. "I'm good." Saying shit like that where everyone could hear was like signing your own exile. If you *were* sick, you kept that shit to yourself and prayed to the moon nobody noticed before you got better.

A ripple went through the pack as the Alpha stepped out of a back room. At six-foot-five, Garrett was possibly the tallest man—or wolf—I'd ever met. He had arms the size of tree trunks the color of walnut, a mean-ass scar scored the side of his face, and looked like he drank the tears of his enemies to quench his thirst. Instinctively, everyone straightened as he took his seat behind a foldout table.

"Right, now that everyone is finally fucking here, we can get started," Garrett grumbled.

Light chuckles flitted around the room like fireflies before being extinguished with a sharp look from our Beta, Devin, who was really just a slightly shorter, paler version of Garrett.

"What have you got for me?" Garrett demanded.

Scott's firm hand on the back of my neck halted my knee-jerk reaction to step forward. I'd have glowered at him if Alpha wasn't watching us so intently.

Garrett snapped his fingers. "The map."

Devin immediately unfolded a map of Kentucky that included several magnified sections of the major cities. Of course, we'd never set up camp in a place teeming with humans and Goddess knew what else, but the outlying areas being magnified was still helpful. When he was finished, he resumed his place by Alpha's side.

Garrett nodded in approval. "I see some good options here. Let's start from East to West."

Megan and her partner exchanged a look. "The Paducah area is more populated than we'd like, but it's an easy ride from there to the Shawnee National Park," Megan said.

Devin narrowed his eyes. "If Alpha wanted to camp in Illinois, we wouldn't be in Kentucky. Next."

Megan shrank inward at the rebuke and her partner, Amy, subtly offered support with a hand on her lower back. I mentally shook my head. Sometimes, the areas we scouted weren't destined to be winners, but the scouting party wasn't to blame. I'd have to find a way to cheer Megan up later.

Next up were Leon and Barb. Their report received a more favorable review, but not by much. The following three met with much the same result and I was starting to wonder what exactly Alpha was looking for. From what I could tell, each location suggested had features we normally looked for—secluded areas to change and run, access to amenities, not overly populated, good riding roads. Granted, Elizabethtown *was* a little too close to Fort Knox for comfort, but it was lush and green.

Finally, it was my and Scott's turn. He gave me a gentle nudge, and I puffed my chest a little. We had a winner. I just knew it. "Knifely," I said. As I hoped, the name alone caught Garrett's attention. He settled back in his seat, giving me his full attention. I quickly went on, trying not to sound too excited. "Relatively isolated. At a cross of county roads, but no other nearby highways or interstates. Good proximity to water. And while the Green River Lake State Park is a bit of a trek, the land in between is mostly uninhabited."

Garrett almost looked... *pleased.* Or he might have, if Elliot hadn't butted his stupid nose in.

"Knifely," Elliot echoed, obnoxiously picking his nails with a switchblade. "Cute name. Let me guess, you saw all the kennels nearby and thought it'd be fun to play retriever?"

I twitched violently. How the *fuck* did Elliot know about the area *I'd* been scouting? "The kennels are nowhere near where we'd be staying and some of them are closed down," I replied, forcing myself to stay calm.

He glanced up. "So you admit it?"

"Admit, what?" I growled.

"That you knew about the kennels and still thought to suggest it as an ideal place for our *pack* to camp?" He may not have been openly smirking, but it shone clearly in his eyes.

A low growl rolled out of Alpha. "I won't have ours anywhere near *dogs*. It's out."

"But they're really not—"

Alpha cut me off with a snarl. "I said *it's out*. Carver, what did you two find?"

Elliot grinned. "Sawyer is perfect. More than comfortable. Plenty of room to run at Daniel Boone National Park. Good roads with enough people around to make it interesting. And best of all, no *dogs*. Well, except for you, Aidan," he finished with a sneer.

Fuck. This. Asshole. I launched toward him, only to be caught by my ruff and forcibly hauled backward. I fought against Scott's hold, but with hair already sprouting along my backside, he had a solid grip. It also didn't help that, unlike most of the Stormfire pack, my hair was nearly gold. It wasn't the first time Elliot had accused me of being more dog than wolf, and I'd doubted it'd be the last. But to do it in front of the Alpha was over the line.

Garrett smacked the map, nearly cracking the table beneath in two. "Enough! Good work, Elliot. Tonight, we settle in Sawyer."

I bared my teeth at Elliot. Motherfucker wasn't supposed to be anywhere near that area. And if I'd had the audacity to talk out of turn, I'd have been dragged outside by my tail. I shrugged off Scott and stormed outside, not bothering to regress my shift before straddling my bike and taking off.

Chapter 2

Zahir

Resentment coiled around my chest, wrapping and squeezing until it felt like I couldn't breathe. This wasn't the life I'd have chosen for myself. But since when had what I wanted ever factored into anything?

Belaboring my disgruntlement at being forced into apprenticeship as a spiritual leader would do no good. I'd made my arguments. Whether they were *heard* was another matter and no longer relevant. I was here now. It didn't matter if it was as a result of some divine vision, because I'd been reckless in my youth and the elders determined I needed to be settled, or simply because the current region's spiritual leader was closer to joining the divine every day.

I took a deep, calming breath and focused on my physical sensations. I began by flexing my cobra hood, stretching the membrane as wide as it could go before relaxing it into a neutral state. From there, I let my awareness drift down the tight muscles of my neck and shoulders, coaxing each one into relaxation.

The scales on my arms itched distractingly, but I pushed the ephemeral irritation aside, choosing instead to tighten and release my core, which was taut from holding my serpentine body at such a straight angle. While Nagas were designed to "stand" upright on our coiled tails, doing so for long stretches of time was taxing.

I inhaled deeply again, allowing the oxygen to expand my lungs to their utmost capacity. Upon the exhale, I released the tension strangling my body and the negativity clouding my mind. With my eyes closed and head bowed, I reached out with my senses. The cavern that held our temple was vast, though removed enough from the roaring waterfall that hid it to be silent...*mostly*.

The great pounding of water cascading into the Cumberland River vibrated through the stone to resonate in my scales. The occasional rivulet of water ran down the walls to drip like chimes into small pools. Precious stones that decorated the walls each echoed with their own perfect harmony.

My soul relaxed as I took in the beauty of this place. It wasn't that I didn't enjoy the temple or held disparaging thoughts about prayer. I embraced our religion whole-heartedly. I just didn't think that I was fit to lead anyone. Least of all, spiritually.

"Gah," I said in frustration, swiping at the calm surface of the water in the bowl before me.

"My dear, Zahir, it seems your practice is suffering today. What is it that steals your focus?" One of these days, I'd discover how a woman that sounded as frail as she looked could move so quietly. Until then, I'd have to deal with her inevitably showing up whenever I was conveniently failing at my lessons.

I placed my hands together in a prayer symbol and inclined my head to the ancient Acharya. "Guru Angira, forgive me."

She chuckled, a sound like dry paper on the breeze. "There is no forgiveness, only understanding." She placed a gentle hand on my shoulder and I couldn't help but relax. "Tell me what thoughts intrude on your practice."

"I'm no good at this," I admitted.

"That is why we practice," she said with a wink.

"Guru Angira, you know that is not what I mean. How can I possibly guide the spirits of others when I cannot even guide my own?"

She nodded sagely as she slithered to the wall containing incense and idols, her yellow scales glimmering in the candlelight. "Your soul is unsettled."

I bit back a groan and moved to her side. There I mirrored her in lighting an incense and placing it on the altar so the thin stream of fragrant smoke could curl around the arranged idols. This wasn't the first time we'd had this conversation, and I doubted it'd be the last. Together, we placed our hands in prayer and bowed to the gods.

"Perhaps it is missing something," she said when she straightened.

"Please, not this again," I implored her. Just because I believed in true mates didn't mean I thought I'd find one. They were rare enough as it was. A special gift bestowed by Vishnu for only the worthiest. They were even rarer for spiritual leaders. Likely because once a spiritual leader was committed to a temple, they never left, I thought bitterly. Hard to find a soulmate when you never went anywhere.

"A mate would settle your spirit."

I fought the rude urge to snort. "Perhaps I should have taken my parents up on the offer to arrange a marriage."

"Zahir, you know that is not what I meant," she said, repeating my earlier statement back at me.

I glanced away from her probing gaze. Unfortunately, avoidance only got me so far. She reached up and softly turned my face back to hers.

"You are troubled because you do not feel you have a purpose."

I stiffened. Her uncanny ability to see through a person to the very heart of them was nothing short of divine.

She lightly patted my cheek. "You will have a purpose when you accept it."

I could have screamed. Railed and thrashed, knocking over the pristine display of idols, wrecking the altar, and dislodging precious stones from the wall. Instead, I placed my hands together and inclined my head. "Namaste."

"Namaste, young one," she replied before turning to slither deeper into the cavern.

Grateful that she hadn't insisted on me persevering despite my unquiet mind, I ventured in the opposite direction, shifting to my human form after traversing the stone corridor and exiting from behind the waterfall. I needed a drink, and I knew just the bar to get it from.

To call *The Oasis* a seedy hole-in-the-wall would be generous. But while the ambience and locale left a lot to be desired, the drinks were strong and the patrons... intriguing. What really made it stand out, though, was that it catered almost exclusively to supernaturals. Not that any of us went about advertising it, but it certainly saved a lot of hassle if you slipped up.

Safe haven aside, tonight I was here for moonshine and entertainment. The real question was: what kind of entertainment? Would I be content people-watching or was I more interested in trying my luck with the harpy at the end of the bar? She had pretty brunette hair and a devious smile that promised all sorts of dark delights. Guru Angira was wrong. I didn't need a mate, just a body to warm my cool blood.

The door to the bar banged open as the latest patron entered. A few of us turned to look, including myself, but the door hitting the wall was a common enough occurrence that most didn't bother. The newcomer banked what looked to be heavy biker boots on the doormat, then straightened his vest like it had done him a personal wrong and raised his head to peer around the room.

Desire shot straight to my dick, and I sucked in a breath at the unexpected force of it. I rarely took men to bed, but I was definitely intrigued enough to find out if he was interested. He was five-foot-nine, give or take, had light brown hair held back by a bandana, scruff on his jaw that made my sensitive scales hum with want, and a chip on his shoulder they could probably see from Canada. Normally, I wasn't so drawn to people who blatantly looked like trouble, no matter how sexy they were, but I couldn't help but be intrigued.

The mysterious man stalked more than walked toward the bar. I subtly licked my lips to taste the air and let out a hiss. A *wolf*. Instant attraction or not, I turned back to my drink. I'd sacrifice my next three incarnations before I tangled with a werewolf. I was still fighting to regain my composure when my senses went on high alert. At this rate, I was going to flare my hood and get myself banned for causing unprovoked trouble. Then again, when a wolf and a serpent were involved, wasn't the trouble always provoked?

Summoning every ounce of calm my spirit possessed, I glanced to my left. *Of course,* mine, the wolf had chosen the seat right beside mine, despite the plethora of other available options. "I don't think you should sit there," I said, reining in the impulse to hiss at him.

He stiffened, then curled his lip as he looked over at me. "I'll sit where I like."

"Apologies. I don't think I was clear. *I* don't want you to sit there. Move."

"I don't take orders from entitled assholes. Get fucked." To underscore how much he was *not* going to move, he pounded the bar to get the bartender's attention.

I could practically taste the venom filling my mouth, but one glance at the bartender lumbering over had me rethinking my desire to teach the *real* entitled asshole a lesson. I leaned a little closer and when I was sure I had his attention, I let my eyes turn to their cobra form. "Didn't anyone ever teach you not to fuck with snakes?" I hissed, infusing the question with all the sinister malevolence possible.

The man instantly snarled and lurched off his barstool, sending it crashing to the ground. "Moon forsaken snake. You won't think you're so hot after I rip out each of your scales one at a time."

"I'd like to see you fucking try," I snarled right back, my cobra hood dangerously close to flaring.

"Hey," a deep gravelly voice said, cutting through our stand-off.

I instantly repressed all the visual manifestations of my naga side and sat up straight. "Forgive me, Arnie, I forgot myself."

"Damn right you did. You been coming here long enough to know I don't put up with that shit in my bar. Your stupid rivalries stop at the door. And you," the barkeep thundered, his voice like an avalanche, "ain't seen you in here before, so consider this your one and only warning. You start shit in my bar and *I* finish it. You hear?"

A low growl emanated from the wolf as he glared at Arnie.

Purely in the interest of preserving whatever goodwill I had left at the bar, it seemed prudent to offer the pissy wolf some words of caution. I cleared my throat, and his amber gaze flicked in my direction. "I wouldn't do that if I were you. Our courteous barkeep is an earth elemental." The wolf's brow pinched just enough to betray his confusion. I lowered my voice so only he could hear and added, "He is literally made of stone. Claws and fangs don't do much against solid rock."

While I offered my sage advice, Arnie continued to stare down the wolf. "I said, Is. That. Understood?"

The wolf took a deep breath and let it out slowly, though it seemed to pain him. It was only then that I realized his face had partially shifted to account for the fangs I'd casually referenced and his hands were equally more claw-like. *Fascinating*. Granted, I hadn't met that many werewolves in my thirty-two years, but I was certain I'd never met one that could do *that*.

"Well?" Arnie asked again, his thinning patience obvious in his tone.

"I hear you," the wolf snapped as he plucked his barstool off the ground and plopped back on it. "You got any real moonshine or just sissy shit you serve to snakes?" I swallowed a snicker. If he put any more S's in that sentence, he'd be the one who sounded like a snake.

Arnie let out a barrel laugh, and the tension dropped several levels, though I still wasn't too happy about having to share bar space with a fucking werewolf. "Ain't no sissy shit here. I got a shine that'll put some hair on your chest." He poured the wolf a glass of the same stuff I was drinking and slid it over. The wolf placed some crumpled bills on the counter which Arnie grabbed, then turned to the next customer, but not before giving each of us a meaningful glower.

I shook my head as I took a sip. "You've got some balls on you talking to Arnie like that."

The wolf picked up his glass and sniffed lightly at the liquid. Apparently satisfied, he knocked back nearly half, then set the glass back down. "Fuck you, scales."

"Fuck you right back, furball," I said and took another drink.

Chapter 3

Aidan

I checked the address Jace had sent me and compared it to the house in front of me. This was definitely the place. I scratched my chin as I continued to study the over-the-top house. It wasn't the *largest* place we'd ever camped, but at almost three stories, it wasn't exactly the smallest either. It wasn't even the lack of bikes parked out front that was bugging me. Alpha would have had everyone park in the back, or even better, in a garage if there was one, to avoid drawing attention.

No, what was ruffling my fur was how fucking *fancy* the place looked. Granted, in that worn down, abandoned way, and at least it had a big porch. But seriously, who needed that much fancy shit topping off each story? It looked like someone's grandma had crocheted it. And what was up with the flat-ass roof? Was it a roof? It looked like it couldn't decide between being a roof or a wall. And why did it look like a reject church?

I shook my head and debated calling Jace just to confirm. Then I remembered how late it was. He'd already be settled down for the night and wouldn't answer. On the one paw, I didn't *think* Jace would prank me by sending me the wrong address. But on the other... *This place*? Well, there was one way to be dead sure. I just hoped it didn't end up with me actually dead thanks to some trigger-happy redneck with a shotgun who thought I was trying to rob him.

I lifted my bike and quietly rolled it around the side of the building. When I saw the line of other bikes, I let out a breath I didn't even realize I was holding. A quick count said I was the last to arrive and I could have kicked myself. It was my own damn fault. I'd let Elliot get under my fur—again—then hared off to the first seedy bar I could find that didn't smell like straight up sweaty human. If I'd stayed longer than I meant to, that was nobody's business but mine.

I cringed as the screen door creaked when I opened it to get to the back door, unsurprised to find it unlocked. Just inside, there was an honest-to-Goddess mudroom cluttered with haphazard pairs of riding boots. I kicked mine off and followed the sound of a television playing deeper into the house. A passing glance told me the place had at least some furniture, though it could go either way if it had been here before the pack arrived or had been "liberated" afterward.

I didn't even bother going up the stairs. All the bedrooms would be taken already, and it wasn't like I'd get one, anyway. When I walked into the room with the noise, it was to the familiar sight of wolves everywhere. Some were curled up with their noses tucked under their tails. Others were sprawled out, their limbs' overlapping their neighbors'. A few were positioned to watch whatever show was playing. And even fewer weren't shifted at all—notably Alpha, Beta, the top lieutenants... and fucking Elliot. Figures he'd get to stay in his human shape to watch TV as a reward for finding the town and probably this fancy fucking nightmare of a haunted dollhouse.

"Nice of you to join us," Devin said without turning to look at me.

"Yeah, my bad. Got lost," I replied with my head bowed and eyes down.

Elliot snorted. "In a bottle. What kind of piss moonshine you been drinkin'?"

I fought the urge to lift my head and bare my teeth at him. The moonshine had actually been pleasantly strong *and* tasty. Best guess I had for what might have given it its unique flavor was some kind of tangy passionfruit. Or maybe mango? Tropical something or other.

"An extra pair of hands would have been useful a few hours ago." I flinched at Garrett's deep rumble and slowly lifted my gaze to find him staring at me.

"Sorry, Alpha. It won't happen again."

He sniffed and turned his attention back to the screen while Elliot sneered at me behind him. Goddess above, how could I be so stupid? It was bad enough I was already in the shithouse for suggesting a location with even the whisper of a dog kennel nearby. But to forget about the rules of move-in day?

I glanced to the side where there were clumps of clothes and started pulling mine off to add to it. Once I'd stripped, I let the change takeover. No matter how many times I did it—partially or fully—it still hurt like fucking hell. Luckily, the feeling of bones breaking and my face elongating didn't take long.

A couple minutes later, I was on all fours and the pain of the change was already fading to a distant memory. I shook out my fur, hating how it was so much lighter than literally every other wolf's in the pack and even more how I couldn't hide it in this form. At least I wasn't scrawny like Jacobs or Darlene. Thank fuck for that.

I delicately padded across the cluttered floor, careful not to step on tails or any other extremities. Starting a fight due to poor paw placement was the last thing I fucking needed today. I was too tired to want to sleep outside, and it smelled like rain.

Finally, I found a spot with enough room to lie down and a halfway decent view of the TV. Looked like Alpha had chosen something that involved a lot of people running, screaming, and getting shot. *Shocker*. But it was better than the singular sound of a room full of werewolves snoring.

I settled down to watch, but lost interest quickly. My mind kept wandering back to the bar—*The Oasis*. Stupid name aside, the place had a decent vibe. Clean, but not spotless. Rough around the edges, but without people getting tossed out left and right. And the drinks were good. I'd have to ask what they made their moonshine with the next time I was there.

My ear twitched as I realized I was already planning to go back. Sure, the pack didn't come across supernatural hangouts often, but there was still plenty of reason for me *not* to return. A pair of onyx black eyes swam before me. I squeezed my eyes shut, but they remained.

Everything about the bar was perfect, except for that fucking snake, with his stupid better-than-you attitude, and shiny hair, and hairless arms. Who the fuck shaved their arms? Weirdo. Maybe it was a snake-thing. Wasn't like I had a shit ton of snake shifters to compare it to, or, well, any. One thing was for sure, I wasn't about to let that asshole scare me off of a good find. He'd learn why snakes avoided wolves. And I was more than happy to be his teacher.

With that pleasantly violently thought, I settled my head on my paws and relaxed into the hardwood floors. Grabbing a spot with some pillows or blankets would have been better, but it was my own fault for showing up so late. I'd be earlier next time.

A sharp pain in my side jolted me awake with a yelp that turned to a growl the second my eyes opened. Fucking Scott. He was an alright dude most of the time, but he was a total prick in the morning.

"Get up, we've got chores to do," he grumbled.

I pushed up to my feet, stretching out the slowly muting pain. Just because werewolves healed hella fast didn't make getting kicked in the ribs with a steel-toed boot hurt any less. I did a few more exaggerated stretches to fuck with him before starting my change back to human. At the top of that list of chores, better be getting his bad attitude some coffee.

Once I was capable of speech again, I cracked my jaw. "Where are we off to?" I asked as he passed me some clothes and my cut. I sniffed the shirt. It wasn't too bad, and it wasn't like anyone else was going to notice that it smelled like a whole damn pack of werewolves. I finished dressing as I followed him to the mudroom at the back.

"We're getting provisions," Scott finally answered, leaning against the back wall.

I froze, my foot halfway into my boot. "What?"

"It's not like that. Just about everyone is out getting supplies. It's a big place and we've got more mouths than ever to feed."

I finished stomping into my boots. I bet *Elliot* wasn't on supply duty. "Then maybe we should stop taking in strays," I replied, pulling the bandana from my cut pocket and absently tied it around my head as we stepped into an already warm morning. Even if I didn't need to color my hair after my shift, I didn't want it in my face as we rode. Maybe I'd luck out and we'd hit up a drugstore.

"Tell that to Alpha," Scott replied gruffly as he made his way down the line of remaining bikes. Seemed some had gotten started extra early, though there were still a few wolves like ourselves getting a slower start to the day. Scott gave me a double take. "Wait. You're serious?"

I shrugged, suddenly wishing I'd kept my mouth shut. Technically, all of us were strays, taken in when our previous packs fell apart for some reason or another. We were lucky the Stormfire pack had come along before the pain of being packless became irreversible. For some, it was already too late. The young ones were the worst. It was a mercy to end them quickly rather than let them suffer the long agony of slowly going mad and withering away.

"Aidan..." Scott said in a low growl.

"What? We could at least slow down. That's all I'm saying," I replied sullenly. "It's getting harder to find places that can hold all of us and not draw attention."

He exhaled heavily through his nose. "Well, I do hear that. At least this house has a yard *and* enough floor space."

"What's the deal with this place, anyway? We squatting?" I asked.

"Renting, if you can believe it." Scott and I turned to look back at the big ass house, which honestly looked even more ridiculous in the daylight. Sure, it was more than big enough to fit the entire Stormfire pack and it wasn't in the best condition with its peeling brown paint, but it was still fancy as fuck and more than we could typically afford.

I glanced at Scott. "Why? How?"

"Elliot found the listing in the local paper. Apparently, someone died inside. Murder or some shit." He shrugged. "They were desperate for someone to take the place. Way I heard it, we're getting it at a steal."

I shook my head. Humans were dumb. Luckily, werewolves didn't give a shit about stupid things like people dying. I swung my leg over the seat of my bike and took in the backyard. It was overgrown and had random broken bits strewn about, but it was nothing we couldn't take care of in an afternoon. I was never going to be Elliot's biggest fan, but I had to hand it to the jerk. He'd done well finding this place.

Chapter 4

Zahir

I walked around the wall separating the kitchen from the living room with my fresh chai, grateful that I wasn't expected at the temple today. Luckily, the ad-segment was still playing, and I hadn't missed any of my show. It was nice that I could catch up on episodes of the baking show that was my guilty pleasure whenever I liked, but the unskippable—and *repetitive*—ads were still a nuisance.

I set my steaming mug down on the side table, then took my time getting situated on the overstuffed extra large couch. If scales could hum in appreciation, mine would have. The house that had been provided for me during my apprenticeship wasn't lavish by any stretch of the imagination. It was a small, fully furnished, one bedroom home that looked much like every other house on the block. But it had desirable amenities, including a laundry room with appliances from this decade and a full kitchen. In short, it was sufficient.

Wasn't like I had friends or even lovers over to impress or accommodate. The couch, however, was a thing of glory. Plush fabric that felt like nirvana against my scales. Deep cushions that could fit the entirety of my naga form without having to coil into tight loops. And so much squishy stuffing that at times I wondered if the elders had employed a witch to spell clouds down from the sky.

I chuckled to myself at the absurd image and snuggled deeper into the dark green couch before plucking up the chai I'd set aside. I let out a content sigh as the spice laden steam curled in my nostrils, then sipped carefully at the scalding liquid. As if by design and not fortuitous timing, the screen changed and rows of contestants appeared.

I'd lost count of how many episodes I'd watched when I realized that I'd drifted into a doze. I stretched my scaled arms high overhead, letting my tail flex, then fall to the ground. A glance behind me revealed the culprit in my foggy stupor. Rays of warm sunlight slipped between the angled blinds to bathe me in a delicious golden pool.

I gave myself a good shake and transitioned to my human shape, watching with vague interest as my sea green scales bled into plain golden skin with yellowish undertones. The human form was pretty in its way, but it could never compare to the luster or vibrance of my iridescent scales.

The man from the bar the other night came to mind, and I suddenly wondered what he looked like in his wolf form. If memory served from my previous encounters with werewolves, his coat would match the hair in his human form, which would make him a lightish brown, possibly with blond highlights. Nope, nowhere near as pretty as a naga's scales. Still, his human form *did* have its merits.

I rolled my eyes at the traitorous thoughts. Pretty or not, wolves and snakes were mortal enemies for a reason—it was in our natures. Two predators, unable and unwilling to cohabitate in the same territory. Snakes at least had the decency to keep to themselves. Wolves, however, walked around like they owned the whole fucking world. My hood quivered in agitation as I recalled the furball's holier-than-thou attitude. As if he could take a fully grown naga.

I'd already showered and was halfway dressed when I realized I was actually hoping he'd be at *The Oasis* tonight. Well, wasn't that some fucked up shit? I really needed to get out more if I was looking *forward* to the prospect of running into the ill-tempered werewolf again. Then again, it might be nice to remind him why cobras were infinitely superior to wolves.

With that rather pleasant thought, I grabbed my wallet and keys, finger-combed my short hair, and headed out. My transportation wasn't fancy—or new—by any stretch of the imagination, but like the house, the elders had provided it and it was sufficient. The engine rumbled to life, and I backed the small SUV out of the drive. A whopping ten minute drive along pock-marked roads found me parking in the poorly lit lot of *The Oasis*. It didn't look like much from the outside, but then, it didn't look like much from the inside either. I turned the engine off and made my way inside.

The bar was surprisingly crowded for a Thursday night. For a second, I feared the wolf had brought his pack to my sanctuary, but a quick taste of the air told me there was only one wolf here. Smiling despite myself, I sauntered across the room, equal parts looking for a seat and searching for the werewolf. When I found neither, I huffed in unexpected agitation.

Right as I approached the counter to order my usual moonshine, my gaze caught on a table tucked into the corner. Or more appropriately, on the table's single occupant. The wolf that had occupied far too many of my thoughts sat hunched over a nearly empty glass. While I wasn't skilled at seeing auras, it was easy to imagine his as a swirling black cloud. A wolf in my bar *and* in a bad mood? Yes, please.

"Don't even think about starting shit," Arnie threatened in his gravelly voice, intruding on my delightful plans to fuck with the wolf.

"Wouldn't dream of it," I crooned at the bartender. "Two moonshines, good sir."

"I mean it. Guy's gotta attitude sumtin' fierce, but he ain't started shit with nobody since he got here."

I raised my hands in a motion of surrender. "And I promise not to change that."

Arnie grumbled something that sounded suspiciously like "fucking *weres* and snakes", then slapped his bar rag on the counter with a loud smack. He continued to glare at me as he poured the paw paw flavored moonshine and pushed the two glasses toward me.

Before he could issue another warning, I dropped the cash owed and grabbed the drinks. "Thank you, Arnold," I said with a sinister smile, then made my way to the darkened corner. Perhaps Gurudevi was right, and I was still unsettled. I was still reckless, that was for sure. It was a testament to the wolf's level of distraction that he didn't notice my arrival until I slipped into the seat adjacent to him.

He flinched and snarled, his sharp gaze zeroing in on me. "What the fuck are you doing here?"

"Well, hello to you too, furball. In case you hadn't noticed, this is a bar." His snarl lowered several octaves into a menacing growl and it took every ounce of restraint I had not to throw my head back and laugh. I slid the extra moonshine over. "This is also the only free seat in the house. I suspect everyone standing is too put off by your bad vibes to venture closer. But I'm not afraid of a furball that's all bark and no bite." I snapped my teeth together for emphasis, loving how his eyes widened, first with surprise, then fury.

"I'll show you bite. Now fuck off, scales."

I pouted. "And here I brought you a peace offering and everything." I nudged the glass closer to him with the tip of my nail.

His nostrils flared, no doubt checking to see what was in my so-called offering. "What is it?"

I quirked an eyebrow. "The same paw paw moonshine you drank the other night."

"The *what*?" His brows pinched together and I couldn't help but notice that they and his hair were darker than when I'd last seen him. Curious.

"The moonshine. It's made with fermented paw paw."

"What the fuck is that?" he asked with his lip curled as he studied the glass like it was a viper that might strike at any second.

The laughter I'd been restraining finally burst free. "I'm sorry, you've been in Kentucky for *how long*? How do you not know what paw paw is?"

"I've only been in Kentucky a week. Fuck you very much," he replied, baring his teeth.

Well, wasn't that a surprise? Didn't werewolves tend to stick to their own territories? "In town for a job?" I hazarded a guess.

"Something like that," he grumbled. Then he polished off the watered-down remains of his previous drink and grabbed the fresh glass.

"To answer your other question," I began, sipping at my drink, "paw paw is a local fruit. I guess you could say it's sort of like North America's tropical fruit. It's Arnie's specialty."

The wolf held up the glass to scrutinize the liquid within. "Well, that explains a lot. It's not half bad." He took another drink and my gaze riveted on his Adam's apple as he swallowed. Fuck, he had a pretty mouth. A mouth that would be even prettier stretched around my cock. I made an involuntary groan at the beautiful image of this spite-filled wolf on his knees for me. His gaze darted to me at the traitorous sound and I blurted the first question that came to mind.

"What's your name?"

He frowned. "What's it to ya?"

I leaned back in my chair and clawed back my composure. I *really* needed to get laid if I was entertaining thoughts like that about a werewolf. "It's a little obnoxious having to refer to you as 'the wolf' in my head," I said with a nonchalant shrug.

"Aidan."

Aidan. I hummed to myself as I took another drink. Such a melodic name. Reminded me of a bell chime. Abruptly, I realized he was staring at me and I was staring back. I set my glass down and fought the sudden need to clear my throat. "No surname?" I asked to distract him. His glower intensified, and I quickly added, "Last name."

"You don't need my fucking last name."

"Suit yourself. Besides, I think I enjoy calling you furball more, anyway," I teased.

"Fucking asshole," he rumbled, and I couldn't help but smile at the obvious irritation I was causing him.

"Zahir."

He paused mid-drink. "What?"

"That's my name. Zahir Khatri."

He searched my face for a moment, as if unsure how to respond. By the time he opened his mouth, there was a commotion at the end of the room from where we sat.

"Oh look, a band. No wonder it's so crowded tonight. Thanks again for the seat." I smiled at him, noting his mounting rage. Unable to resist the temptation to see how far I could push him, I trailed a finger through the condensation on my glass and flicked it at him. I hadn't really been aiming, so it was pure kismet that the drop of water landed perfectly on the tip of his nose.

Someone stepped up to the microphone and the resulting feedback loop made everyone wince. It also drowned out my unwitting companion's threatening growl. I leaned back in my seat, propping my feet on the table and caught sight of Arnie scowling in our direction. I saluted him with my glass, then turned my focus to the band gearing up for their first song.

I couldn't say whether the music was any good or even to my taste. By the end of their set, I couldn't even have told you the genre, let alone the name of the band. I also didn't look back over at Aidan. I didn't have to. For every second I stayed, I could *sense* him fuming. And it was fucking delicious.

Chapter 5

Aidan

I watched as Jace unloaded the last box from the haul Scott and I'd brought in. Sweat poured down my back from the heat and exertion of being at this bullshit all morning. I fucking hated supply runs. Half the time we couldn't even ride our bikes. We had to drive the rundown pickup. It was a piece of shit that wasn't worth the parts or the labor it took to fix it. Not that anyone gave a shit since I was usually the labor.

Scott emerged from inside the house and tossed a towel at me. I caught it before it could hit me in the face and shot him a look. "Get out of your funk, already," Scott grumbled, his voice muffled by the towel as I rubbed it over my head. "It's bad enough having to put up with your shitty attitude on a normal day, but you've been extra pissy."

"He's got a point," Jace chimed in, dusting his hands on his worn jeans.

"Look, I get you're mad that Elliot shit all over the place you scouted," Scott said, and I gritted my teeth against a growl. The place *I* had scouted? Last I checked, we were partners. He'd

30

vetted the locale too. But I didn't see anyone giving *him* shit about it. "You probably shouldn't have bowed-up to Alpha like that, though. What the fuck possessed you to challenge him? I'd be glad you're just on a few weeks of supply duty if I were you," Scott said, looping his towel behind his neck and leaning against the back of the house.

"Could have been worse. You could have ended up in the doghouse." Jace glanced to the far corner of the yard where a literal fucking doghouse sat, complete with a chained leash. I shuddered and absently rubbed my neck like I could still feel the rusted collar pressing against my skin. Alpha thought that shit was funny. It had been three years since the last time I'd had to endure that humiliation—stuck out in the cold without food or water to be laughed at by every member of the pack. Definitely not an experience I wanted to repeat. *Ever.*

I grunted as I pushed off the wall and headed inside, the sound of Jace's and Scott's voices trailing after me. Those fuckers would never understand. Wasn't like *they'd* been on Alpha's and everyone else's shit list since they'd been brought into the pack. Maybe things would have turned out differently if the other pups they'd brought in at the same time had survived the change.

I paused and looked at the gross towel in my hand. I didn't remember any of their faces. Three of us had remained after a moonstruck wolf had destroyed the pack. I remembered that. Another pup my age—a girl maybe—and someone older. I shook my head. They couldn't have been that much older, surely, because everything had gotten so much worse when we'd had our first change. At least we'd made it that far. We'd have been ripped to pieces too if the Stormfire pack hadn't shown up when they did.

My hands ached, and I suddenly realized I'd been wrapping the towel tighter and tighter around them. I dropped it on the floor. Mights and maybes wouldn't change anything in the here and now. The fact was, they *hadn't* been strong enough. Their changes had been twisted and painful, going on for what felt like an eternity. It was a mercy they were dead and didn't have to suffer anymore.

I toed off my boots in the mudroom and peeled off my disgusting clothes, tossing them into the laundry area before grabbing a fresh set of clothes and the plastic bag I'd hidden earlier. Then I stomped upstairs in search of an available shower.

Miraculously, the one on the third floor—the most isolated, if smallest—was open. I didn't even have to wait for someone else to finish first *and* the water was warm. I sighed in relief as I stepped beneath the spray. Sweat, grime, and grease cascaded down my body to pool at the bottom of the tub before finally draining.

I scrubbed at my scalp, hating the grungy feeling beneath my nails as I worked out the grease I'd used to darken the color. The last few supply runs I'd gone on with Scott hadn't gone anywhere near a place with the dye I needed, but we'd lucked out today, which meant no more having to use oil from the engine.

Once I was sure my hair was clean-clean, I went to work on the rest of me, savoring not having to rush and that the water stayed warm. While I washed, my mind wandered to the snake at *The Oasis*. He was... weird. He was a snake, so that really went without saying, but he was *more* weird? I couldn't put my finger on it and that ruffled my fur. Then, so did the fact that I'd run into him at the dive bar several times now and that... didn't bother me?

"Zahir," I said aloud. Even though I didn't shout it, the name still filled the steam-fogged room. I liked the way the sounds rolled around my tongue. They were different, unique. *Just like him.*

I shook my head, splattering water into the side wall and curtain. I didn't have time to worry about some stupid snake that didn't know when to leave well enough alone. I needed to worry about *me*. Speaking of which... I focused my hearing to see if anyone was waiting for their turn in the shower or stomping up the stairs. When I came up with nothing, I decided to be extra indulgent and rub one out while I had some peace and fucking quiet.

I was only a little surprised to find that I was already half-hard. I shrugged it off, owing it to just the idea of having privacy. Much as I would have loved to savor drawing out my strokes, nothing ever stayed private for long where the pack was involved. Which was all the time. I pushed that out of my head and focused on just how good the tight grip on my shaft felt. Way too soon, I was grunting my release and painting the tiled wall. I'd have been embarrassed with how quick it was if I wasn't so determined to actually *have* a release.

I did another quick rinse, then toweled off, getting my hair as dry as it was gonna get. Then I stepped up to the sink, wiping the mirror with the towel before discarding it and opening the plastic bag. I snapped on the cheap gloves that came with the boxed dye. Luckily, it was one of those all-in-one kits that didn't require mixing. That shit was a mess and a total bitch to clean.

My reflection stared back at me, my hand frozen inches above my hair. Why did it have to be blond? Not just blond, Labrador-fucking-Retriever blond. I'd never met another werewolf with hair like mine. I flashed back to my long dead pack. Had any of them looked like me?

With a growl, I dismissed the thought. I *never* thought about that time in my life. Most of it was a blur, anyway. Right now was what mattered. And right now, dying my hair was a necessary evil, even if I did have to re-do it after every shift. At least when it was dyed in my human form the rest of the pack forgot to give me shit. More than worth it in my opinion.

Feeling more relaxed than I had in weeks, I made my way down to the kitchen in a damn good mood. Didn't hurt that my hair was finally dyed a nice chestnut brown, or that we were making lasagna. It was true that there were a lot of jobs in the pack that I hated, mostly because they were considered low-man work. Oddly, working the kitchen shift wasn't one that had ever bothered me, though plenty in the pack sneered at it. Probably had something to do with that I was actually *good* at it.

My good mood brightened even more when I rounded the stairs and learned I was working this shift with Megan. We'd hooked up a few times in the past, but that had been before she'd gotten with Amy. While I didn't personally understand being attracted to the same sex, more power to 'em. Amy was cool, and she made Megan smile. That was enough for me.

"Hey, you," I said, walking up behind her and squeezing her trim sides.

"Hey, yourself," she replied with a laugh, smacking my hands away. "You remember how to make the sauce?"

I snorted. "Do I remember? I'm the one who taught *you* how to make it from scratch."

"Yeah, yeah. Quit your bragging and get to cookin'." She flicked flour at my face.

I briefly flashed to Zahir doing something similar with water, the way his mouth had tilted in a smirk, his dark eyebrow raised in challenge, and it took me a second to laugh. Megan and I lowkey flirted all the time. We never meant anything by it. There was no way *a snake* had been flirting with me. Was there?

"Hey, lazybones, get a move on!" Megan hollered, then smacked my ass, leaving a flour handprint. My laugh came easier this time.

"Yes, ma'am," I drawled to match her Mississippi accent.

"You did *not* just *ma'am* me!" she screeched. I was still laughing when she grabbed a handful of flour and threw it at me.

I spluttered, sending a cloud of the white dust everywhere. "Hey, I just showered!"

She stuck out her tongue and reached for the small heap of flour that remained by the forgotten dough.

"Don't do it," I warned, still smiling.

"Do what?" she asked coyly. "This?" She lifted her hand full of flour and held it in front of her face. Then she blew out a big breath and sent it flying toward me.

"That's it. Now you're gonna get it!"

She let out a squeal of delight as we chased each other around the small kitchen, tossing tidbits of flour at each other. We were wrestling in the disaster we'd made and laughing up a storm when Amy walked in.

"Alright, break it up, you two." She tsked as she surveyed the flour-covered room. "I hope you know being on kitchen duty also means you have to clean this mess up."

Megan disentangled herself and swayed over to her stupid-tall girlfriend. "Aw, baby. Won't you help me?" She batted her eyes and trailed a fingertip between Amy's breasts, leaving a trail of flour on her deeply tanned skin. "Just a little bit?"

Amy sighed and tugged her close, heedless of the flour. "What am I going to do with you?"

Megan smiled mischievously. "I have a few ideas."

I heaved myself up from the floor, pretending I wasn't jealous as hell of what they had. "Yeah, yeah. You can tear each other's clothes off later. Dinner first. This pack won't feed itself."

Amy chuckled and dusted the flour from Megan's face before giving her a quick kiss. Then she stepped away and looked at me. "Okay, chef, where do you need me?"

I smiled at her, still genuinely happy for the pair of them, if a little sad for myself. Wasn't like I'd ever find someone who looked at me the way they looked at each other. Fuck, I couldn't even imagine bearing to be that close to someone for long enough to *catch* feelings. "Let's start by wiping down the counters so we can chop the veggies. We can save the floors until after. Megan, see if you can salvage that dough for the rolls and I'll get started on the sauce."

Neither of them argued or questioned what I'd asked. Yeah, a lot of my packmates didn't like kitchen work. But me? I fucking loved it.

Chapter 6

Zahir

I set aside the ancient scripts detailing how the naga had been influential in maintaining the balance in ages past. From there, we'd become spiritual leaders, not just of our own people, but for all who might seek a meaningful path within the universe, forever guiding others toward enlightenment. Hinduism was beautiful that way, especially as the naga had practiced it for millennia. It was also the current source of my headache.

Smoke from the jasmine incense I'd lit what felt like hours ago wafted in my face as I leaned forward to rub my tired eyes. I absently waved it away and ached for the exceptionally long day to be over. I craved a reprieve from my studies.

A pair of pretty blue eyes swam in my mind's eye. I waved it away just as fervently as the irritating incense smoke. I wasn't going to *The Oasis* on the off chance I'd see Aidan. The wolf, I forcibly corrected myself. The *furball*. I wasn't. Even if he was easy on the eyes and incredibly entertaining to fuck with.

"At this rate, your brow will be more wrinkled than mine," Gurudevi teased with her characteristic dry raspy laugh. I'd long since given up trying to anticipate or listen for her approach. She was surprisingly quiet—and spry—for a 750-year-old-woman.

"Have you no sympathy?" I asked, my voice ragged.

She laughed again and tapped my scaled shoulder with her papery hand. "Only for those who are in need of it. You, child, are not. Bemoan your situation as you like. You are where you are meant to be. Someday you will see that."

"I don't know why anyone thinks you're nice. You're a cruel guru," I grumbled.

"Ah, now you know my secret," she said. "For that, you must pay penance."

Startled, I glanced up at her. "What?" Penance held no place in our faith. I shouldn't have been surprised to see mischief in the crazy old naga's smoke-brown eyes.

"You are late for your monthly call with your parents."

"Vishnu protect me," I said, quickly swiveling around to head deeper into the temple, where through some miracle of magic, there was a tech room set up, complete with video monitors. Her cackle followed me as I slithered out of the temple proper, down the long hall and into the room, shifting back to human just in time to collapse on the rolling chair.

Per usual, my parents were dressed as if they'd come to the temple in person. My father, Pavan Khatri, wore his usual beige linen suit, which was quite striking against his severe features. But any who knew him knew better than to believe he was a hard man. Pavan was much more soft-spoken than his gruff exterior would suggest. My mother, on the other scale, was a woman sharp in both wit and personality. Uma Khatri was truly the embodiment of bright colors-equal-danger. The stunning yellow scales of her naga form should give the clear message to proceed with caution, though I couldn't think of anyone who had ever heeded that warning.

"Pati. Maa. You're looking well," I said, doing my best not to sound out of breath and failing.

My mother arched a dark eyebrow, but my father spoke first. "It is good of you to join us, beta. You are looking equally well." His soft smile set my heart at ease, as it usually did. We'd never had much in common, but we got on well. Alas, I was my mother's son in more ways than one.

I subtly inclined my head, both in humble acknowledgement of his praise and in apology. "A thousand pardons. I was wrapped in my studies and lost track of time. I did not mean to keep you waiting."

"Your studies," Maa sniffed, and I cringed inwardly.

"Uma," my father implored her in a harsh whisper, "let him be. He—"

My mother held up her hand, cutting off whatever else he planned to say. "Guru Angira tells us that your practice has lacked focus. That perhaps you would benefit from being married." She gestured absently toward Pati. "We can easily arrange a marriage if that is the case. Maybe then you could devote more purpose to fulfilling your duties."

I blanched. "Ack, Maa! I do not need an arranged marriage. My studies are fine." I couldn't *believe* Gurudevi had thrown me under the bus like this. Actually, scratch that. I could *absolutely* believe that conniving old woman would pull a stunt like this, then wait to inform me of the call so I'd be scrambling and defenseless.

"And what is wrong with an arranged marriage?" She squared her shoulders, lending her petite frame an imposing imperial air. "Do you doubt our ability to find you a suitable life companion? We are friends with many influential families in the community that would be *honored* to have their child partnered with a spiritual leader." I didn't miss the subtle dig that *I* should feel more honored to be in my situation... more grateful.

We could go back and forth about this all day. Had before. Though it had been several years since she'd threatened me with an arranged marriage. Not that she would ever see it that way. Sadly, I was too mentally exhausted not to repeat the same mistakes I'd made the last time we'd had this conversation.

"Pati, please, tell her I am capable of finding my own life partner. Not that I need one," I added, because I'd never learned to leave well enough alone.

He cringed while my mother released an indignant huff. "Beta," he began, but my mother quickly overrode him.

"Do not *need* one?" she challenged, and I had to restrain myself from openly wincing at her sharp tone. "Then why does Gurudevi tell us you are unsettled? That *this* is the reason your practice is suffering? It was she who suggested you have a companion."

A distant call drifting through the tunnel caught my attention, and I turned away from the monitor. I could have sagged with relief when I realized it was Guru Angira calling me back. Though how relieved I should be when this whole mess was her fault, I couldn't say.

"Forgiveness," I said, turning back to the contrasting image of my irate mother and apologetic father, "Gurudevi is summoning me back to the temple. I will try to call again before our next scheduled time to catch up. I can regale you with the results of my latest studies," I suggested with a forced smile.

"This conversation is not finished, Zahir," Maa threatened, clearly not buying my false cheer. Then her face relaxed into a more neutral expression. "We look forward to hearing more about your studies. In the meantime, I will see what suitable matches might be amenable to moving to the States."

My father cleared his throat and offered me a wan smile. "Try not to study too hard." I couldn't help but return his smile as my mother rolled her eyes.

"You indulge him too much. This is why he is so unmoored," she muttered.

"Love you, Maa. Love you, Pati," I said.

"Love you, beta," they said in unison and ended the call.

I stared at the blank screen a moment before pushing away and exiting the room with a heavy sigh. They meant well, and I knew they loved me, but I already chafed beneath the weight of their expectations. I didn't need to add an arranged marriage on top of that. Aidan's pretty blue eyes flashed through my mind again and, to my shame, I didn't dismiss them as quickly as I should have.

"Interesting conversation?" Gurudevi asked as I approached the rear entrance to the temple.

"You could say that," I grumbled, shifting back to my naga form to match her. "Thank you for saving me from it."

She let out a raspy chuckle. "Is that what I did?"

I narrowed my eyes at her. Actually, no. Most of that clusterfuck had been of her making. Now I'd be dodging proposed matches from my mother for the next year... or ten. "Why did you tell them I needed to marry?"

"I did nothing of the sort," she said, swiveling on her tail to lead the way.

"Then why did my mother spend the whole time threatening to arrange a marriage for me to improve my 'focus'? She said it was *your* idea," I challenged, hot on her scales.

She shrugged her slim shoulders. "I merely suggested that you could benefit from a mate. I mentioned nothing about you needing to be married. Your studies are suffering more than I thought if you do not know the difference."

"Yeah, well, that's exactly how my mother took it." Of course I knew the difference. A spouse was a partner you chose to spend your life, a friend if you were lucky, possibly someone you could grow to love. A mate... A mate fit you so perfectly as to create the ultimate balance, a true harmony of souls. Fat chance I'd ever find one of those locked away to rot in this temple.

The glittering entrance of the temple opened before us. I took a deep breath and envisioned expelling all the negative energy within me upon the exhale. It took more than one, but eventually, the tension in my shoulders lessened. Feeling moderately more at peace after the trying conversation, I slithered to Guru Angira's side.

"Why did you call me away?" I asked softly.

She came to a stop and smiled at me, which I immediately found suspicious. Then she gestured toward a pair of nagas standing in the entryway that I'd been too distracted to notice. "Mr. Kumar and his daughter Shakti have come in search of guidance today. I told them they would be in excellent hands with my disciple."

I fought to keep the panic from my face as I accepted each of their hands in welcome. "It is a pleasure to meet you and I am honored to provide whatever guidance I may to help you on your path," I said by rote.

Gurudevi rested her hand on my arm and smiled warmly at the father and daughter. "Swami Zahir will take good care of you. I'm fortunate to have such a dedicated disciple to help a frail old woman."

I nearly swallowed my tongue, adding mortification to the long list of things going horribly wrong today. She was going to *abandon me* to offer spiritual guidance to these people? *Alone?* What if I fucked up? Sent them on the wrong path? I wasn't ready for this. Hadn't she *literally* just been ratting me out to my mother about how my practice had been lacking?

The young woman batted her long lashes at me and smiled shyly. "Guru Angira speaks very highly of you, Swami Zahir." I winced internally at her breathy tone, as well as the honorific I in no way deserved. She had pretty maroon scales that almost looked black at certain angles and a perfectly oval face. She was also at least half my age, if she was anything.

I smiled awkwardly and turned my attention to her father, who didn't look nearly as put out about his teen daughter openly flirting with a grown man as I thought he should. My mother's words that many parents would be honored to have their progeny wedded to a spiritual leader came to me unbidden. Fuck, maybe she just *looked* young. It hadn't even occurred to me I might need to worry about being hunted like some prize trophy from *supplicants*.

"How may I offer guidance today?" I asked, sending a silent prayer to Vishnu that my voice didn't sound strained. Shakti's smile widened and her father nodded approvingly as I guided them toward an area laden with floor pillows where we might discuss their spiritual matters in comfort.

"My daughter has received many invitations to prestigious universities," Mr. Bhakti said with pride as he made himself comfortable on a red, oversized cushion. "She seeks guidance as to which would best suit her path."

I groaned inwardly. Like my studies weren't demanding enough. Now I was supposed to be a guidance counselor? As if I should have any bearing on this girl's future. Why did my words have any more weight than her friends'? Her parents'? Her *actual* fucking college counselor? Whatever my feelings on the matter, they both stared at me expectantly while Gurudevi deposited a tray of fresh tea, then left me to fend for myself.

Four hours, an unholy amount of tea, and seven college acceptance letters later, I was more than willing to forego a hot shower in favor of a stiff drink. I didn't even bother stopping by my place to change before heading straight to *The Oasis*. Thankfully, the bar wasn't crowded. Not that it should be on a random Wednesday. But it was one less irritant to my already shit-tastic day.

Arnold was behind the bar, along with one of his usual staff. He must have picked up on my obvious bad mood, because he raised his eyebrows in question as I approached the counter. Rather than answer the unspoken query, I plunked myself on a stool and looked around the room. I drummed my fingers absently on the worn wooden bar top as I waited impatiently for him to bring me my usual.

"He's not here," Arnold said, sliding an extra tall glass of moonshine toward me and startling me into popping my cobra hood. It was a terrible habit and one I'd never quite outgrown. Most naga didn't allow their forms to bleed into each other so much. Then again, wasn't it that type of reckless behavior that had landed me as an apprentice to the oldest fucking guru alive?

"What?" I asked, reaching for the cool drink, my gaze still sweeping the bar.

"The wolf. He's not here. Hasn't been for the last couple of nights," Arnie clarified.

"Why would I care?" I snapped, irritation prickling along the back of my neck along with something I didn't want to look too closely at.

Arnie shrugged and went on his way without replying.

I took another long drink while my eyes confirmed what he'd just told me. Aidan wasn't here. The fucking furball was nowhere to be seen. I wasn't disappointed. I wasn't. I was fucking furious.

Chapter 7

Aidan

I made my way down the two flights of stairs with a spring in my step. Halfway down, I caught my reflection in a spotted mirror and paused long enough to fix my hair and flash myself a grin. The latest dye I'd found—okay, stole—was perfect. A good, rich brown that completely hid my natural blond, *and* it was super fucking easy to apply. Who knew they had single day hair dye? Me, that's who. Well, now I did, at least. And it was going to make my life a breeze.

I didn't even bother with the last few steps, just vaulted over the railing to land with a loud thud in the short hall leading from the front of the house to the back. A good hair day like this deserved to be celebrated. Maybe I'd hit up that bar again. *The Oasis* had a good vibe. The moonshine was on point. The patrons were chill. Fuck, even the snake wasn't too bad.

Zahir.

An involuntary shudder ran through me, just like it did every time the guy's name floated through my mind. Which was a hell of a lot more often than I would ever willingly admit. I chalked it up to my wolf's natural aversion to another predator. Snakes were dangerous and best avoided. But then, when had I ever avoided danger?

One of my packmates burst through the backdoor covered in mud and I barked out a laugh. Steph shot me a dark look. "Fuck you, Aidan. Are there any bathrooms free?" they asked irritably.

"Should be," I said, absently running my hand through my hair. "You planning on spreading mud all over the stairs?"

"Why? Worried you'll have to clean them?" they snapped as they stripped out of filthy clothes.

"Nah. More like wondering if I should sell tickets to when Alpha makes *you* do it. With your tongue."

They huffed a laugh, their animosity easing, and finished tossing their clothes aside, then made their way to the stairs. "Thanks for the heads up about the bathrooms. Stupid fucking pop-up shower came out of nowhere. Riding drenched and getting pelted by rain was bad enough. But then I hit a pothole the size of the Mississippi and went flying into a mud pit."

I winced at the awful image Steph painted. "That sucks. Want me to take a look at your sled?"

They paused a few steps up and looked down at me, indecision clear on their face. And honestly? I got it. Not counting the fact that I had a tendency to piss off just about everyone, your ride was sacred. Steph let out a breath and nodded with an almost smile. "Actually, yeah. That would be pretty great. You don't mind?"

"Not at all." I hiked a shoulder in a shrug. I was in a good mood and feeling particularly generous. Besides, doing favors could go a long way. They finished stomping up the stairs to hopefully catch the shower before someone else claimed it, and I made my way outside.

It was a fucking beautiful day. Not a cloud in the sky or any other evidence of the so-called pop-up shower besides the faint scent of rain and heavier than normal humidity. If I hadn't just dyed my hair, I'd have seen if anyone wanted to go for a run.

Oh well, I could run another time. Right now, I had a bike to inspect. Even if I didn't already know what Steph's bike looked like, I'd have been able to know which one was theirs. I walked up to what should have been a shiny blue roadster, but nearly dry mud caked all the metallic paint. Kentucky summers didn't fuck around.

Shaking my head, I peeled off my shirt and set it safely out of the way in the hope that it'd stay clean enough to wear later, and grabbed the hose. I was less worried about getting mud on my jeans. With how hot the sun was beating, they'd dry in no time. And if they didn't, I'd just help myself to a pair from the laundry room. The shirt, however, was one of the few that fit me well and looked halfway nice.

It didn't take long to hose off the bike and even less time for it to dry. I grabbed a toolbox from the back of the pickup and pulled up an empty crate left over from the last supply run. Once I was situated, I took my time checking over each nut, bolt, and gear. Motorcycles were a blast to ride, but they could be temperamental as fuck. All it took was for one piece of machinery to be out of whack for you to bite it.

Sweat dripped down my back and chest as I got lost in the methodical work. Of all the things we got to learn in the Stormfire Pack, I was most grateful for this. I loved working on the machines and I was *good* at it. I was tightening a lug on the kickstand when someone shoved my head into the side of the engine.

"What the fuck?" I snarled, dropping the wrench and lurching to my feet. My head hurt something fierce where it had struck the unforgiving metal and I was pretty sure the hot liquid running down my cheek *wasn't* sweat. I spun around, making myself a little lightheaded, but wasn't remotely surprised to find Elliot with a sneer on his face.

"Poor puppy hit his widdle head?" he asked in a baby voice that made me want to tear his throat out.

I dragged my forearm across my face, clearing the sweat—and, yep, blood—away. "What's your fucking problem, man?"

"Just making sure you're not tampering with shit you shouldn't be."

"Yeah, well, I'm not. I told Steph I'd look at their sled after they ate dirt," I replied defensively.

He walked slowly around the bike as if assessing it, and I had the sudden fear that he'd push it over and try to blame me when something broke. "Looks alright to me," he said, a dangerous look in his eye that I didn't trust as far as I could throw him.

"Yeah, Steph was lucky. Only a few loose bolts. Tightened 'em up and figured I'd do a once over while I was at it," I replied cautiously, my mind sending up red flags for danger as Elliot continued to circle like a damn shark. One of these days, I'd listen to that little voice in my head when it told me to get the fuck out. In the blink of an eye, Elliot was on me, fingers wrapped tightly around my throat, lengthening claws digging into the side of my neck.

"Yeah? Well, I think you're fucking with shit you shouldn't. I think you're out here sabotaging bikes," he snarled, so close to my face I could feel his spit.

"Fuck you, asshole!" I shouted, scrabbling at his arm.

His grip tightened, and his claws pierced the skin. "Why anyone would trust a low life dog like you to touch their sled is beyond me. Mangy mutts should be put down." His gaze flicked to my hair, and he huffed. "You're not fooling anyone with that shit. You're a freak and a fuckup and you always will be." As abruptly as he'd grabbed me, he shoved me back.

I coughed a breath, my werewolf healing already working to ease the strain of my bruised throat. "Fuck you, Elliot," I growled. "I'm as much a part of this pack as you are. You should show some fucking respect."

He smirked and held out his arms. "Oh yeah? And who's gonna make me?"

My ribcage convulsed, then expanded as it shifted shape and grew a smattering of hair. I barely even registered the painful crunch as my jaw elongated or the twinge of agony as my fingers twisted into brutal claws. The partial shift was as much instinct as it was pure animal rage. I launched at Elliot, clearing the dozen feet between us in a heartbeat and slamming into his equally partially shifted body. I hit him square in the middle, taking us both down in a tangle of claws and furious growls, backdropped by a loud metal clang.

We snapped at each other's faces, thick ropes of saliva dripping from our misshapen jaws—not human and not quite lupine. My claws got stuck in his shirt while his raked across my chest. I yanked mine free, shredding his shirt in the process and could have howled with satisfaction at seeing the long lines of blood scoring his torso. We rolled and tousled, only managing superficial wounds.

"Enough!"

Both of us jerked violently and froze, still snarling in each other's faces, as the Alpha command wrapped around us. My whole body shook with the force of trying to fight it, to close the distance and finish Elliot off for good.

Someone fisted a hand in my hair and dragged me off of him, pulling a few strands out in the process. I flailed to get free of their grasp until Garrett walked into my line of sight. He shot me a look, and I instantly stopped moving aside from the heave of my chest as I fought to catch my breath and bring my heart rate back down.

"Shift," he commanded in a low growl.

Taking a gamble, I released the partial shift, easing back into my human state. A few feet away, Elliot did the same as he got to his feet. It looked like Alpha was about to demand we shift to our wolf forms when Steph came tearing out of the house in nothing but a pair of loose shorts.

"What the hell did you do to my bike?!" they screeched, naked fury turning their face a dark red. It was only then that I realized that when I tackled Elliot, it had been *into* Steph's bike. The once beautiful Harley now looked more like a reject scrap metal sculpture than an actual motorcycle.

I glanced from the understandably pissed Steph to Elliot, who was wiping the blood from a cut on his mouth that had already healed. His eyes glittered with pure malice and I knew without a doubt he'd goaded me into that fight for this exact outcome. Not that it would do me a damn bit of good to point that out. No one would believe me.

Jace joined the inner ring of this shitshow and cleared his throat. "Why don't you take some time to cool off, Aidan? We'll work on a plan for you to fix Steph's bike later," he said, looking at me with a mix of pity and disappointment.

"Good idea, Jace," Alpha said, slapping him on the back, then glanced at me. "Go straighten your tail and know what awaits you when you get back."

I fought the impulse to look past him to the dog house baking in the sun without so much as a leaf of shade around it. This stupid fight wasn't *that* bad. Right? Then again, judging by the angry expressions on everyone's faces, it probably was. Well, everyone except Elliot's face. Bastard had the nerve to stand there and look smug.

"Fuck this," I grumbled, finally pushing off the hand holding my hair tight. Should have known it was Scott. Without another word, I stomped over, snatched my shirt up, then made my way to my bike. I shoved the shirt haphazardly into the saddle bag then cranked the engine all beneath the watchful gaze of my pack yet again witnessing what a fuckup I was.

Once I was on the open road, I slammed my hand against the handlebar and shouted "Fuck!" The wind whipping around me stole the sound, and I pushed to go faster. I knew better than to get into shit with Elliot. Why couldn't I learn? Why did I let him get under my fur? I was the only one who ever faced any consequences for the stunts he pulled.

I followed the county road, not even thinking about where I was going until I pulled up at a red light. A small gasp drew my attention. I turned and scowled at the uptight woman idling in the minivan beside me. She quickly looked forward and pretended like she couldn't see me as she rolled her windows up.

Faced with my reflection, I understood her reaction. Blood and dirt covered nearly my entire top half. Most of the underlying wounds had already healed, but some were much deeper. Not to mention, injuries from a werewolf took their sweet ass time to heal up, and they usually left a scar.

I returned my focus to the road in front of me and peeled out of the intersection the microsecond the light turned green, employing another partial shift to speed along the healing process. By the time I pulled up at *The Oasis*, the sun was just setting. I yanked out my miraculously clean shirt and went inside, stomping halfway across the bar before the door had even closed.

"Oy! I warned you. Don't be starting shit in my bar!" the barkeep hollered after me.

I shot him the bird and dipped into the restroom to see what I could do to clean up. It was even worse than I thought, and I ended up using damn near every towel available and even stole some from the other restroom.

When I was positive I wasn't bleeding anymore and wouldn't get my shirt dirty, I pulled it on. The only saving grace to the whole fucking disaster of a day was that *somehow* my hair had stayed dyed through two partial shifts. Satisfied that I looked at least moderately presentable, I returned to the bar, ready to get absolutely piss-ass drunk.

Chapter 8

Zahir

I pulled up to *The Oasis* just as eager for an escape from my studies as I had every other day. Given how often I felt like I needed a drink these days, I should probably be more concerned that I was becoming an alcoholic. I snorted to myself and shoved the door open, then made a beeline for what was fast becoming my customary seat at the bar.

"Don't even fucking think about it," Arnie growled from behind the counter, forcing me to hover with my ass inches above the stool.

"Excuse me?" I hissed, barely repressing the urge to go full cobra on his ass. We'd see how well an earth elemental could stand up to naga venom when I sank my fangs into his throat.

He shook his head and continued scowling. "Not tonight. I'm over your shit. Your two bad attitudes can keep each other company tonight." He pointed aggressively deeper into the bar.

My brows pinched together, betraying my confusion as he waved for me to keep walking to the far side of the bar. I was tempted to coil around the damn stool out of sheer obstinance, but admittedly, part of me was curious what the fuck he was talking about.

I hesitantly walked the length of the bar, which was fast filling up given it was a Saturday night. If Arnie was fucking with me and cost me my seat, I was going to be pissed. Given how shitty my week had been, I might throw caution to the wind and *actually* bite him. A cluster of people finished grabbing their drinks and walked away from the counter, offering me my first view of who the barkeep was likely referring to.

Aidan.

A tightness in my chest eased, which I had absolutely zero interest in evaluating. He sat at the same table we'd been at the last time he'd been here. There were four empty glasses decorating the top, and he was staring sullenly into a fifth. As I got closer, he lifted his head, his gaze landing unerringly on me as if he could sense me staring. His brown hair was mussed like he'd run his fingers through it repeatedly. He wore a dark teal shirt that was remarkably close to my scale color with a subtle V-neck. His mouth was pursed in his characteristic pout that I was sure was meant to be intimidating. He looked fucking incredible. I was seriously torn between sinking my teeth into his pouty bottom lip or drawing it into my mouth to suck on until he moaned.

His sharp blue gaze tracked my steps as I closed the distance to his table. When I got close enough, he kicked out a chair with a scowl. I slowly lowered myself into the aggressively offered chair, wary of a trap. It wasn't until I scooted the chair closer that I realized that one of the glasses I'd thought was empty was still full.

He took a gulp from the half-empty glass clutched in his hand and shot me a sidelong look. "If it's watered down, then you should have been here earlier," he grumbled.

I blinked at him and turned my attention to the *very* watered down moonshine. "You bought me a drink?" He'd been expecting me?

"Don't be weird about it." He tossed back the last of his drink, then raised his arm to signal for another. The empty glass clanked against the others as he slid it across the round top. "You may be a snake, but drinking with you is still better than drinking alone."

"Uh, thanks?" I still couldn't make heads or tails of what was going on right now. Maybe I *did* need to reevaluate that strange feeling from earlier...

He snorted and gestured for the bar hand—noticeably *not* Arnie—to set the drink down. Before I could remove my glass from the literal pool of condensation that had developed beneath it, Aidan snatched it up, swapping it with the fresh glass. I was still trying to find my voice when he stuck his index finger in it and stirred.

I stared with rapt attention when, rather than wipe off the liquid on his jeans, he stuck his finger in his mouth and sucked it clean. His tongue curled around the digit, ensuring not a single drop escaped. Unbridled lust raced down my spine and immediately had my cock twitching.

A frown pinched Aidan's beautiful face. "What?"

I shook my head and grabbed my drink. "Nothing. Thanks." I saluted him with the glass and took a hefty swallow. Okay, this promised to be an interesting evening. I eyed the plethora of empty glasses. It took *a lot* to get a werewolf drunk, and he looked like he was on a mission. "Shitty day?" I hazarded.

"Yeah. You?"

"Shitty *week*," I said, polishing off the fresh drink in a few gulps and signaling for two more. "Wanna talk about it?"

"No. You?"

"Nope," I said, popping the "P". A crooked smile tilted his lips. I wasn't sure how much of it was the alcohol or the shared shittiness, but I'd take it. Actually, I'd take a hell of a lot more of it. This wasn't the feral smile he'd given me before, or the one when he'd bared his teeth at Arnie. It was soft, playful, almost sweet. I decided right there that smiling should really be Aidan's default. He had a face made for it. "No vest tonight?"

He chuckled into his drink. "It's called a cut. And it's out in my saddlebag."

"You have a motorcycle?" I asked, not that it should have surprised me. Though, I suppose it was possible he was talking about a horse. We *were* in Kentucky.

His grin grew, and my stupid traitorous heart did a ridiculous flip. "Yeah. A Harley Roadster. I'm hoping to upgrade it, eventually."

"Why?"

"She's a beauty, but she's old. She'd be a classic if anyone had taken care of her before she got to me. But now it's a minor miracle I can even keep her running." He shrugged. "You ride?"

"Nah." It was on the tip of my tongue to add that I didn't mind being ridden, though. Aidan smirked like he could hear the unspoken thought. I cleared my throat and settled deeper into the chair. "You do stunts on it?"

He threw his head back and let out a rich laugh. "Yeah, not so much. I might be a werewolf, but I'm not a daredevil. Some in my pack do stunts like jumps and wheelies, but mostly, we just ride. Wind in your face, the open road... there's not a better feeling of freedom."

"Sounds like a good time. It's pretty cool your whole pack rides."

A shadow flitted across his face, darkening his previously jovial expression. I wanted to hunt down whatever had spawned that shadow and strangle it with my tail. "It can be. But I don't want to talk about that. I'm a lowlife biker, no news there. What about you?"

"Well," I began with a heavy sigh, "once my mother tired of my reckless behavior and 'impulsive youth', I got shipped off to become a spiritual leader. Now I spend my days studying dusty tomes, memorizing ancient prayers, and generally trying not to go insane."

"You're a... priest?"

"*Fuck no*. Things are different in my religion. I'm apprenticed to become a Guru, but that's fucking *centuries* away," I finished with a miserable groan.

Aidan arched an eyebrow, but mercifully didn't push. He seemed to pick up on that I didn't want to discuss my depressing lot in life any more than he did and shifted the topic to something more innocuous. "What would you do if you weren't studying all day?"

I thought about that a moment, stubbornly pushing away answering thoughts of *him*. I sure as hell wasn't about to confess my guilty pleasure of baking shows. So what did that leave? Finally, I chuckled as the obvious answer came to me. "Probably sunbathing."

He tipped his head back, releasing a hardy laugh. I watched completely enraptured, like he was actually one of those charlatans that called themselves snake charmers. "I don't think I've ever heard a more snake response."

"Stow it, furball," I said, but there was no bite in it. I couldn't even keep my mirroring smile at bay. "How about you? If resources weren't an issue, what type of motorcycle would you upgrade to?"

"Honestly?" He cast me a furtive glance as he trailed his finger slowly through the condensation on his glass, a small smile still playing on his lips. "I'd love to restore her. Rebuild her from the ground up."

"Sounds like a lot of work."

He shrugged. "It would be, but I've never shied away from hard things." I smothered a snicker at his undoubtedly unintended double entendre. He rested on his forearms, batting his half-empty glass between his hands. "Tell me about these supposedly reckless years," he said with a sharp glint of challenge in his bright eyes.

"I didn't go to jail, if that's what you're insinuating."

He huffed a laugh. "That makes two of us."

I lost count of how much we drank while we traded stories and asked questions. It wasn't until a loud clap of thunder eclipsed every sound in the bar and the lights flickered that we looked up.

"Fuck," Aidan snarled as he pushed away from the table and unsteadily made his way to the door. I followed, slightly steadier, stopping beside him to stare at the absolute deluge coming down outside.

"Maybe it'll let up," I said hopefully. On cue, another peal of thunder rolled over the bar. Lightning flashed close enough to illuminate the entire parking lot in bright white. Then the lights cut out. "Or not."

"Right! Listen up!" Arnie hollered as he came around the bar. Between the steady flashes of lightning and the fact that most of the supes in here likely had some variation of nightvision, we didn't have any trouble tracking his movement to the center of the room. "You can either cash out with actual cash or you can comeback tomorrow or whenever the fuck the power's back and settle up then." He glowered and pointed aggressively at the mute crowd. "And don't even think about stiffing me."

Aidan and I shared a look. I doubted anyone here wanted to find out what would happen if they tried. At the very least, they'd get banned from the bar. And seeing as how it was the only exclusively supernatural bar for at least a hundred miles, that was bad enough. Grumbles surrounded us as some people moved to the bar to toss down cash, while others gravitated toward the door to ponder the mad dash to their vehicle.

To my surprise, Aidan was among those who dropped cash. He had a short, heated conversation with the barkeep, then made his way back to where I was still standing. I tilted my head toward Arnie. "What was that about?"

"I settled our tab and asked if I could wait out the storm here. He said no. Actually, he said 'fuck no, get your shitty attitude out of my bar'. I even asked nicely." He huffed, crossing his arms over his chest, and glowered at the torrential rain falling a few feet away.

I side-eyed him. Nothing about their brief exchange looked like it had involved "asking nicely."

He ran his hands through his hair, causing it to stick up in all directions. "Fuck. What am I supposed to do? Riding in that is as good as driving off a cliff."

I snorted a laugh, which he echoed. Then inspiration struck, much like the next bolt of lightning. "Come back to my place."

He looked at me like I'd lost my mind, which to be fair was, well, fair.

"I don't live too far from here. You can wait out the storm and I'll bring you back to get your motorcycle." Why was I pushing this so hard? It had to be the alcohol. While I was confident I was fully capable of driving home, it was clearly messing with my judgment in other areas. Drinking with a wolf was one thing. But bringing one home?

Aidan continued to stare at me. Finally, he hiked a shoulder. "Fuck it. Why not? You know we're going to get drenched, right?"

I scoffed. "The car will dry and once we get back to mine, we won't need to worry about clothes." I realized half a beat too late how that would sound. Heat—or what I was pretty sure was heat—flared in Aidan's eyes, and suddenly I was really glad for my Freudian slip. The idea of Aidan naked sounded fucking *amazing*. My cock thickened painfully behind my zipper as I imagined running my tongue over the pulse point in his neck while I wrapped a hand around his dick and his heavy breaths teased my ears.

He faced the doors once more, snapping me out of the haze of lust. "Which one's yours?"

"The gray SUV on the far right," I replied, unable to tear my gaze away from him or stop thinking about what he would taste like.

He snorted. "You would park all the way in the back." He rolled his shoulders and hopped in-place before catching me with a wry smile. "Alright, let's do this."

I barely registered his words before he was out the door. I barrelled after him, though it didn't occur to me until I was unlocking the vehicle that our "run" to the truck would have been much easier in my naga form. I certainly wouldn't have slipped and landed on my ass.

"Woo!" he shouted after he closed the door. I couldn't help but laugh at the joy emanating off of him. Then he shook out his shaggy brown hair, sending water everywhere.

"Ew," I complained, shielding my face from the onslaught and turning on the truck. He simply laughed. A crack of thunder split the air as a bolt of lightning struck close enough to bathe everything in white and leave an afterimage of multicolored dots.

"Fuck!" Aidan exclaimed. "Let's get out of here."

I stared back at him while an electricity that had absolutely nothing to do with the deadly lightning filled the SUV. "Yeah, let's go," I said, my voice suddenly low and thick, and put us in reverse.

When we pulled up to the small house, I expected Aidan to say something, but he hopped out before I'd even pulled the key from the ignition and bolted for the door. I quickly joined him, crowding us underneath the meager awning to prevent us from getting any more drenched than we already were. Not that there was any point to it.

My hand was surprisingly steady as I unlocked the door, given how aware I was of Aidan's body heat pressed against my back. I licked my lips and tried desperately to get ahold of the anticipation flooding through my system. We practically fell inside, and I quickly forced the door shut against the invading rain.

I stole a moment to shake the water off my arms, then pushed my hair back, squeezing the water out as I lifted my head. The second I met Aidan's gaze, time seemed to stand still. My heart thundered in my ears and the erection the storm had tempered returned with a vengeance.

Without a second thought, I reached out whip-fast, fisted my hand in the front of his shirt, and dragged him toward me. Our mouths crashed together with bruising force, as much teeth as it was a firm press of lips. Aidan gasped, and it was all the invitation I needed to snake my tongue into his mouth. I swallowed down his groan as our tongues slid over and around each other, fighting for dominance. He tasted even better than I imagined—like mango and sunshine.

As abruptly as I snared him, I pushed him back, already kicking off my waterlogged shoes. He stumbled a step, but the heat didn't leave his eyes as he mirrored me. "Bedroom," I ordered, closing the distance between us again before he could finish getting his last shoe off. He was already reaching for me as I slammed back into him. We stumbled into damn near everything on the way to the bedroom—the coffee table, the sofa, the *wall*—but couldn't break apart long enough to avoid them.

Finally, we staggered into the bedroom where mercifully I'd left the lamp on. I fumbled to undo the button on his jeans and push the clinging material down his toned legs, which fought me for every exposed inch. At last he could kick them aside, and I coasted my palms over the coarse hair of his legs as I straightened, pausing to grope the firm globes of his ass. He hooked his fingers in my shirt and tugged me forward, then buried his face in my neck and groaned while I continued to massage the firm muscle. His fingers were still curled into the hem of my shirt, trying to get it off me when I pushed him back on the bed. He made a sound of muffled surprise that oddly resembled a huff of laughter.

I took a moment to appreciate how fucking edible he looked splayed out before me. His brown hair sticking up in odd directions, his lips swollen and shiny from our fevered kisses, his gorgeous cock bouncing against his stomach from the fall and the bead of liquid already pearled at the tip. I was going to absolutely *wreck* this fucking wolf.

His eyes glowed yellow as they caught the lamplight, tracking my every movement with an undeniable hunger. I peeled off my shirt and tossed it aside before stripping out of my pants and briefs in one go. In my head, it was a lot sexier than the execution ended up being. By the time I stumbled free, we were both laughing, but the heat had yet to leave his eyes. It was that exact heat that had me crawling up the bed and up his body to snare his luscious mouth again.

I ground my hips against him, dragging the length of my dick along his. He grunted and bucked into me, continuing to snatch at my lips. I roved my hands along his chest, reveling in the way the hair felt against my sensitive hands, then followed the same path with my mouth. Aidan continued to grind against me as I nipped at his jaw, then ran the flat of my tongue over his pulse point before sucking out a bruise that vanished almost as soon as I made it.

As much as the slick precum was helping our mindless frotting, it wasn't enough. I abandoned his mouth to angle toward the nightstand. His mouth closed hotly on my neck, kissing and sucking, and I blanked on what I was doing for a second. I got my wits back enough to secure the lube and blindly poured some into my hand before discarding it by the lamp.

I awkwardly shimmied back to tangle my tongue with his once again, then angled myself up enough to slip my hand between us. His hips jerked up when I wrapped my hand around both of our dicks, and he dropped his head back with a gasp.

"Fuck, Zahir. *Fuuuuck*," he moaned, making my already hard cock even harder.

"You like that, furball?" I asked, stroking us in tandem with a tight grip.

He growled something that might have been a curse and thrust into the tight channel of my hand while he dug his fingers into the mattress.

"Don't even think about putting holes in my sheets," I warned, my voice low enough to be dangerous. Rather than quip back, he released his white-knuckle hold on the bed to dig his fingers into my shoulders, dragging me closer and sealing his mouth over mine.

Our breaths became ragged and our kisses sloppy as we rutted against each other in search of release. I shuttled my hand faster as that release danced closer and my hips lost all sense of rhythm. Pleasure built at the base of my spine until it exploded. I groaned into Aidan's neck as my dick pulsed stream after stream of cum, coating my hand and making the glide even more incredible.

I continued to milk my cock, riding out the wave of the toe-tingling orgasm. Right at the cusp of overstimulation, Aidan gripped my ass, pumped his hips off the bed, and grunted as he spilled between us. I let my dick slip free of the hold, but kept stroking him through his release while I peppered kisses along his neck and chest.

After a few seconds, he made a small whimper at the back of his throat and pushed my hand away. Taking the hint, I released him and rolled onto my back, still panting for breath. I thought about stumbling to the bathroom to clean up, but that required way too much movement and I was positive I wouldn't make it with my legs in their current shaky state.

Using the little energy I had left, I groped around for the shirt I'd discarded, suddenly glad the damn thing was still soaked. I wiped the cum from hands and abdomen, then tossed it onto Aidan, who also had yet to move. He made an indignant sound, but used the clothing to wipe off and tossed it away on the other side of the bed. Feeling more satisfied than I had in weeks, maybe months—who the fuck was I kidding? *Years*—I shuffled closer to his warmth and slipped into a heavy sleep.

Chapter 9

Aidan

I wasn't sure what woke me up, the pounding in my head, the black hole in my stomach, or my body's internal clock. But when I dared to crack my eyes, the headache won. A soft groan drifted out of me as I rolled onto my side, my eyes squeezed shut against the invasive early morning light. If I wasn't sure that I'd had *way* too much to drink the night before, the fact that I had werewolf healing and *still* woke up with a hangover sealed it.

I debated shifting to eliminate the painful remnants. Then it hit me—I wasn't in wolf form. I rocketed the rest of the way back to awareness, braving the light to get a better idea of where I was. Not only was I still in my human form, I was in a bed. A really nice bed. My eyes drifted shut as the weight of what I'd done last night settled over me. I'd hooked up with a snake. Not just a snake. A *male* snake. Suppose there was a first time for everything.

And honestly? I wasn't even mad about it. Arguably, the snake part was weirder than the dude part. Probably didn't hurt that he'd been really fucking hot. A smile twitched my lips as I recalled the heady drag of Zahir's thick cock against mine, the way he'd pressed me into the mattress and dominated my mouth. Unsurprisingly, my dick swelled as I continued to relive the interaction. Yeah, I definitely wouldn't be opposed to another round with the snake.

On cue, I heard the subtle squeal of a door hinge. I opened my eyes enough to peer toward the sound. There, in the opening of what I assumed was the bathroom, stood Zahir. His golden face was slack with shock as he stared at me lying in his bed. I fought a grin as I let my gaze slide down his naked body. His muscles were clearly defined without being grotesque—smooth and lickable. Which, okay, I'd literally never once in my life had a desire to lick another guy, but here we were. My dick was getting harder and Zahir looked like he was preparing to bolt.

I slipped an arm free of the warm cocoon of covers and pulled them back in invitation. "I'm not ready for the freak-out portion of this morning."

"Uh..." Zahir replied uncertainly.

"Come on. Twenty more minutes, then we can freakout all you want," I suggested. When he continued to stand there waffling, I wiggled the sheet.

At last, he made his way back to the bed with jerky steps, then slipped beneath the covers. He seemed subconsciously to shift closer while also trying to keep his distance. I wiggled a foot close enough to brush his leg and immediately recoiled.

"Fuck, why are you so cold?" I asked.

He rolled his head to glower at me. "Snake, remember?"

I couldn't have held back the chuckle if I'd wanted to. Oh, I remembered all right. "Then I guess it's a good thing *weres* run hot." He continued to stare at me, doubt clear in his deep brown eyes. I scooted closer until my erection bumped his thigh and I'd draped a leg over his. When I ran the palm of my hand over his flat stomach, his eyes fluttered shut and he released the softest moan I think I'd ever heard.

Emboldened, I scooted closer to him, pressing a hot, open-mouthed kiss to his shoulder. When he rewarded me with another of those tiny moans, I did it again on his collar, then his neck, then his throat. I nipped lightly at his quickly warming skin and continued laying kisses to the background of his encouraging moans until I'd practically crawled on top of him. I couldn't get over how he didn't seem to have a single strand of hair anywhere on his body below his eyelashes. That was probably a snake thing, too.

He rested his hands on my hips as he angled his head to give me more room to work. I licked a stripe along the column of his throat, then gave into the impulse to straddle him. I shifted my focus back down to his chest to suck out a few more bruising kisses. He gasped, and I sensed as much as felt him turn his head. When I lifted my head to meet his gaze, my heart was running at a steady gallop, my breathing was heavy, and I was fully hard... and I wasn't the only one.

Want pulsed through my chest as I stared into Zahir's lust-blown eyes. My gaze darted down to his parted lips, where soft pants of air escaped. Pure instinct had me closing the distance before I could even think to worry about morning breath. There was a split second where it was just the soft meeting of our lips. Then Zahir tangled his fingers in my hair and deepened the kiss.

I groaned hungrily as he speared his tongue into my mouth. Just as eager to touch him, I roved my hands everywhere my position would allow. Carding my fingers in his short, dark hair. Dragging my nails over his strong shoulders. Pressing against his firm chest. And damn near humping him as I got lost in kiss after kiss.

Eventually he released my hair to give my body the same treatment, gripping, grabbing, and squeezing, until he dug his fingers into the meat of my ass. I gasped as a level of want I'd never experienced before rolled over me.

"Put your finger in my ass," I panted, without pausing to think about what I was actually saying.

He pulled back enough to look at me, his confusion obvious even through the haze of lust. "What?"

Smirking, I reached for his hand and brought it to my mouth. His breath hitched as I sucked his first two fingers, getting them good and wet, before removing them. "I didn't stutter." I released his hand and captured his mouth, sweeping my tongue boldly inside to glide along his.

He shifted slightly beneath me, but it wasn't until I felt the light brush of his finger against my hole that I fully registered what I'd just demanded from him. Determined not to let on that I was *way* out of my depth, I continued to kiss him like my life depended on it while the blunt end of his finger circled and teased. I shuddered as the new sensation rippled through me. Who the fuck knew your hole was so damn sensitive? I didn't even have the wherewithal to tense when his long finger slid inside.

"Fuck your hot," he hissed as he slid his finger slowly out then pressed back in. "So fucking hot."

"Uh-huh," I mumbled incoherently, dropping my head to his shoulder and getting lost in the steady glide of his finger in and out, in and out. It wasn't long before I was pushing back to meet each thrust of his fingers, my cock painfully hard between us, and sporadically capturing his mouth. But it wasn't enough. It was nowhere near enough.

Need itched almost painfully beneath my skin until I couldn't stand it. I pushed his hand away and stole a quick kiss before reaching out to slide my hand through the lube that had spilled onto the nightstand from the night before. Then I rocked back on my heels and wrapped my hand around his thick cock, coating it in as much of the lube as I could. Hopeful that most of it had made it onto his dick, I angled the fat head toward my clenching hole. I was so damn close when Zahir's fingers dug sharply into my hips and diverted my attention. I turned to see him looking back at me with surprise and uncertainty.

"Do you know what you're doing?" he asked, breath ragged.

I cocked an eyebrow. "Do you?"

"Yes," he replied without missing a beat.

"Good, then lie back and watch me ride this snake dick," I said with all the bravado I could muster, while hoping like hell he didn't call me out.

"Aidan..."

"What? I figured if I was going to do the whole gay experience thing, I might as well check most of the boxes."

He shook his head, a small smile playing on his lips.

Didn't he understand? I *needed* this. I didn't even know why. Just that I desperately did. Before he could decide whether he was going to stop me after all, I shifted back to take him. To my embarrassment, I immediately yelped at the sharp sting and jerked away. Not that I got anywhere, considering the flare of his cockhead caught on my rim, which only intensified the sting.

His grip tightened once more, and I forced myself to meet his gaze. To my surprise, he wasn't mad or judging me for being incompetent. His gaze was soft, and the slight crinkle between his dark brows oddly concerned. "Easy. Go slow, okay?"

I nodded, reflexively relaxing at his gentle words.

"Nice and steady." To emphasize his point, he subtly pressed down on my hips.

Better prepared this time, I slowly worked my way down, giving the burn of the stretch a chance to dissipate before gaining another inch. Thank fuck for werewolf healing, was all I had to say. I maneuvered so I could lean back on my arms and let out a deep moan as the last of him slipped inside. I'd never felt so much like I was being split in two and that was saying something, given what the change was like. And I never knew it could feel *so fucking good*.

Zahir babbled something that sounded a bit like a prayer, the only part of which I caught was, "Hot, so hot."

Using my newfound leverage, I raised my hips and slowly took him down to the root again. The burning need finally subsided, and I did it again and again. Fuck, why had I never done this before? I was clearly missing out.

Zahir's hands roved over my legs and stomach, occasionally stopping to stroke my cock as it bounced obscenely over me. "Cant your hips," he said suddenly, disrupting my concentration.

"Huh?"

"Tilt your hips. Towards the ceiling. Just a little," he said through harsh pants. No sooner did I adjust like he said than he thrust up. Pleasure radiated out to consume every nerve. I had no clue what he was doing except that it had to be magic—snake magic—and I didn't want him to stop. And he didn't. He pounded up into me and I clenched around him, all of it too much and not enough all at once.

I shifted my weight to one arm and wrapped my free hand around my leaking dick. The ridiculous amount of precum dribbling out of me provided more than enough lubrication as I furiously stroked my cock in time with Zahir's thrusts. Between one heartbeat and the next, the wave of ecstasy I was riding crested and my orgasm slammed through me so hard I lost feeling in the rest of my body. I came and came and came, suspended in a world of overwhelming pleasure. If it wasn't for his hands firmly gripping my sides, I probably would have fallen over.

His hips faltered, and he thrust hard a few more times before coming with a grunt that made my spent cock twitch valiantly. Werewolves had impressive stamina, but even I was going to need a minute. And when the fuck had grunts become sexy? Zahir gave a few more half-hearted thrusts as my mind continued to float and wander in the post orgasmic haze. Even that didn't stop my groan of disappointment when he finally slipped out, my stretched hole already healing.

I collapsed in a sweaty heap beside him, aching to curl into him, but unable to convince my limbs to move. Werewolves might be notorious cuddle sluts. I couldn't help but wonder how snakes felt about it.

"That... was not how I expected this morning to go," Zahir said, still a little out of breath.

"Oh yeah? And how did you expect it to go?" I asked, angling my head enough to look at him out of the corner of my eye.

He huffed a laughed. "Honestly, I kind of figured I'd wake up to find you gone and my wallet empty. No offense," he added, turning his head fully to look at me.

I smiled and leaned forward to steal a kiss. "None taken. That does sound like something I'd do." He chuckled, filling my chest with a lightness I hadn't felt in years, maybe ever. Grudgingly, I rolled up to sit on the edge of the bed and reached for my pants. "Though I should get going. Goddess only knows what state my bike is in."

"Shit. Right. I'll drive you over."

Before he could do more than twitch his muscles, I turned and placed a hand on his chest to keep him pinned to the bed, giving him a smile. "Don't worry about it. The bar's not far and a run will do me good."

"Okay. If you're sure..." he said, relaxing back into the mattress. He looked like he wanted to say more, but didn't add anything. I suddenly had the insane desire for him to ask me to stay. Not like I could, given the pack, but the desire was there all the same.

"I'm sure."

It took every ounce of willpower I had to force myself to get up and finish getting dressed. Once I had my boots on, I snuck a glance back at Zahir to find him passed back out. Shaking my head, I moved to go when my gaze snagged on his discarded jeans. Like mine, they were still damp from the downpour the night before. Chuckling to myself, I leaned down and snagged his wallet, then removed all the single bills, including some colorful ones, and leaving the large ones. Couldn't very well disappoint his expectations, now could I?

Outside of Zahir's house, I gave myself a good stretch. My joints popped and I let out a contented hum. I glanced around to make sure the coast was clear, then made my way to the stretch of woods around the back of his place. When I could no longer see the house or the road, I stopped and stripped again, taking time to bundle my clothes tightly and secure them with my boot laces.

That done, I dropped to all fours and let the change take me. The process of all of my bones breaking and reforming would never not be painful, but this morning it was hard for anything to eclipse my good mood. In a couple of minutes, I'd shifted fully to my wolf form. I snatched up my makeshift rucksack with my teeth and took off through the trees, heading toward *The Oasis*.

The bar ended up being a little farther than I expected, but I wasn't complaining. It had been too long since I'd run. Fuck, had it really been since the last full moon? I shook out my coat and silently vowed not to wait so long next time before starting the shift back. My body was still shaking as I collapsed on the grass, reminding me just how long it had been since I'd eaten, not to mention how much energy a full shift took.

Even then, I couldn't be bothered to care. I felt fucking incredible. And apparently I liked dick. *A lot.* Maybe not all dick, but definitely Zahir's thick cock. I was almost sad that werewolf healing had eliminated any hint of sting in my ass. The reminder would have been nice.

A faint whiff of his scent tickled my nose, and it hit me—there was no way I could go back to the pack smelling like him. There'd be questions. They'd want to know where I was, who *he* was, why the hell I was fraternizing with a snake, and I had zero interest in answering any of them. Zahir was *mine,* and I planned on keeping him that way.

I sniffed around until I found a pungent patch of wild growing herbs and rolled around in it until it was the *only* smell on me. Then I rubbed the rest of my clothes in it, but hesitated at my shirt. It might not be the smartest thing, but I couldn't bring myself to eliminate every trace of Zahir's subtle scent, like the air after a spring rain, soft and full of promise. Instead, I put on everything else except for the shirt and made my way to the parking lot of *The Oasis.*

Thankfully, aside from a shit ton of mud on her, my sled looked no worse for wear. She'd probably need a tuneup, but I should be able to get back to the house where the pack was staying easily enough. I opened the saddlebag and traded the Zahir-infused shirt for my cut. In a matter of moments, I was rumbling down the road, ready to face retribution for my actions.

I wasn't dumb enough to think they'd have cooled off or, even better, forgotten. Add to that my skipping out all night and most of the morning without checking in and I had a world of trouble headed my way. If I had to guess, a few days in the doghouse, at the very least. But much like waking up and realizing I'd slept with a guy—a snake—I did not Give. A. Fuck.

Chapter 10

Zahir

I wouldn't go to *The Oasis* tonight, I decided, lifting an ornate statue from the altar to dust beneath it. It wasn't like Aidan would be there, anyway. After two weeks of showing up every night and not so much as a hair of him, you'd think I'd get the hint. We hooked up, that was all, nothing more. So why did it *feel* like more?

I snarled to myself as I replaced the hand-sized statue and plucked up another. Fuck, I was pathetic. Werewolves were trouble, I *knew* that. I never should have taken him to my place, shouldn't have kissed him, shouldn't have explored his body with greedy hands, and I definitely shouldn't have had sex with him. *Twice.*

Cold washed through me as I considered another possibility Aidan hadn't been around. Maybe he felt like I pushed him into something he wasn't comfortable doing. He wasn't gay or bi or pan or anything fucking else. He as much as said so by referring to our hookup as "The Gay Experience". But then he'd been the one to initiate the following morning. So what was the *real* reason he was ghosting me? I shook my head. Thank fuck I'd forgotten to get his number, otherwise I'd probably be blowing up his phone like a desperate tween.

A discreet cough at my side lurched me out of my spiraling pity-party. "Might I inquire how Lakshmi has personally wronged you?" Gurudevi asked, stepping into my periphery.

I frowned and quickly replaced the idol. "What? No, of course not. Why would you ask such a thing?"

"Because you were staring at her rather intently with a scowl that has deepened every time I've looked at you." She placed a hand on my scaled arm. "What troubles you, young one?"

I shrugged her off and slithered away to replace the cleaning supplies before I did something thoughtless—*like* accidentally chuck an idol across the temple. "Nothing is wrong. I'm fine." Just pitifully obsessed with a furball that clearly wants nothing more to do with me.

"Zahir." Gurudevi's firm tone brooked no nonsense.

I reluctantly looked back at her. "I'm fine. Really."

She tsked and flicked out her forked tongue as if tasting my lie in the air. "Keep in mind that I have been providing guidance to lost souls for centuries. Perhaps you could benefit from *receiving* the guidance rather than merely observing it." That honestly sounded like the absolute *last* thing I wanted, and yet I found my mouth opening and words spilling out.

"I... met someone. Sort of. It's a poor match from the start, but he's... diverting."

She nodded along, as if none of this was news to her. Part of me wondered if I'd ever develop that kind of wisdom or at least acting ability. "Go on," she prompted. "So far, I do not see the source of your distress."

"We... spent an intimate evening together," I edged.

"You had sex," she deadpanned. "There's no need to appear shocked. I'm old, not celibate."

I shuddered. That was not something I wanted—or needed—to know, and it would probably take centuries to scrub the involuntary images that came to mind. "Anyway, it's been weeks since I've seen him."

"And you fear he is avoiding you."

"Maybe?" I admitted begrudgingly. "I feel like a fool showing up every day only for him not to be there."

Her aged features softened into an expression I struggled not to interpret as pity. "You are not a fool. Stubborn, yes. But foolish? I think not. Is it possible that he was simply passing through and is no longer in a position to meet you?"

While I *hadn't* considered that, I still vehemently shook my head. "No, he would have..." What? Told me he was leaving town? Said goodbye? Fuck, I really was pathetic. My shoulders sagged. "I barely know him."

"And yet, you're confident he would not disappear without seeing you."

"But I'm... not?" I wasn't even sure who I was trying to convince with that bullshit.

Gurudevi hooked her thin arm through mine and guided us toward the array of cushions. "Let's assume your gut is correct and he would not go without informing you first. Perhaps something beyond his control has kept him away. We often forget amidst our busy lives that others also experience trials and tribulations. Has he shared these with you?"

"No," I replied, ignoring the sudden blossom of optimism in my chest. "In fact, we've made a point not to discuss the troubles of the day."

She gave me a knowing smile that maybe wasn't as irritating as it normally was. "Then, after tea, I suggest we take time to pray this afternoon."

I accepted the cup she poured. "But wasn't someone coming for guidance this afternoon?"

"Yes, and I provided it," she replied with a grin that twinkled in her eyes. Okay, maybe the smile was still irritating as fuck, but that didn't prevent me from returning it. I took a sip of the scalding liquid, letting the spices flow over my tongue and soothe my spirit. One more night. It couldn't hurt to go to the bar one more night.

Hours later, I only had to walk a few steps in *The Oasis* to confirm what I'd expected—Aidan wasn't here. Obstinately, I walked deeper into the bar until I was standing in the center and could see every table, stool, and patron. My gaze met Arnold's as I searched the bar for Aidan's familiar flop of brown hair.

Arnie subtly shook his head, an undeniable glimmer of pity in his dark eyes. Unlike the other times I'd come only to be disappointed, anger didn't rush to fill my chest and cloud my vision. It was something far more insidious—hopelessness. I never should have let Guru Angira talk me into coming tonight. It was ridiculous to believe that he'd show when he hadn't any other time.

I nodded at Arnie and turned to go. No way could I bear nursing a drink for hours while I waited for someone who was making it abundantly clear that he didn't want to see me again. It was time to move on. Maybe I could find another bar to go to for a while, meet someone who didn't get under my scales, who could help me forget.

"Oh good. I was hoping you'd be here."

My gaze riveted to the source of the voice that had been haunting me. "Aidan?"

"Who else would I be?" he asked, already two-thirds of the way to me, and the door to the bar hadn't even finished closing behind him. At his cheeky smirk, the anger that had abandoned me flared with a vengeance.

"Where the fuck have you been?" I hissed under my breath, knowing damn well he'd be able to hear me.

He grabbed my wrist without responding or slowing and proceeded to drag me toward the back of the bar.

I caught movement by the bar and realized Arnold had taken out what looked suspiciously like a nail-studded baseball bat. I quickly shook my head even as I struggled to keep my footing. His gaze narrowed, but he put down the bat and turned to a customer.

Down the hall that led to the restrooms, Aidan hesitated only for a moment before choosing neither door. Instead, he reached for a third door that I was pretty sure was locked until he snapped the mechanism. In one motion, he pushed the door open, flicked on the light, and dragged me inside. I had all of a second to process what was happening before he kicked the door shut and mashed his mouth against mine.

My anger guttered and went out as he swept his tongue inside my mouth. I pressed him into the wall with a moan, the heat of his body against mine, addling whatever was left of my senses. I devoured his kisses like he might vanish any second. Desperate to touch more of him, I squeezed my hands between us, sliding them under his shirt to coast them over his chest and rucking up the fabric.

"Where have you been?" I asked between frantic presses of lips as I pulled his shirt over his head.

His low chuckle should have been infuriating, *not* sexy as hell. "Was in the doghouse for a few days, then had some biker shit to deal with," he said, more than a little out of breath. "Why? Miss me?" His cheeky grin had me smiling back at him before I could stop myself.

"No." I kissed along his jaw until I could whisper in his ear, "Why would I miss a furball?" I pulled his earlobe between my teeth. His resulting groan when I tugged on it went straight to my dick. As if sensing my struggle, he thrust his hips off the wall to rub against my erection and betraying how turned on he was as well.

"Oh, I don't know. Just a feeling," he quipped, entirely too coherent for my liking.

I had the perfect way to fix that. We'd see how many words he could string together when I sucked his brain out through his dick. I slashed my mouth over his once more as I lowered my hands to his fly. A few deft movements had the button flicked open, the zipper down, and my palm cupping his cock over his briefs.

His breath hitched, and he moaned into my mouth as I gave him a light squeeze. I ran my thumb over the damp spot blooming on the fabric before pulling it down and freeing his cock. I leisurely stroked his hot shaft as I decorated his jaw, his neck, and then his chest with kisses.

"Fuck, I can't wait to have you in my mouth," I said, continuing to work my way lower. His cock twitched in my hand, letting me know exactly how he felt about that. Which only intensified my surprise when he tightened his hands in my shirt and halted my progress.

"Wait," he gasped. He untangled his fingers from my now very wrinkled shirt and dropped them to my fly. After only a little fumbling, he managed to shove my trousers down enough to wrap his exceedingly warm hand around my dick. "I want you like this."

He captured me with another kiss, then pushed my hand away from his erection. Before I could question what he was doing, he dropped a liberal amount of spit onto his dick and shifted his grip to take both of us in his hand. Between the copious amounts of precum we were each leaking, and the improvised lube, the glide of his hand was smooth, tight, and absolutely perfect.

"Oh, fuck!" I cried as he twisted his hand over our heads and stroked back down. I clung to his shoulders, nipping and sucking at his jaw and neck, while he worked us over. He rubbed his thumb over my slit, dipping in to steal the latest surge of precum, then swirled it around my swollen head. I mindlessly thrust into his hand, my balls tightening and starting to tingle. "Aidan. Oh, fuck, Aidan. I'm close," I panted.

He quickened his strokes, squeezing and twisting in all the right places until I couldn't hold back anymore. I buried my face into the side of his neck and grunted my release. A scant half second later, Aidan groaned, his cum spurting between his fingers as he milked both of us dry. When we had nothing left, he leaned forward to rest his forehead against mine. By some miracle, he'd caught most of our combined release with only a few rogue drops decorating his abdomen.

"Full moon at midnight, I needed that," he muttered, his breath ghosting over my lips, swollen from our fevered kissing.

"Yeah?" I grabbed his hand coated in our release and brought it to my mouth. I watched his face as I licked his fingers clean with my serpentine tongue, savoring the salty taste of us.

"Whoa," he breathed as I unraveled my tongue from his middle finger and licked at his palm.

"Regretting you didn't let me blow you?" I teased.

His gaze snapped to mine, his blue eyes bright with laughter. "Sounds like you are," he said with a goofy grin that I was positive was supposed to be a smirk. Whatever it was, it still made my heart do a ridiculous flip. Fuck, this wolf and his smiles.

"Come back to mine?" I whispered before my brain had a chance to catch up with my mouth.

He gave me a crooked smile, but there was a sad light in his eyes. "You have no idea how much I want to say yes. But I can't stay for too long. I'd rather avoid being chucked in the doghouse again."

I let go of his hand and reached to drag his mouth back to mine. My fingers were centimeters from brushing his neck when he flinched. I frowned. "Are you hurt?"

He let out a huff of laughter that sounded more forced than genuine. "I'm good. Werewolf healing and all. The feel of the chain just lingers." He dropped his gaze like he couldn't meet my eyes anymore and my stomach gave a sickening twist.

"Aidan," I said, my voice suddenly hard. "What do you mean when you say doghouse?" Surely he wasn't referring to a *literal* fucking doghouse. And he definitely wasn't implying that someone had *chained* him to it like... like some *animal*. Hell, that was considered cruel to *actual* animals.

"Hey, I'm fine. I promise. Besides, I did kinda bring it on myself." He pressed his lips against mine, but I could barely return the sweet kiss. I was so distracted with rage.

What kind of pack tolerated its members treating each other like that? I had half a mind to go find the entire nest of mangy furballs and take out my bubbling fury on them. Not even werewolf healing could stand up against naga venom.

"Zahir." He gave me a light push, giving himself enough room to pull his shirt back into place and pulling me back from the dark thoughts. Though now I wanted more than ever for him to come back to my house, ideally where I'd lock him up and never let any of those bastards near him again. "Still with me, scales?" he prodded.

I let out a stuttering breath. The fact was, I didn't actually know who had done what—if anything. I was simply leaping to the worst case and getting myself all worked up like I always did. "How long do you have?" I finally asked. His slow smile made my heart hurt.

"Maybe another hour before I need to head back."

"Let me buy you some drinks?" I asked, tipping his nose with mine.

"Yes. And I can cover the tip." He pulled out a cluster of folded bills, the distinct color of an Indian rupee wrapped around them, and gave me a smirk.

"Wait a second. That's *my* money!" I shouted as I followed him out of the storage closet.

Chapter 11

Aidan

I fiddled with my phone as I scooted further down the aisle. Today's supply run was a little unusual, and not just because we planned on actually *paying* for most of what we left with. On top of that, there were five of us instead of the usual two and we'd ventured so far south-east we were practically in North Carolina. But I didn't care about that. The others could grab what we came for. I was more interested in the Wi-Fi signal from the shop next door and that for once I was in charge of one of the pack's shared cell phones.

Finally, I was close enough to pick up the signal. An excited squeak slipped past my lips. I quickly glanced back into the store, scanning to make sure no one had heard and was coming to investigate. Reassured that none of my nosey pack brothers had heard, I retreated to my shadowy corner. I chewed on my bottom lip as I pulled up a browser search.

<GAY SEX>

I hit enter and a loud moan from a pop-up ad immediately poured through the small speaker. I scrambled to mute the obscene—*and hot*—sound. Okay, maybe something less generic. I needed insight, not porn. At least, not right now. I ran a hand over my face and let out an awkward chuckle.

Zahir and I had hooked up a few times since I'd gotten out of the doghouse, mostly quickies in the backseat of his SUV. Nothing as intense as what we'd done at his place, but enough to keep me panting for more. What I wouldn't give to have the freedom, the time, to get lost in him again. Having him inside me felt better than I ever could have imagined. I was borderline desperate to experience the toe-curling, star-inducing sensation again. But as amazing as it felt, it'd be nice to understand *why*.

Maybe that was where I should start. I triple checked the volume was all the way down this time *and* on mute, before typing:

<WHY BUTT SEX FEELS GOOD>

This time I was ready for the "sponsored results". I skimmed past them and kept going until I found an article titled <u>The Magic of the Male Prostate</u>. Eyebrow raised, I opened the link and scanned the page. I skipped over the words that I didn't have a prayer of understanding, let alone pronouncing, but I got the general idea. It was some kind of spongy cluster of nerves that felt like fucking heaven when touched right.

Apparently, all guys had this "pro-state" thing, some even referred to it as the "P-spot". I chuckled at the obvious play on a G-spot. So... *not* snake magic, after all. Except snake magic sounded way cooler. I'd just stick with that. I kept scanning the article for any more helpful tidbits until my gaze caught on a sponsored link on the side of the page: <u>The Ins & Outs of Anal Sex</u>.

A little dubious about the title *and* the name of the website, I warily clicked on the link. Much to my surprise, the site was not only *not* a porn site, but actually looked really fucking legit. Now we were talking. I periodically glanced toward the entrance to my aisle as I read through the different pages and chewed on my nail.

I understood better why going too fast that morning had been an epic mistake. Why it eventually felt so fucking good. The monumental importance of lube, which boiled down to "there's no such thing as too much lube". I chuckled to myself again and skipped the links about dicks. Figured I had a pretty good grasp on those since I had one. If all else failed, I could come back to the site next time I was near Wi-Fi and had a modicum of privacy.

My thumb coasted over the smooth screen as I continued to scroll down. Then my gaze caught on a term I hadn't heard of before: Rimming. My eyes got wider and wider until I was positive they'd fall out of my head. Could werewolf healing fix popped eyeballs? I shook my head. More importantly, how did I convince Zahir to do this to me? Rimming sounded fucking *next level*.

I swallowed thickly, imagining the long tongue he'd used to clean my fingers sliding inside of me, teasing, tasting, *taking*. I stuffed my fist in my mouth to stifle a moan and closed the browser, reflexively clearing the search history. Communal phones *sucked*. Now I just needed my insanely hard dick to calm the fuck down before someone noticed and accused me of perving in the local market.

Once I was fairly confident that I had my situation under control, I slid the phone into my back pocket and ventured out of the aisle. I glanced around for one of the others to figure out where we were at with things. I still didn't understand why Bree, Carver, and Eliott needed to be here or why they'd chosen a place so far out of our way. There were plenty of markets closer to where we'd set up camp.

I spotted Scott's head, towering over a display, and was lifting my hand to get his attention when I caught the scent of an unfamiliar werewolf. I dropped my hand and twisted around, inhaling deeply to get a better heading. Cliche as it was, I followed my nose until I found the source a few aisles down. I stared in wonder at the slim, brunette woman with light tan skin that looked to be in her early twenties, by human standards, anyway.

Despite the smattering of strays the pack took in, I'd never actually met a werewolf that wasn't part of the Stormfire Pack. Most prospects were too young to be with the main pack, and there was always an adjustment period. Some chose not to stay. They vanished in the night without a word, never to be seen or heard from again. Whatever. It was their loss. If they wanted to wander around packless and slowly wither away into nothingness, that was their business.

I was still trying to figure out what to do with this unprecedented opportunity to *talk* to a werewolf from another pack when she turned and caught sight of me. Her delicate nostrils flared, and she yelped, clearly startled.

"Sorry, I didn't mean to spook you," I said, holding my hands up. "Hi, I'm Aidan."

She curled in on herself as she studied me with open wariness. My big ass grin probably wasn't helping the situation, but hell, if I could do anything about it. Finally, she unwrapped her arms from around her torso and I realized her right arm was a prosthetic. She tentatively raised her left hand in greeting. "Hi. I'm Pri."

"You from around here?" I asked, repressing the urge to ask about the arm. I'd never met a werewolf that had lost a whole limb before.

"You could say that. And you? Passing through?" There was an edge to her question that I couldn't place. "Where are you headed?" she pressed when I didn't immediately reply.

I shook off her strange tone, chalking it up to her obvious nerves. "I'm not headed anywhere. My pack set up a few towns over." I smiled broadly as a thought occurred to me. "Looks like we'll be in the area for a while. Maybe we could... bump into each other again sometime?"

Her walls immediately went back up, and she narrowed her gaze.

"Not like that!" I quickly added. "I just thought it'd be nice to chat with a wolf outside my pack."

Despite my reassurance that I wasn't awkwardly asking her out, her distrust continued to waft off of her, making my nose hair curl with its sharpness. "Who did you say your pack was?"

There was that edge again, and now *I* was getting nervous. Why wasn't she as excited as I was to bump into another *were* in the wild? "I'm with the Stormfire Pack." Confusion shone in her eyes, but didn't entirely replace the distrust. "You could say we're kind of nomadic. We pick a place, settle down for a while, then move on to the next," I added.

She took an angry step toward me and dropped her voice. "Does Alpha know you're here?"

"Of course, my Alpha knows I'm here. Why wouldn't he?" I replied, my face scrunching at the weird turn this chat had taken. "He knows all of us are here."

Her eyes widened, and she took a step back, the sour tang of fear suddenly tinging her scent. "How many is 'all of us'?"

Now I was really weirded out. Sure, I'd never talked to a *were* outside the pack before, but this couldn't be normal. Right? "There's just four of us here today. Five, if you count me." I caught sight of Scott's head off to the side and turned to flag him down. "I'll introduce you. Hey, Scott! I've got someone I want you to meet!" I huffed when he didn't respond and moved to go get him. That's when Pri screamed.

A few aisles over, Scott turned at the noise, then started making a beeline toward us. My hackles went up, and I spun back to face the young woman.

She shrank back against the shelving and held out an accusatory finger. "You... You're... You're one of *them*."

"What the fuck are you talking about?" I asked, stepping closer to her.

"Get away from me!" she screamed. I froze in my tracks, and her panicked gaze slipped over my shoulder. "You too. Don't come any closer. I mean it!"

"Would you stop yelling?" I asked under my breath. "Do you know us?"

She barked a laugh that sounded more like barely suppressed terror than humor. "Know you? I'll never forget you. And I'm never going back! Not ever!"

I was about to ask why she was freaking out when the hair on the back of my neck stood on end.

I turned enough to realize the rest of our party had gathered behind me. When I faced Pri again, her pupils were so dilated her eyes were nearly black and pure terror was rolling off of her in waves.

"I won't go back. I won't," she whispered, shaking her head and taking a step backward toward the unblocked end of the aisle. I felt as much as heard the others advance behind me.

"Would you cut it out? You're scaring her," I snapped.

"Be quiet, Aidan." I bristled at Scott's order and attempted to step toward Pri, only to have his meaty hand wrap around my bicep. At the move, Pri's fear seemed to crystallize.

"I'll die before I let the Order cage me again!" she shouted, inching farther down the aisle.

"That can be arranged." Eliott's sinister voice made my skin crawl, and the reality of the situation finally hit me. They had no intention of letting her leave alive.

I ripped my arm out of Scott's grasp and lurched forward. "Run!" I shouted, shoving Pri into motion.

She stumbled slightly, but didn't waste any time spinning on her heel and taking off down the aisle. The slap of her running feet on the linoleum floors filled my ears as I swiveled to face my packmates.

"Stop her!" Eliott shouted. "We can't let her leave!"

"Like hell you can't," I snarled and launched myself past him to barrel into Bree. We went down in a heap of limbs and angry shouts. By now, we were drawing attention from the other shoppers whose curiosity had won out over caution. Normally, I'd bitch about the stupidity of humans, but right now, I needed that stupidity. It would keep anyone from shifting and give Pri the best chance to get away.

Pri let out another ear-piercing scream, and I looked up to see Carter had blocked off her exit at the other end of the aisle. Bree took advantage of my moment of distraction to claw at my face. Pain burned along my cheek as one of her nails pierced skin. I rolled off of her, kicking at her ribs, before pushing off the ground to tackle Eliott.

His face slammed into the ground with a loud crack that would have made me grin if I wasn't so desperate to keep him and the others from killing Pri. Who'd. Done. Nothing. Wrong.

"You'll suffer for this!" Eliott screeched, writhing to get out of my grasp. "The doghouse is too good for you. I'll see your head on a spike!"

I kept his face pressed against the ground and risked a glance up. Pri was struggling to get past Carter's larger frame in the narrow aisle and looked on the verge of a shift. Desperate to help her get away before the others followed through with Eliott's dire promise to kill her, I flailed blindly for something to throw. My fingers bumped into smooth plastic and I clutched at what turned out to be an economy-size shampoo bottle.

Eliott nearly slipped free, forcing me to bear all of my weight down to keep him pinned. I just hoped the angle of my throw wasn't too off as I lobbed the bottle as hard as I could at Carter. I held my breath as it tumbled through the air in slow motion, then crashed into Carter's shoulder hard enough to explode.

He snarled, shooting a glare in my direction, and Pri mercifully took the opening. Unfortunately, even distracted and dripping shampoo, Carter was fast. Pri barely managed two steps before he grabbed her arm. I couldn't help but grin as I realized which arm he'd snagged. Between one blink and the next, Pri had ripped free and Carter was left holding her prosthetic arm, looking dumbstruck.

I had exactly one second to appreciate that she was actually going to get away when firm hands yanked me off of Eliott. I flailed in the air, but there was no escaping Scott's hold. "Let me go!" I howled.

Eliott flashed Scott a scathing look. "So much as a hair of him gets free and you'll be paying the same price," he snarled. "Take him outside."

I had half a mind to ask about the supplies we were supposedly here for, but not even *I* was that stupid. So I kept my mouth shut as Scott "escorted" me out to the truck. No sooner did he shove me into the cab than Bree and Carter jogged up.

"Well?" Eliott barked.

The two shared a look. "She got away," Carter said, sloughing shampoo off of his arm onto the ground.

"Her car was already halfway down the road by the time we got out here," Bree added, sparing me a nasty look. I bared my teeth at her in return.

"Fuck! This is going to change our timeline. Garrett will *not* be happy." I had exactly two seconds to wonder what the hell Eliott was talking about before his face filled the open door of the cab. "You're going to pay for this. I'll make sure of it."

"Go fuck your—" Scott's fist slammed into my face, cutting me off and plunging me into darkness.

Chapter 12

Aidan

When I regained consciousness, I was in a dark room. Not that the dark bothered me, especially since I had nightvision. The pounding in my head was another matter. Scott must have broken more than just my nose for my face to still be hurting this badly. That asshole had some serious payback coming his way.

I took a step toward the door and the clink of metal on metal turned my blood to ice. With shaking hands, I reached up to feel my neck, already knowing what I would find. My fingertips brushed against unforgiving metal already warmed to my body temp.

A howl of despair ripped free of my throat as I clawed at the thick metal. "No, no no no no," I panted hopelessly. In my desperation, my fingers lengthened to claws. But for every sliver of metal I gouged out, I lost a claw, until only bloody, half-healed nubs remained.

I gave up trying to rip off the sturdy collar and let my hands return to normal. The tang of blood clouded the air as I hooked my raw fingers over the jagged edge I'd created and held it away as far from my throat as I could manage while I tried to get a handle on my breathing.

I fought back the sting of tears and rising panic as I looked around the room for any hint of where I was. My first guess would have been a closet, but the space was too big and had a concrete floor. Some kind of shed, maybe? I listened intently to see if I could pluck out any sounds to clue me in. But no matter how I strained my ears, nothing stuck out. No voices, no steady hum of traffic, not even the subtle sound of bodies moving around.

The weight of how wrong this was dropped me to my knees. Why wasn't I at the house? Even the doghouse would at least have been familiar. This isolation had me even more anxious than the industrial collar. What was happening? At a loss for what else to do, I threw back my head and let out a long, mournful howl.

A few seconds later, the door opened and light spilled in. I flinched away from the sudden brightness, blinking rapidly to bring the backlit figure into focus.

"You can cut that shit out," Elliot said, leaning on the frame.

I snarled and barely remembered that lunging at him would be a horrible mistake with the chain around my neck. "Fuck. You."

He bared his teeth at me. "I've waited for this a long time. Looks like you've finally fucked up one time too many. I can't wait to see what Garrett does to you. I heard he has Devin mixing up a batch of the training serum."

Cold settled over me despite my naturally elevated body temperature. That shit hadn't been a picnic when I was twelve. I'd been relieved when I'd finally mastered my shift enough not to need it. I swallowed hard and fought to shake off the sudden spike of fear. If I could survive it then, I could survive it now.

Elliot cocked his head to the side and gave me a sinister grin. "Did I mention it won't be the kiddie stuff? It's a special batch. Just. For. You." He stepped deeper into the room, stopping just out of my reach. Even with the lack of light in the room, I could see the hatred shining in his eyes. "I'm going to enjoy every second of your suffering. Maybe I'll even get Garrett to let me participate. I'd love nothing more than to cut into you until you scream for mercy."

"What the fuck is your problem?!" I finally snapped. "I've never done *anything* to you!" Well, nothing that he didn't start first. I tugged slightly at the chain holding me to the wall before stopping. "Why do you hate me so much?"

For all the nasty looks Eliott had given me over the years, I'd never seen any that came close to the unbridled hatred that twisted his face now. "Because it should have been you. *She* should have lived and *you* should have been put down like the dog you are," he said so forcefully, spittle actually hit my face.

I was still struggling to understand who or what the hell he was talking about when another figure darkened the doorway.

"We're ready," Devin declared in his gruff voice.

Sick glee replaced Eliott's twisted snarl. "This is going to be fun." He stepped back to let Devin and someone else into the room. Scott's familiar scent of oil and charcoal hit my nose as the chain holding me was disconnected from the wall.

"Scott?" I whispered in disbelief. I'd always known he was my keeper, but I'd also thought he was at least a little my friend.

"Shut your traitorous mouth, or I'll shut it for you," Devin threatened. He waved for Scott to go ahead. Scott yanked on the chain and I stumbled after him in a daze out of the dark room.

I winced against the bright sun as we exited what turned out to be an old barn. Once my eyes adjusted, I glanced around in search of the rest of the pack, but the only people I saw were my grisly escort and the cluster of lieutenants waiting by a post topped with a metal ring. I didn't need to know what they planned to do to me or why a "special" batch of the training serum had been made. I knew I didn't want any part of it and I definitely didn't want to be tied like an animal for slaughter.

Self-preservation kicked in and I fought against Scott's firm hold, clawing once again at the metal encircling my throat. Blood slicked my neck, though it was a toss up if it was from the shredded edges of the collar or my own claws digging into the flesh. A steel-toed boot cracked into my back and I went sprawling into the dirt mere yards from the hitching post. I scrambled frantically to get my footing back under me while I fought a tide of panic.

"Enough!" Garrett's deep booming voice cut across the otherwise empty yard.

I stopped moving, frozen in a hunched position while uncontrollable shaking wracked my body.

"Bring him here," Alpha ordered, unmistakable fury lacing his voice.

It wasn't until the chain holding me rattled through the ring that I found my tongue. "Don't do this. They were going to kill her! I didn't do—"

A hard fist slammed into my mouth, sending shockwaves of pain through my jaw and loosening a few teeth. "What did I say?" Devin growled.

I whimpered, but wisely kept my mouth shut this time. I felt as much as heard Eliott's snicker, but I was way past having pride. It'd be a miracle if I survived this punishment. Something deep down told me I wouldn't, that I wasn't supposed to. Eliott would finally get what he'd always wanted—me gone *for good*. Knowing that he apparently had a *reason* didn't do shit for me now.

"Stand him up," Garrett barked.

No sooner was I fully upright than another fist landed in my gut, causing me to double back over. Someone yanked my head back, and I awkwardly stared at Alpha, the *were* who was supposed to protect and guide the pack—*me*—and who was currently looking at me like I was worse than dog shit on his boots.

He grabbed my chin with a bruising grip. "You have put this entire pack in jeopardy. By helping that wolf escape, you have put every last one of your packmates' lives in danger. You've betrayed your pack, and I have no tolerance for traitors." Garrett's growl rolled through me, making me queasy.

I desperately wanted to argue that I hadn't done any of those things. I loved my pack. I was *loyal*, dammit. But most importantly, I wanted to know how preventing the death of an innocent wolf was betrayal.

Garrett held out his free hand, and someone—Devin, probably—placed a syringe in it. I reflexively jerked as Garrett brought the obscenely thick needle to bear on my neck. He tightened his hold on my jaw, his eyes dark with barely banked fury, and sank the needle into the soft tissue that had only recently healed from my misguided attempt to escape.

I cried out as he ruthlessly pushed the cool liquid into my body. The warped metal of the collar sliced into my neck again as I spasmed, painfully aware of every drop of the serum as it flooded my system, burning like acid and instantly making me feel weak. Eliott hadn't been exaggerating. This was *not* the same stuff I'd been exposed to when I first joined the pack. It was a thousand times worse.

My veins felt like someone had set them on fire. But what was worse was that the feeling kept going. It didn't subside as my werewolf healing kicked in. Almost as if... My eyes widened in horror as I realized my enhanced healing wasn't kicking in at all. I willed my hand to grow claws, my arm to sprout fur, my teeth to elongate... *anything*. But no matter what I tried, no matter how hard I concentrated, nothing happened.

Blind panic seized me and I thrashed against my restraint, mindless of the metal cutting into me or Garrett's unforgiving hold on the verge of shattering my jaw. No. This wasn't right. I hadn't done anything wrong! I opened my mouth to say exactly that, only to have Garrett twist my head to the side so I could vomit all over the ground. The others sneered in disgust, but none moved to intervene.

"What do you have to say for yourself?" Garrett asked, his voice every bit as hard as his gaze.

I panted through my mouth, still reeling from the effects of the suped-up serum. "She... she... didn't do... anything."

"Maybe not. But you did. I was hoping it wouldn't come to this. We can't afford to lose any of our kind, but you never could get it. I gave you chance after chance, and you kept finding ways to fuck it up."

My gaze darted around in search of support, anyone who could say that he was wrong, then my gaze landed on Eliott's smug face. I snarled. If I'd fucked up, it had been because he made sure of it.

Garrett released my face, which immediately began throbbing. "Don't kill him. Get me when it's time to give him another dose."

"Sure thing, Alpha," one of the lieutenants replied. I was too distracted learning that I'd be given *more* of the serum to notice who. Garrett stepped back and the rest of them closed in. I couldn't say whose claws ripped into me first, but I'd put money that it was Eliott's.

My feet dragged along the ground as I was taken out of the tack room for the latest round of beating. Not a single inch of me had been spared. Dried blood crusted barely healed wounds that ripped open with every breath. I'd stopped trying to inventory broken bones or how many times I'd been injected. At least I'd stopped puking every time they administered the serum. Though that might have had just as much to do with not having anything to throw up.

The guys carrying me dropped me in the dirt at the foot of the post. I squinted through swollen eyes, grateful that it was later in the day and not so bright. There was no telling how long they'd been holding me. All I knew was that no one else from the pack ever came here and I'd seriously underestimated Eliott's mean streak. Besides taking part in the torture, he regularly popped in to taunt me. He talked more about this girl that should have lived instead of me, but I still didn't know how that was connected. The only girl that came to mind was the one that had joined the Stormfire Pack when I had, but hadn't survived the change. I couldn't even remember her face, let alone how I could be responsible for her death.

Metal clattered through the ring on the post, and the tightening of my chain jerked my head upward. I didn't bother to try standing. Even if I could muster the energy, what was the point? They'd just knock me back down. Then they'd beat the ever-loving shit out of me like they did every day, but only after shooting me up with the serum again, which I swore was getting more potent with each dose.

"Stand him up," Alpha ordered.

Immediately, strong hands yanked me up by my arms. It took my feet a second to remember how to hold me and I vaguely registered I'd lost one of my boots. I swayed in place and stared bleary-eyed at the scar running across Garrett's face. The firm grip on my biceps remained. Without them, I probably would have collapsed back to the ground.

"I've got the latest dose. Though I think we might be pushing how much monkshood we can use without outright killing him." Devin's voice sounded distant, like he was underwater or something. Or maybe I was the one under water.

"So be it. I grow tired of this. I was planning to kill him soon, anyway. He's already ruined our timeline enough as it is," Garrett grumbled, sounding bored and irritated.

I could have sagged with relief that it would finally be over if I wasn't being forcibly held up. I'd made my peace that this would be how it ended. My only regret was that I didn't get to see Zahir one more time. I doubted he felt the same, but it was a nice fantasy imagining that someone actually liked me enough to wonder where I was, maybe even worried.

"Wait," Eliott said as Garrett reached for my head, presumably to snap my neck.

Alpha paused and shot him an angry glower. For one tiny second, I actually thought he'd smack him for daring to stop him. Then I realized *Eliott* was advocating for me *not* to die?

Eliott cleared his throat and moved into my line of sight. "No disrespect, Alpha, I just know you want this traitorous dog to suffer as much as possible before dying. And honestly, death is too good for him." The considering look on Garrett's face made my stomach turn.

"What did you have in mind?" he asked.

I held my breath in anticipation of whatever fresh horror Eliott was about to suggest. Because of course he didn't want to spare my life. He wasn't done torturing me yet.

"Exile." At his single word, all the air left my lungs, leaving me even more lightheaded than I already was.

No. *NO.* I summoned strength I didn't even know I still had and attempted to launch myself at Garrett. Maybe I could force his hand.

"See?" Eliott continued as he watched me struggle uselessly. "I vote we give him the latest shot and set him loose." Garrett's responding growl raised my hackles, but didn't phase Eliott in the least. "Think of it like a head start. We'll shift with the rest of the pack tonight and circle around. It's not like he'll get far in his condition. We can hunt him down like the pathetic dog he is. Worse case, somehow he gets far enough away and still dies a slow and painful death from being packless."

Garrett clapped him on the shoulder, and I could have screamed. "I like the way you think. Do it," he ordered, angling his chin at Devin. I didn't even have a chance to brace myself before he stabbed the needle into my arm.

"What about this?" Devin asked, tapping the empty syringe against the metal holding me in place.

"Leave the collar. I want anyone who sees him to know him for what he is."

The rough metal bit into my raw neck as someone gripped the chain and broke it a few links from where the lock held the collar in place, causing me to choke. I collapsed to the dirt, coughing and spluttering. When I looked up, it was to see a collection of disgusted expressions. Then Eliott's face filled my vision.

"Better run along, little doggy. We'll be hunting you later." He patted my cheek and straightened. Then he and the others turned and left without so much as a backward glance.

I waited, huddled on the ground, for them to return. With each second that passed, the sun sank lower behind the trees and dread grew from the pit of my stomach to encompass my whole being. I glanced around and cautiously got to my feet, clinging to the post for support. After another long pause, I took a shaky step toward the woods. When no one immediately appeared to stop me, I took another, and another, until I was stumbling as fast as my abused body would go in the opposite direction. East. Toward the bar. Toward Zahir.

Chapter 13

Zahir

I finished my latest circuit of the living room and picked up my phone for the millionth time. It had taken some doing—namely going to *The Oasis* and begging Arnie for information—but I'd finally tracked down another werewolf in the area. Ezra Thatcher owned a local garage that served everything from diesel trucks to motorcycles. When I'd first heard that, I'd gotten excited that maybe, just maybe, I'd found a place where Aidan would have been seen. Then I recalled Aidan mentioning offhand that he did a lot of the repairs and maintenance for his pack's bikes. Also, apparently, Ezra had never heard of Aidan or anyone even remotely matching Aidan's description. Nor had he ever heard of a werewolf motorcycle gang.

None of that mattered after three weeks of increasingly desperate searching turned up nothing. I was next to useless at the temple. My studies had taken a serious hit. Truth be told, it was a miracle my mother hadn't been hounding me, or worse, flown from India to put me back on track. I suspected Guru Angira had something to do with that, though there was no telling how long she'd extend her enlightened level of patience.

Suddenly, it was all too much. I couldn't take it anymore. I tossed the phone at the couch, where it bounced off and landed with a thud on the floor. "This is insane. *I'm* insane! I just need to accept that he's done with me. Fooling around was fun, but that was all it was ever going to be." Except my heart didn't believe that. We may not have known each other long, but I was convinced that even if Aidan was done with hooking up, he'd have the decency to tell me rather than ghost me.

I laced my fingers behind my head and released a guttural sound of frustration. If I was being honest with myself, I was more than frustrated—I was worried. Yes, Aidan was a fully grown werewolf, more than capable of taking care of himself. Still, I couldn't shake the soul-deep feeling that something was horribly wrong. My eyes stung, and I quickly tilted my head back in an attempt to prevent the imminent tears from slipping free.

"Why didn't I get your number?" I asked the empty room, my throat tight with suppressed emotion. I couldn't afford to lose it if I wanted even a prayer of ever finding him again. "Fuck," I groaned, the despair wrapping ruthlessly around my chest, "I don't even know your surname."

Defeat weighed me down until I wasn't sure how I was still standing, let alone breathing. Maybe him being MIA wouldn't have been so bad if I wasn't so sure that he was in trouble, that he *needed* me. I huffed a bitter laugh. That sounded ridiculous, even in my head.

I closed my eyes and whispered a prayer. "Vishnu, please let me find him. Let him be—"

A thump against the front door cut me off mid-plea. I dropped my hands and warily approached the door. It was well past dark, and I wasn't expecting anyone. It wasn't like I knew a ton of people in the area and those I did would have called or texted. Plus, that had definitely *not* been a knock. I took a steadying breath and peered through the peephole.

At first, all I could see was darkness. I flicked the switch for the front porch light, then cursed under my breath when I remembered I hadn't gotten around to replacing it. Movement caught my eye and something scraped along the door, making my skin ripple with the urge to bring out my scales. I was about to give it up and retreat deeper into the house and probably pre-dial animal control when the clouds outside parted and the light of the full moon flooded my front yard.

I sucked in a shocked breath. Whatever was at my door was definitely not an animal. In fact, it looked almost like... I was undoing the locks and ripping back the deadbolt before my brain could even finish the thought. I threw open the door and stared in horror at the blood-covered sight of a man.

The figure swayed in place as if fighting to remain upright, then slowly raised his head. He peered at me through eyes damn near swollen shut, the sliver of bright blue confirming what my heart already knew. This wasn't just any man, it was Aidan.

"What happened?" I asked, desperately wanting to drag him inside and wrap him up, but terrified of hurting him even more.

"I didn't know where else to go," he croaked, his voice so dry and rough I half expected him to cough out rust. When he did cough, a fine mist of blood coated his lips, then he collapsed.

I lurched forward to catch him, but only succeeded in breaking his fall. I carefully maneuvered him around so I was cradling his head and brushed the hair back from his face. I choked back a pained sob when I realized it was matted to his face with blood and lodged in open wounds. "Aidan, what happened?"

His eyes remained firmly closed and his breathing was so shallow I could barely make it out over my thundering heart. A light breeze drifted over us, reminding me we were sitting in the

open doorway. I needed to get him inside, cleaned up, and call...
someone.

I shifted beneath him, prepared to drag him inside as carefully
as you can drag an unconscious body. My gaze caught on his
bloody feet. One shoe was split like it had been put through a
shredder and there wasn't even a shoe on his other foot. Had he
run here?

Cold washed over me as I slowly lifted my gaze from his
battered body to the moon hanging low in the night sky. The
full moon. Aidan was a werewolf and he was still in his human
shape. Granted, I knew little about the intricacies of being a
werewolf, but even I knew that wasn't right.

"Aidan," I said, trying and failing to keep the rising panic
from my voice. "Aidan." I shook him gently, then more forcefully when he didn't respond. "Aidan, sweetheart, look at me.
Aidan!" my voice cracked on the pained shout, even then he
didn't so much as twitch.

With significantly more determination, I looped my arms
under his shoulders and dragged him inside. Picking him up
probably would have been a hell of a lot easier, but I was worried
attempting to do so would cause more damage. I was all set to
drag him clear across the house to the bedroom when I noticed
the smear of blood his body was leaving in its wake.

I carefully laid him down in the living room, then hurriedly
shut the door, ignoring the streaks of blood now coloring it. For
a second, I just stood there, dragging in sharp breaths, unsure of
what to do next. My gaze caught once more on the trail of blood.
I raced into the kitchen and soaked every towel I could find, then
took the soggy pile back to the other room where I dropped
them unceremoniously next to where Aidan still hadn't moved.

I knelt beside him and picked up the first towel with a shaking
hand. As carefully as if I was touching the world's finest glass, I
brushed the damp cloth across his cheek. I bit back a sob when,

after only a few passes, fresh blood replaced the dried I'd cleared. This was wrong. So wrong. Why wasn't he healing? Why wasn't he in his wolf form?

I nearly fell over in my hurry to secure my cell phone from where it had ended up beneath the coffee table. Thankfully, I'd called this number enough times by now that it was the first to pop up.

The line rang and the second the call connected, I blurted, "Ezra, don't hang up."

"What the fuck do you want?" Ezra asked gruffly. "Haven't you badgered me enough in the last two weeks?" Okay, so he wasn't wrong, but he was also the only werewolf contact I had.

"I found him. Aidan. He's at my place now."

"Thank fuck! Now you can leave me the hell alo—"

"He's not healing. He's hurt really badly, but he's not healing, like at all." Abruptly, I realized I was on the phone with a werewolf during the full moon. "Shouldn't you be out running or something?" I asked, momentarily sidetracked.

He huffed. "I just got back from my run. But more importantly, go back to the other thing. What do you mean, he's not healing? How severe are the wounds?"

"Uh..." My gaze flicked over Aidan, but between the blood, mud, and who knew what else, it was difficult to tell the extent of his injuries. "I'm going to go with severe-severe, but it's not those that have me worried. Well, not just those. It's the superficial cuts. He has some on his face, but they won't stop bleeding. Why isn't he healing, Ezra? Have you ever heard of something like this? Can werewolves be hemophiliacs?" I asked, grasping at straws. I didn't think Aidan was given I'd seen him with healed scratches before.

"No, I've never heard of anything like this before. Um..." There was a muffled noise on the other end, like Ezra was moving around. "Okay, keep cleaning him up and do what you can to stop the bleeding. I'm going to make some calls and see if I can find anything out."

I nodded.

"Zahir? Did you hear me?"

"Y-yeah. Clean him up. You'll call back." I was fairly sure Ezra said something else, but it was taking every ounce of willpower I had to keep it together. The line died, and the phone fell from my numb fingers. Clean him up. I could do that. I picked up a fresh towel, still mercifully damp, and resumed carefully trying to remove the grime from Aidan's face. I was almost out of clean towels by the time I got to his neck.

I delicately wiped at the hard edges of scabbed skin. My finger brushed against something smooth and for a terrified second, I thought it was bone. I quickly reined in my overactive imagination and wiped with more purpose, though the rag I was using was solid red now. Finally, I managed to clear enough of the blood—old and fresh—to see the source of the mysterious smoothness. Metal. No, not just metal. A collar.

What was left of my control shattered. An unearthly wail filled the room that I only vaguely recognized as coming from me. I didn't even register that I'd shifted to my naga form until I reached out to rip the metal from around his neck. But no matter how hard I tried or what angle I came at it, I couldn't get a good enough hold. What was worse, every failed effort caused the shredded metal to cut into his neck more. Still, he didn't move. He didn't even cry out in pain, though it had to be immense.

My entire body shook as I did the only thing I could think of. I curled around Aidan in my naga form, carefully cradling his head in my lap, and waited for Ezra to call back.

Chapter 14

Zahir

I lost track of time as I listened to Aidan's struggling breaths, my hand placed over his heart so I could feel each pained beat. I'd tried to categorize his injuries, but there was too much blood to make out much of anything. My living room looked like a murder had taken place and I couldn't have cared less. I just wanted Aidan to wake up.

A few feet away, my phone hopped and buzzed with an incoming call. I plucked it up with my tail and brought it closer. A relieved breath whooshed out of me when I saw Ezra's name on the screen. I stopped stroking Aidan's cheek with my free hand and answered.

"What have you found?" I asked without preamble.

"Hey, I'm sorry it took me so long to get back to you. I called a few friends, then called my Alpha to see if he had anything."

"And?" I asked, not liking the tightness of his voice.

"And..." He let out a heavy breath that sounded far too much like a resigned sigh for my liking. "And we've got nothing. No one has ever heard of something like this or has any idea what could cause it. Alpha still has people searching the Pack archives, but doesn't expect to find anything."

It took me a moment to realize the high-pitched whine wasn't coming from the phone, but from me.

"I know. I know." There was a muffled sound like Ezra had run his hand over his face. "If Alpha finds something, he'll let me know ASAP. Is there anything I can do? Is he conscious?"

"No. He passed out shortly after arriving and hasn't stirred since. As for help..." I glanced at the shine of metal encircling Aidan's throat and swallowed thickly. "Do you have bolt cutters? I can text you my address."

"Bolt cutters? I mean, I have some, but what do you need them for?"

"There's a... there's *something* around his neck. I tried to get it off but..." I trailed off, recalling how my fingers had slipped on fresh rivulets of blood and the awful squelch of the metal tugging free of where it had embedded in the flesh.

A hardness entered Ezra's already gruff voice. "What is around his neck, Zahir? Zahir, answer me. Is he wearing a collar?!"

I winced at the word. "You'll see when you get here." I hung up without waiting for a reply, sent him the address, then dropped the phone on the blood-stained carpet and curled back around Aidan. "Help is coming," I whispered. "I'm going to take care of you, sweetheart. You're going to be okay. Just stay with me." I placed a kiss on a miraculously still clean patch of skin.

It could have been a couple of minutes or a couple of hours when a knock came at the door. I lifted my head and stared at the door a moment before registering that I hadn't responded.

"It's open," I called, my voice raw and weak, probably from all the wailing. I was about to try again, louder, when the knob turned and the door opened. To my surprise, Guru Angira stepped inside the small house.

She stood a few feet inside, taking in the scene. She'd pulled her wispy gray hair into a bun and wore a baby blue kurta pant set that at once made her look ancient and oddly youthful. It occurred to me I'd rarely, if ever, seen her in her human form. She looked at Aidan's still form, her gaze traveling over him as if assessing the extent of his injuries.

"What are you doing here?" I asked.

"You have been absent from your lessons," she replied. I wasn't sure if that was intended to be a statement of fact or a criticism. Her gaze finally reached me and I curled tighter around Aidan, as if some part of me feared she might try to take me away from him. "I am glad Mr. Thatcher called, though I can't help but wish you had."

The words sounded like censure, but there was only compassion in her brown eyes. "Ezra called you? Why would he do that?" I croaked. I wanted to ask how he even knew her, but that was a question for another time.

"Because I was hoping she'd have a better idea of what the fuck is going on than I do," Ezra replied, walking through the front door carrying an industrial pair of bolt cutters. He nudged the door shut with the heel of his boot and walked over. He sucked in a breath as he took in Aidan's state. "Mother of the moon, this is awful. What the hell happened to him?"

I absently stroked Aidan's hair back. Not that it moved much, since it was still matted with blood. "I don't know. Thank you for bringing the cutters. I noticed a lock on the back when I was trying to get the... *it* off earlier."

Ezra squatted down beside me. "This is fucking barbaric," he whispered harshly, then glanced over his shoulder at Gurudevi. "Sorry about the language."

"Oh no, I believe this situation warrants a good deal of 'what the fuck'."

I blinked, taken aback at her unexpectedly crass language.

"You do what you must. From the look of things, it seems more towels are in order." She nodded curtly, then held up a hand when I shifted to retrieve them. "I will see to it. Stay with your wolf."

A little relieved that I wouldn't have to leave Aidan's side, I turned to Ezra. Given my reaction to discovering the collar, I probably shouldn't have been surprised by the rage darkening his face. "What can I do?"

Ezra shook his head, though his eyes remained tight. "Could you lean him forward so I can get a better look at what we're working with?"

I carefully maneuvered Aidan like he asked, prompting several wounds to start freely bleeding again. I kept my focus trained on where Ezra was inspecting the collar.

"Here," Gurudevi said, handing down a cup of warm water. "Try rinsing the area." I could have tail whipped myself for not thinking of that sooner.

Using a combination of poured water and freshly rinsed towels, we painstakingly removed a fair amount of blood—dried and fresh—to reveal the collar in all its gruesome glory. Ezra let out a low, menacing growl as he delicately traced jagged scores in the thick metal. The collar had to be at least an inch thick and weighed a ton. It was also those scores that had continued to slice Aidan open when I tried to remove the collar myself.

"One thing is for sure, he could still shift when they put this on him. Looks like he tried to tear it off. Unfortunately, that's also means the metal has fused to the wounds." Ezra glanced at me. "Taking this off won't be pretty. We'll need to go very slowly so we don't cause more harm and to prevent him from bleeding out."

I swallowed thickly and nodded my head, my throat too tight for words. I'd suspected as much. "Have you heard anything else?" I asked, not really expecting a response.

Ezra paused in positioning the bolt cutters to take out the lock. "Actually, yeah. It's not as helpful as I would have wished, but it's something." He finished lining up the wicked sharp cutters, and I had to bite my tongue from demanding he tell me what he found. We all winced at the brutal clang of the lock snapping. Ezra set the bolt cutters aside and met my gaze with a heavy sigh. "Some of my pack came to us after getting away from some really bad people. Not *weres*," he added, as if sensing my unspoken question.

"Was their account similar to what we are seeing now?" Gurudevi asked, pausing in her efforts to clean more of Aidan.

"That's where it gets weird. Yes... and no. This kind of violence was definitely done by another *were*. And they didn't mention anything about collars, but they're also still working on recovering from the trauma of what they went through. What *is* similar is the lack of healing. Some recalled being injected with something that slowed and sometimes even stopped their natural healing abilities."

I shifted, my tail curling in anticipation while a small ember of hope burned in my chest. "And? Do they know what it is? How to stop it?"

Ezra's defeated look said it all. "No, and no. They said it eventually wears off. So our biggest hurdle right now is keeping your guy alive long enough for his body to metabolize whatever he was given. Not knowing more, that could be a few hours... or a few days."

My face crumpled as despair sat heavily on my chest, crushing the air from my lungs. "And the collar?" I asked, my voice so faint, it was a wonder he heard it even with werewolf hearing.

"We'll have to go really slowly, use a lot of fresh water, and," he glanced at the veritable mountain of cloth Gurudevi had accumulated, "probably all of those."

"Okay." I took a deep breath and released it slowly, mentally preparing for what we were about to do. "Okay," I said again. Ezra nodded. Then the three of us worked together to remove the warped collar.

When all was said and done, we'd not only gone through every towel, but had to rinse and reuse them multiple times. In addition, while Aidan was still a mess, we'd managed to get him clean enough to dress some of his more glaring wounds. The claw marks decorating most of his body were alarming, to say the least, but the raw skin peeking from the bandage around his neck made my stomach turn.

We took a break to eat—not that I could stomach much of anything—and cleaned the living room so it looked a little less like a crime scene. Through it all, Ezra kept an ear out for Aidan's breathing. No one said anything, but we were all equally surprised that Aidan had never once stirred during our ministrations... and that he was still breathing at all. It was shallow and labored, but it was *there*.

The early morning light that I normally loved to bathe in, especially while I was in my naga form, filtered through the windows. I stared at the blinds, struggling to understand when night had turned to day. Finally, I blinked and looked down at Aidan's arm, which I'd absently been petting, though I'd be lying if I said it wasn't more to comfort myself.

It had been difficult to find any part of him that felt safe enough to touch. Just because he was unresponsive didn't mean I was willing to cause him additional harm. I sighed quietly as I stroked the surprisingly soft hair of his arm and suddenly wondered why it was so much lighter than his brown hair. Unsurprisingly, my gaze drifted to one of the shallower cuts criss-crossing his forearm. No sooner did I register the wound was no longer trickling blood than it slowly came together. The skin fused until all that remained was the faintest blemish of a scar. I sucked in a breath and the other two immediately raced over.

"What is it?" Ezra asked.

"Has he bled through one of the bandages again?" Gurudevi asked at the same time.

"He... he *healed*. Right there." I pointed to the barely visible, thin line on his forearm.

Ezra scrubbed his hands over his face and dropped his head back. "Thank the moon."

I glanced up as Gurudevi placed a gentle hand on my shoulder. "It will likely still take time, but this is a good sign. His healing is returning."

"She's right, but this is what we were hoping for. I think... I think he's going to be okay." Ezra gazed dubiously at the multitude of towels obscuring the horror that had been inflicted on my cocky fur ball. "Or as okay as anyone can be after being through whatever happened to him."

Gurudevi nodded sagely. "His wounds will certainly be more than skin deep. He will need care." Abruptly, her gaze turned sharp and demanding, reminding me uncomfortably of a look my maa gave me. "Care that you cannot provide if you are dead on your tail. Once we have gone, I expect you to rest. As for your practice, it will keep for the meantime. But you *will* call me immediately if things here take a turn or if you need any assistance. Is that understood, Zahir Khatri?"

I swallowed hard. Clearly, I wasn't getting away with not calling her. "Understood, Guru Angira," I responded humbly, bowing slightly over prayer hands, then turned to Ezra. "Sorry for blowing up your phone and thank you for coming."

He shrugged. "I don't know how other packs do it, but in mine, we look after our own. But, yeah, call me if you need anything and I'll pass on anything I hear from the pack."

We finished saying our goodbyes, and they left. As much as I wanted a shower and to pass out for a week, I dallied, watching the steady rise and fall of Aidan's chest from where we'd moved him to the couch. Something Ezra said kept playing in my mind, and each time it ran around, it bothered me more. *His pack looked after their own.*

Where was Aidan's pack? And why had they let this happen to him?

Chapter 15

Aidan

Everything hurt. Which could only mean one thing: I was alive. Which was great and all, except I had no clue how. Or where I was, for that matter. I cautiously cracked my eyes and was more than a little surprised to see dust motes dancing in soft sunlight. It took me a second to pinpoint why that felt noteworthy, then it all rushed in. The darkness, the pain... the exile.

My stomach cramped violently, but there was nothing in it. Hadn't been for some time. On cue, my stomach released a savage growl. I quickly glanced around for the tormentors that had never been too far. My packmates. My *former* packmates, I mentally corrected myself and tried to ignore the sharp pain slicing across my heart. I may not have gotten along with everyone, but they were still my pack, my family.

Suddenly, my surroundings registered. I was in a house, possibly an apartment, lying on the biggest, squishiest couch ever. I fought back the anxiety threatening to strangle me at waking up in an unfamiliar place, even if it was an improvement over the shuttered tack room. The harsh smell of cleaning chemicals wove through the air, so potent that it almost completely eclipsed the iron tang of blood. I wrinkled my nose at the sour undercurrent tainting the blood. On a whim, I plucked at what remained of my shirt and sniffed it, then promptly gagged. Finding food could wait. I needed this awful smell off of me before my stomach could find something to toss up.

It wasn't until I'd sat up and stood on shaky legs that I realized I recognized the room, which was definitely in a house. A smirk twitched at my lips. Small wonder it had taken me a minute. I'd been pretty fucking distracted with getting a certain snake naked the last time I'd been here. Now that I finally knew *where* I was, I just had to figure out *how*. Most of the journey—if it could be called that—was a blur. And while I was at it, where the hell was Zahir?

I scrubbed at my face, immediately regretting the decision, as it became uncomfortably clear that while my face was somehow magically clean, my hands were not. Thoroughly disgusted, I carefully peeled off my clothes, mindful of the millions of tender spots decorating my body. Once everything was in a heap that I vowed to burn as soon as I could, I set out for the bathroom.

Of course, the only restroom I knew of was the one off the bedroom. So I padded naked across the house and quietly opened the door. Even after everything I'd been through the last several days—fuck, I hoped it was just days—my heart stuttered and my breath caught at the sight of the man sprawled across the bed. Zahir truly was a beautiful man, even fully clothed, his arm flung over his eyes to block the light, and a light bit of drool pooling on the pillow from his parted lips.

I flicked a glance at the bathroom. Even though I was positive he already had, I didn't want Zahir to see me like this—injured, pathetic, tossed aside. I darted into the bathroom with the grace of a startled chipmunk, closed the door, then strained to hear the telltale signs that I'd woken him. When I was satisfied that he was still firmly out, I sagged against the door and looked up. Unfortunately, it was right into my reflection.

I grimaced at seeing my sorry state. Alley strays were in better condition. My eyes were sunken and shadowed. Blood covered so much of me it almost doubled as the clothing I'd ditched. And I didn't even want to think about how much weight I'd lost. I wasn't the biggest *were* on the best of days. Goddess, help me if I had to be in a fight. Which reminded me. I glanced down at my hand and willed it to shift. A faint tingle buzzed beneath the skin, but nothing happened.

I bit back a growl and stubbornly refused to think about if it was permanent, just like I stubbornly refused to look at the raw pink encircling my neck. The tingle was significantly more than I'd managed in a while. The ability to change would come back, just like the evidence of the collar would eventually fade. Until then, there was no use dwelling on it.

I turned to the shower and cranked it as hot as it would go, but didn't wait for it to finish heating before stepping beneath the spray. I had every intention of violently scrubbing myself clean, but my body betrayed me. My head swam from all the movement and I braced my forearms against the wall beneath the showerhead to keep from falling over. I lost track of time as the water drummed against my shoulders and back, heating to the point of scalding. When I was fairly sure I wouldn't do something as embarrassing as collapse in the tub, I leaned back and reached for the soap.

It took five washes of my hair and body before the water finally ran clear. The tantalizing scent of soft jasmine and sandalwood fogged the small space every bit as much as the steam. I still felt like shit, but at least I was clean. I was mid-wrapping the towel around my waist when I suddenly froze. Noise was coming from outside the bathroom. It was probably stupid to think that I'd be able to shower, steal a change of clothes, and slip away without waking Zahir. Because he was *definitely* awake, and moving around.

A sudden flush of anxiety squeezed my lungs. It wasn't that I was self-conscious of walking out naked. Far from it. Nudity lost most of its shine when you were frequently naked around people you had zero sexual interest in. No, what had me freaking out was that I had no clue how I was going to explain any of this. Randomly showing up at his place. The blood. Fuck. *All the blood*. And the collar.

I reflexively reached up to touch my neck before hastily dropping my hand. *Someone* had gotten it off, and it wasn't me. Then a new worry dawned on me. I swiveled to face the mirror so fast I nearly went down in a heap of limbs and swiped at the fogged glass. Yep, just as I feared. The horrendous blond was back. I'd just thoroughly washed out every bit of mud, oil, and blood that had been darkening it.

The noise beyond the door got louder, and I scrambled to figure out how to hide what had kept me on the fringes of my pack for as long as I could remember. The thing that singled me out as a freak. Low on options, I removed the towel from my waist, then muttered a curse.

"How the fuck do women do that twisty shit with towels?" I grumbled to myself. After the third try, I gave up and just draped the damn thing over my head. Then I took a bracing breath and opened the door with exactly zero ideas of how to explain anything.

"Aidan." Whatever I'd been expecting, it wasn't the soft sigh of my name wrapped in worry.

I looked at Zahir's face, surprised to see it pinched with the same concern. "Uh... hope you don't mind. I used your shower. And, uh, most of your shampoo." My cheeks burned at the confession. Sure, I'd used a lot of the stuff because I was fucking gross, but it had also smelled really nice. I doubted my hair had ever been this clean or soft, but, again, that was a problem.

"Thank fuck you're okay," Zahir said, his voice strained. Then, faster than I knew a snake could move, he rushed me, only to lurch to a stop inches away. The tips of his fingers lightly brushed my face, pecs, and arms. His hands hesitated over my neck, confirming what I already suspected. He'd absolutely seen the collar. His touch became more deliberate as he continued to check me over, then he reached for the towel hanging on my head.

I grabbed his wrist firmly to stop him, startling both of us. "I'm fine."

Anger darted behind his dark eyes. Even though I knew cobras didn't have rattles, I could swear I heard one shaking in warning.

"I *will* be fine," I added, gentling my grip on his wrist. Sadness swept through me when he removed his hand and stepped back. I cleared my throat to hide the flash of disappointment. Zahir wasn't worried about *me*. He was more than likely pissed that I'd crashed at his house looking like I'd fled a massacre, then used all of his fancy shower soap. "Um..."

He took another step back and dropped his gaze to the floor. "There are clothes on the bed and I've almost finished unpacking the food," he said, gesturing absently to what looked like a pair of sweats and a t-shirt. "I'll be in the other room when you're ready."

I watched him turn on his heel and leave, not sure what to make of the strange interaction. I continued to stand there at a loss until the smell of food filling the air got me moving. It took less than a minute to pull on the clothes, which hung awkwardly on me thanks to us having completely different body types, not to mention I was currently super underweight. Now I just had to figure out how to hide my damn hair. I spotted a beanie shoved behind a stack of dust-covered books on the floor and promptly popped it on my head.

As I ventured out of the bedroom, it struck me that there was no blood anywhere that I could see. I shied away from thinking about how much of it there must have been or how much cleaning it would have taken to get rid of it. It wasn't exactly like I had any way to pay Zahir back to make up for it, either. My wallet was gone and my bike was still with the pack. I'd have to get out of here ASAP before he thought I was some kind of leech.

"Why are you wearing a ski hat?" Zahir asked, startling me out of my depressing thoughts. I glanced at him, not really surprised to find him giving me a funny look. After all, it was the height of summer and way too fucking hot for the knitted cap.

"My ears were cold," I lied, tugging the hat further down. Unfortunately, the move caused Zahir's gaze to drop to my neck. I quickly dropped my hands and cleared my throat. "That's a lot of food. Did I crash a party?" I tried for a smile that fell flat.

"Werewolves need a lot of food, right?" His hands flurried around the impressive collection of takeout containers. "It helps when healing. I'm sure I read that somewhere. Or knew? Maybe Ezra told me... I *knew* I should have fucking waited," he muttered to himself, probably not thinking about the fact that I'd be able to hear him clearly.

"Whoa, hey, easy there. You're right." I shoved my hands into the pockets of my borrowed sweatpants and shrugged. "Werewolves eat a lot. Even when we're not total disasters, just barely the right side of dead." The same anger I'd seen in the bedroom flitted through his eyes, gone just as quickly as before. "I'll just, uh, grab a couple of those boxes, if that's cool, and get out of your hair. And, uh, sorry about fucking up your place," I finished awkwardly, ducking my head so I wouldn't have to see how eager he was to be rid of me.

"The hell you will," he snapped so fiercely that I actually took a step backward.

"What?"

"Listen here, furball. You're going to sit your furry ass down at this table and eat until you think you're going to pop, then you're going to *rest*. Or so help me, I will fucking bite you and put you on the *wrong* side of dead."

"Kinky," I replied cheekily to cover how freaked I was by his intensity.

He arched an eyebrow. "You think so, do you? I suppose you've conveniently forgotten that naga venom is lethal to damn near everything on the planet, supernatural or otherwise." He crossed his arms over his sturdy chest and glowered at me. "Well?" he prompted when I wasn't quick enough to respond.

"Don't get your scales in a bunch," I grumbled, trudging over to the table and sinking into the closest chair. "You didn't say you'd be using your fangs."

"I'll be using my fangs," he said, slamming a carton of food in front of me so hard that some of its contents exploded out the top. To emphasize his point, his face shimmered and a pair of very snake-like fangs descended from the roof of his mouth. Fuck, those things were big. And yet I wasn't afraid. Part of me wanted to goad him into biting me—obviously the suicidal part of me that was convinced I'd finally lost my mind and was actually still chained up in that dark room.

I watched him slowly retract the wicked points and suddenly I really wanted to know what he looked like in his naga form. I snickered to myself as I reached for a fork. He was probably every bit as beautiful in that shape as he was in this one.

"What's so funny?" he demanded as he pulled up a neighboring chair and sat. It was almost like he didn't trust me to eat. If anything, I was more worried about hoovering the food so fast that I choked.

I shook my head and took a massive bite. "Nothing," I said around the mouthful of savory pork.

He snorted and dragged a different container closer to himself, then began plucking things out and eating with his fingers. I blinked in surprise, but he didn't act like it was in any way unusual. Well, at least I didn't have to eat by myself. That was nice.

Time went by and the food gradually disappeared. By the time I was polishing off the last container, I really did feel like I was about to pop and couldn't have told a soul what I'd just devoured like it was my last meal. I slumped back in the chair and resisted the urge to rub my overfull belly. Zahir let out a sigh, and I glanced over at him. He'd been remarkably quiet while I ate, despite finishing long before I did. It seemed that was done now.

"I really want to ask you what happened." He paused for a long moment before continuing. "But I don't think that would be wise. Not right now, anyway. What I will ask is, how are you feeling?"

"Full?"

He narrowed his eyes at me, then let out a sharp laugh. "I suppose that's sufficient. At the very least, you're well enough to act like an ass." He pushed away from the table and started clearing things.

My heart sank into my *very* full stomach, making me queasy. I guess it'd been too much to hope that we'd be able to go back to the easy banter we'd had before. "So, I'll just... get out of your hair then," I said as I stood.

Zahir shot me a sharp look that was every bit as lethal as his fangs. "Get in the fucking bed, Aidan, and stay there."

"What are you gonna do to make me? Tie me down?" I teased.

His eyes softened. "No," he whispered.

I wanted to say something, preferably another smart-ass remark, but I couldn't find any words. When my eyes started to sting, I turned on my heel and scampered back into the bedroom, where I practically dove under the covers, sweats and all.

Chapter 16

Zahir

There were a million questions I wanted to ask Aidan, but every time I got close, my tongue stuck to the roof of my mouth. It certainly didn't help that he'd been at my place three days now and aside from sleeping like the dead, the most he'd done was scuttle around avoiding me. And. I. Didn't. Know. Why. And it wasn't all in my head either. He seemed determined to bounce as soon as possible. If he insisted on getting out of my hair one more time, I was going to lose my shit.

My grip on the teaspoon tightened until my knuckles turned white. Like I hadn't been out of my mind worried about him. Like I wasn't terrified that if he left my sight, he'd vanish forever. Realistically, I knew I couldn't put off asking him about what happened much longer. Especially not now that Ezra was blowing up *my* phone with demands to talk to Aidan.

I glowered at the cabinets in front of me. Telling Ezra when Aidan had finally regained consciousness was a mistake I wished I could go back and undo. I understood his desire to know, but

I wasn't about to inflict a strange werewolf onto Aidan without first knowing what had happened myself.

"Your drink piss you off or something?" Aidan asked from the entrance to the small kitchen.

I forced my hand to relax, tapped the spoon on the rim, and set it aside. "What makes you ask that?" I asked, blowing on the steaming cup of chai before taking a sip and turning to face him.

"Because if you held that spoon any tighter, it'd be bent in half. So what gives?" He crossed his arms over his chest and I was relieved to see that more of the bruising and larger cuts had vanished. Though I still couldn't make heads or tails of why he continued to wear the damnable beanie.

"How are you feeling?" I replied, blatantly avoiding his question. His shoulders instantly stiffened, just like they had every other time I'd asked. At least I'd dialed it back from asking every hour.

He shrugged and averted his gaze to somewhere over my left shoulder. "Mostly healed. Think I'll be able to fully shift today."

"That's great!" I exclaimed a hair too excitedly. I couldn't imagine how disconcerting not being able to shift would be, and I knew it had been bothering him, even though he refused to talk about it.

"Yeah. I guess." The defeat in his voice clawed at my heart. And why wouldn't he look at me?

"A full shift helps with healing, right?" I hazarded, taking another sip of my chai in an attempt to project a casual air. "Something about the magic inherent in *weres*? I admit, I know little about how werewolves actually work. Hearsay, really." The color rose in his cheeks, and I winced internally at his dejected expression. Then his distant gaze dropped to study the floor. My heart sank with it. What was I doing wrong? Why was he being so standoffish? "Aidan..."

"I'll, uh, just leave you to your drink." He ducked his head and angled to leave.

Before I could second guess myself or even formulate a plan, I reached out for him. The exceptional warmth of his arm suffused my fingers, and I released an involuntary sigh. "What if I don't want you to leave?" I asked softly.

His head snapped up and surprise flashed in his pretty blue eyes. "Why?" he asked, his voice soft and hoarse, like uttering that single word was painful. Vulnerable was not a word I would ever associate with werewolves, or Aidan for that matter, yet he looked ready to shatter into a thousand tiny pieces at one cruel word.

My heart threatened to break in two. Did he really not know how much I wanted him here? I set my cup aside and stepped into his personal space close enough that he had to look up at me with his doubt-filled eyes. I stroked his cheek, which was finally looking less drawn, and leaned down so our breath could mingle. "Why do you think?"

His breath hitched, and he went still as a statue as I brushed my lips lightly over his. The sound of our collective heartbeats filled the small space as I waited. I was about to step back, admit that our connection was more one-sided than I wanted it to be, when he tilted his head and pressed his lips delicately against mine. An uncontrolled moan slipped out of me. I slanted my mouth for a better angle and kissed him like I'd been aching to do for days. He made a small sound of surprise, then curled his hands around my waist, pulling us flush against each other.

The heat of his fingers burned through my clothes, and I wanted nothing more than to tangle my fingers in his hair as I tangled my tongue with his. But I wasn't about to yank off that damnable wool hat without understanding why he insisted on wearing it in the first place. So I made do with clinging to him every bit as tightly as he clung to me.

"Yeah, in case it wasn't clear before, I don't *want* you to leave," I said when I could finally pull myself away from his plush mouth. He looked back at me with a slightly dazed expression, doubt still swimming murkily in his eyes, and it seemed prudent to clarify further. I trailed the tips of my fingers down the length of his arm, but kept my gaze locked on his. "In fact, I would really like it if you stayed." I bit off adding "forever" for fear of scaring him off, though if I was being honest with myself, I was equally terrified of how badly I *wanted* to say it.

"I think I'm going to step outside and see if I can manage a shift," he said quietly, his gaze searching mine.

"Okay," I replied, equally gently, while I willed myself not to thread our fingers together *or* insist on going with him. What if he walked into the woods and never came back? I didn't think I could go through that again.

Suddenly, his wary expression softened into something that looked like tentative hope. "Maybe afterward we could have some lunch together, maybe even watch something?"

The tension that had slowly been wrapping around my chest eased so abruptly it was a wonder I didn't gasp. "I'd really like that. Anything in particular you're craving?" The heat that flashed in his eyes was gone so fast, I'd have missed it if I wasn't already lost in his gaze.

His slow smile held a hint of the mischief I'd come to associate with him in the brief time we'd known each other. "Meat."

A laugh burst out of me. "I think I can make that happen." I leaned forward to brush my lips over his again, simply because I could. "Come back soon?" I hadn't meant for it to sound like a question, but apparently my own doubts were not so easily assuaged.

"Guess it depends on how quickly you can get that food here," he replied cheekily.

"I'll have it here in thirty," I promised boldly.

"Then I'll be back in thirty." He stole a quick kiss, then turned on his heel and headed for the back door.

I had to check the impulse to see if my heart was still in my chest and not flapping about the kitchen like a moth chasing the light. Aidan was stunning when he smiled like that, and even better, he said he was coming back. For food, at least, if not for me. But I wasn't about to split hairs.

To my chagrin, both the food *and* Aidan took forty-five minutes to show up. I had to remind myself that he needed time to shift, or at least that's what Ezra had said. Something like an average of ten to fifteen minutes to complete the transition. So, perhaps thirty minutes had been a little over ambitious. What mattered was that Aidan had returned, and he'd eaten his weight in the barbeque I'd had delivered. Ezra had also mentioned that a healthy appetite was a good thing for recovering *weres*. Far as I could tell, Aidan's appetite was plenty healthy.

"Not a fan of barbeque sauce?" I teased as he polished off the last of the pork ribs.

He snorted. "If the meat needs sauce, it wasn't done properly," he said, gathering the now empty takeout containers and taking them to the trash. Suppose I'd have to get used to never having leftovers if I was going to be living with a werewolf. My heart gave an excited flutter at the thought that I prayed didn't show on my face.

"So, you mentioned watching something? Did you have anything in mind?" I asked, relocating to the cushy sofa, my body already tingling in anticipation of cuddling.

"I'm not picky. Just no extreme action films." He shuddered.

"How do you feel about baking competitions?" I asked tentatively.

He finished clearing the table and wandered to the front room, where I was waiting. "Yeah? You like those?"

I refused to be embarrassed as I snuggled deeper into my corner of the couch. "They're kind of my guilty pleasure." Okay, so I was a little embarrassed. Would he think I was ridiculous? Besides, it wasn't like *I* could bake.

His face brightened. "I actually love those shows. Not that I ever get to watch a whole season from start to finish. Still, there's something..."

"Relaxing?" I filled in for him.

He chuckled and more of the tension that had been riding me the last three weeks evaporated. "Yeah, but only the British one. The American one is too cut throat to be considered chill."

At the mention of throats, my rebellious gaze flicked down to Aidan's. I'd tried so hard not to stare at the horrific marks when he was awake, so I wouldn't make him selfconscious. To my infinite relief, the red puckered skin was gone. I couldn't even tell if it had left scars behind. I cleared my throat and plucked up the remote. "You're in luck. I have all of this season's British Baking Challenge recorded. Now get comfortable and get over here already."

His brow furrowed slightly. "Really? On the couch?"

"Yes, *really*. Now come on already. I've watched most of them, but I don't mind starting from the beginning again." I patted the seat beside me to emphasize my point and exactly where I expected him to sit.

"Um, okay." He shrugged and pulled off that contemptible beanie—*finally*—and I did a double-take.

"Your hair. It's... blond."

His face flamed. "Yeah, I guess you were going to find out about it eventually." He ran a hand over the jagged locks that were bright as sun-spun gold.

"It's nice," I replied awkwardly, adjusting my focus to the television screen. Truthfully, it was a lot more than nice. It was *gorgeous*. I burned to know why he felt the need to hide it, but

I didn't want to make him more uncomfortable than he clearly already was. I'd just selected the recording of the first episode when I noticed out of the corner of my eye that Aidan hadn't stopped at the beanie—he'd stripped off his shirt as well and was currently kicking off his sweats. "What are you doing?" I asked, distracted by the unexpected nudity.

"I need to change."

It was on the tip of my tongue to ask "Hadn't he just done that?" but I wasn't a werewolf. What did I know? Maybe he wasn't referring to shifting at all, but something else. Then his body began to *change*. My jaw dropped at the same time his hands hit the ground. I watched as his bones took on new shapes with a mix of horror and morbid fascination. I'd never seen a werewolf shift before. And I was pretty sure I wasn't supposed to be watching either. I ripped my gaze away from his mutating form as golden fur sprouted across his body. Within a couple of minutes, the transformation was complete and a massive wolf with the prettiest coat I'd ever seen in my life stood in Aidan's place.

He shook out his fur and leapt onto the coach, causing it to groan. I fought to keep my shock to myself as he maneuvered into a comfortable position and flopped down beside me. From what I'd found in my research and the little I'd dragged out of Ezra, that was *not* typical. The change was private, excruciating, and *long*. But Aidan had just... stripped and changed. What. The. Fuck.

He shuffled closer and nosed my hand holding the remote. I startled, nearly dropping the damn thing, and he made a noise that sounded suspiciously like a laugh. Grumbling to myself, I hit start and set it aside, then was confronted with a new dilemma as the intro played. What the fuck did I do with my hand?

Taking my life in my tail, I tentatively laid my hand on the back of Aidan's head. Sweet Vishnu, his fur was soft. Aidan snuffled, pressing more firmly against me as if to signal his acceptance and encouragement of the touch. Well, okay then, this was a thing that was happening. I was sitting on the couch, watching my favorite show, with a fully shifted werewolf curled against my side. How was this my life?

Chapter 17

Aidan

It was a little pathetic that curling up on the couch and binging a baking show with Zahir ranked in my top ten best afternoons. *Ever.* Ugh. Who was I fooling? Top five. Easy. Hell, maybe even top three. But pathetic as that was, it didn't beat passing the fuck out on said couch so hard that I didn't notice when he turned off the tv. Or got up. *Or* laid a blanket over me.

By the time I woke up in the small hours of the morning to shift back and pee, I was embarrassed *and* alone. Which, honestly, the alone part sucked way more than I cared to admit. I was used to going to sleep and waking surrounded by my pack. And, sure, I didn't get along with all—most—of them for one reason or another, but they were still my pack. My family. But that was all gone now.

I rubbed at the sudden sharp ache in my chest and wondered how long it would take me to deteriorate now that I was packless. Maybe I'd go mad instead. Everyone knew that a werewolf couldn't last long without a pack. But no one *knew* what happened to you. There was the oddball "lone wolf", but I wasn't sure how much of that I believed. What wolf *voluntarily* struck out on their own? Didn't miss the closeness that came with pack? Didn't want it? Didn't *need* it?

Shaking my head to clear the gloomy thoughts, I pushed up from the couch. I absently reached for the beanie lying on the ground, then thought better of it. Zahir already knew about my hair. What was the point except to shield his eyes from the awful pale yellow? Then again, he'd said it was nice. So, maybe he didn't think it was all that awful? Weird. But he was a snake and snakes, by definition, were weird anyway.

I glanced around the room, noting how everything seemed to have a place. It wasn't obnoxiously perfect or anything like that, just... neat. The thin rays of morning light that pierced the blinds lent the small space a dreamlike quality, catching tiny dust motes as they drifted aimlessly through the air. It was even quiet, though if I focused, I could just make out Zahir's steady breathing from the other room.

It was that weird in-between time of day, when night was receding and the dawn was taking its first breath. All the nighttime insects had gone to ground for the day to come and not even the birds had picked up their song yet. I'd always secretly loved this time of day. There was something magical about the stillness in the air. The sense of endless possibility that the day could bring. And most importantly, nothing had gone wrong yet. But it had. So much had gone horribly wrong, and I still didn't understand it.

I scrubbed at my face to clear away the lingering traces of sleep from my eyes and determined to be useful today. I looked around the room again, dismayed not to find *anything* that might spark inspiration at what form that usefulness might take. Then my stomach growled, and a smile split my face. I may not be able to clean anything, but I could cook. It hadn't escaped my notice that all the food Zahir had generously provided had been ordered. Maybe he'd been pressed for time, or maybe he didn't like to cook. Either way, making the man breakfast was the least I could do after everything he'd done for me.

Except his fridge was empty. Like, *bone dry* empty, and the cabinets weren't much better.

"What does this guy even eat?" I muttered to myself as I rechecked everything, but their mostly barren state remained unchanged. "Well, fuck." My gaze caught on Zahir's wallet and keys chilling on the counter. It wasn't technically stealing if he was going to spend it on ordering food anyway, right? Before I could dwell too much on the ethics of taking yet more of his money, I snatched up the wallet and keys, slipped on the pair of shoes by the door, and headed out.

Nearly two hours later, a big bowl of fluffy eggs, a mountain of pancakes, and a pitcher of fresh-squeezed orange juice cluttered the counter. And if that wasn't enough delectable heaven, the smell of perfectly crisped bacon filled the air. My stomach rumbled in appreciation as I sampled some crispiness that had fallen free.

I was on the verge of getting Zahir out of bed myself so we could eat when he poked his head into the kitchen. He was adorably sleep-rumpled with his dark hair sticking up at odd angles and a pillow crease still lining his cheek. Truthfully, he looked every bit as edible as the bacon.

"That smells amazing," he mumbled, shuffling deeper into the kitchen.

I flashed him a grin as I finished wiping my hands from cleaning the last pan and turned to lean against the counter. "Good morning to you too, lazy scales."

"Where did you order this from? I don't know of any place that delivers breakfast that looks *this* good."

I snorted, but a part of my chest warmed at hearing that he thought it looked. "I didn't order anything."

He stopped surveying the spread and looked at me with wide eyes. "How..."

"I may have borrowed your wallet. And your car," I added with a slight wince, suddenly wishing I'd taken more than half a second to consider my scheme. My impulsiveness had gotten me in enough trouble over the years. You'd think I'd have learned by now. "I, uh, hope that was okay."

"Okay? This looks amazing, *and* I didn't have to cook. I'd say it's more than okay." He plucked a piece of bacon from the paper towel covered plate and bit into it with gusto, then made the most sinful sound I'd ever heard.

I coughed to clear my throat and angled away so I could attempt to discreetly adjust myself.

"Sweet merciful Brahma! Are those *pancakes*?"

At his sudden gasp, I swiveled around, my inconvenient erection momentarily forgotten. I gave him a dopey smile, my chest warming again at his open enthusiasm. Not many people loved food as much as a werewolf, but it was looking like Zahir might be a kindred spirit. Especially when you took into account our shared love of baking shows. "Sure are."

"Gimme," he said, his mouth full of bacon and his hands making grabby motions.

Okay, Morning Zahir really was adorable as fuck. I grabbed the plate of pancakes, prepared to take them to the table, and took a step forward, only to have his grabby fingers hook in my shirt and tug me close. It was a moon blessed miracle I didn't drop the plate as his mouth sealed over mine. The saltiness of the bacon he'd eaten filled my mouth as he claimed me with a kiss that left me breathless and *really* wishing I wasn't starving... for food.

"Sorry," he said with a smirk that didn't look even remotely apologetic when he pulled away. "Had to show my appreciation somehow."

"Won't hear me complaining." My stomach, of course, chose that exact moment to growl loud enough to wake the damn dead. "Traitor," I grumbled, glaring at my stomach.

He laughed and took the plate from me. "There's plenty of time for... other things later. Maybe after we eat?" An unexpected wariness shadowed his darker features, and my heart sank. I already knew what he was going to say before the words left his mouth. "And maybe, if you're up for it, after you tell me what happened?" Yep. Called it.

I wanted to take the out he'd given me, but I knew it would just be kicking the can down the road. Either way, sexy times would definitely *not* be happening after breakfast. "Yeah, I need to fill you in on... things." I swallowed thickly and tried not to look as defeated as I felt.

Abruptly, his hand was cupping my cheek, and I looked up into his deep brown eyes. "Breakfast first," he said with a smile.

Breakfast didn't last nearly long enough, though I was more than happy to note the relish with which Zahir enjoyed the meal. I'd never in a million years admit to my pack that the biggest reason I liked cooking so much was getting to see them *enjoy* something I made. It was one of the rare times no one had anything shitty to say to me. Not even fucking Eliott. Granted, they weren't exactly showering me with praise like Zahir kept doing, but it was a nice reprieve from the usual dynamic.

Sadness suddenly gripped my heart as it sank in yet again that I didn't have a pack anymore. I was alone. And being without them would be the death of me—probably sooner rather than later.

"Hey, is everything alright?" Zahir asked as he returned from rinsing the dishes. He'd insisted that since I'd cooked, it was only fair for him to clean. He crossed the living room to join me on the couch, the cushion sinking beneath him. "If you need more time before sharing, I understand."

I shook my head. "Waiting won't change anything. Now's as good a time as any." I glanced at him out of the corner of my eye. The concern on his face wouldn't be there once he knew the truth. I couldn't help but wonder how long it would take after my ugly story before he demanded I leave. Panic squeezed my chest like a vise. "Before we get to that though..."

In less than a heartbeat, I straddled his lap, held his face between my hands, and kissed him for all I was worth. There was a clear moment of surprise in which he didn't move. Then his tongue was pushing past my lips and his hands were grabbing and pulling me closer. I let myself get lost in the heated moment, knowing it would eventually end, but longing for it to go on forever. Finally, I had no choice but to pull away for air. Stupid oxygen.

"What was that for?" he asked, his breath every bit as ragged as mine.

"Sorry. I know you said talking first. I just..."

"Just what, Aidan? And for the record, not complaining. More curious."

I rested my forehead against his, unable to meet his gaze. "I just wanted to do that one more time before you know..." *What a total loser I am.* "Everything. And you decide you don't really want me around," I finished, slinking back to my end of the couch.

His hand whipped out lightning fast to encircle my wrist, preventing me from getting very far. "Unless you're some kind of deranged serial killer, I don't see that happening. Like, at all." He tugged lightly on my captive arm. "Do you hear me? My wanting you here, wanting you to stay, isn't going to change. I only want to know what happened to you. I was worried out of my damn mind. I thought..." He trailed off and seemed to fight with the urge to say more. It was all well and good for him to say that *now*, but I knew better than to get my hopes up.

"I'm not even sure where to start." I ran my hand over my hair, briefly forgetting that it was blond again until Zahir's eyes tracked the motion. I quickly snatched my hand back down. "So, my pack is called the Stormfire Pack." Another painful stab in my heart. "Well, it was," I corrected myself.

He frowned, his thick eyebrows coming together. "What do you mean 'was'? Did something happen to them?"

"No. I... I'm not part of the pack anymore. They, uh, banished me." My shoulders slumped inward at admitting the truth out loud.

"What? Why?"

"Because I defied the pack," I mumbled. "We were on a supply run and I bumped into another werewolf. The others with me wanted to stop her from leaving, but I... helped her get away. I don't remember getting back to the house, but when I woke up, I found myself chained in a dark room. Then...then I was punished. A lot." My cheeks heated, and I ducked my head to hide my embarrassment. "So, yeah, I don't have a pack anymore."

"I'm sorry," Zahir said, but where I expected to hear pity, his voice was laced with something that sounded more akin to angry disbelief.

I risked a glance at his face and, to my surprise, found equally furious storm clouds darkening his face. "What?"

"You're telling me that *your pack* did that to you?"

"Yes?" I fidgeted, my comfort increasing with each second he stared at me. Abruptly, he stood and the sudden shift in weight had me careening toward the vacuum he'd left. "What are you doing?"

"I'm going to fucking kill them," he spat, the area where his neck met his shoulders doing something weird. I was trying to figure out what could cause the skin there to flatten and expand when his words sank in and I lurched to my feet.

"You can't."

"Watch me." He took a decisive step toward the door.

On instinct, I repeated the same move he had earlier and grabbed his wrist. He stopped walking, but seemed to vibrate with the effort of staying put. "You *can't*. Even if naga venom is the deadliest on the planet, there are at least thirty *weres* at the house. They'd tear you apart before you could do much damage." To my surprise, I was far more concerned with what they would do to Zahir than what he might do to them.

I watched as the fight left him as quickly as it had taken him. He ran his free hand over his face. "I hate that you're right."

I tentatively released his wrist. "I don't see why it matters. After all, I'm the one that fucked up. Truth be told, I fucked up a lot. They were bound to get tired of it, eventually." I cringed inwardly, wishing I'd kept that little tidbit to myself. Then again, I couldn't very well have Zahir marching off and getting himself killed.

"Why it matters?" he echoed, slowly turning to face me. "Aidan, they *tortured* you. Chained you up like an animal. Gave you something so you couldn't shift or heal. And they Kept. Doing. It. Do you have any idea how freaked out I was when you stopped coming around *The Oasis*?"

I shrugged, suddenly self-conscious. "I wasn't gone that long."

Horror exploded across his face. "You were gone for *weeks*. Weeks, Aidan. Then you show up at my door out of the blue, covered in blood, on the verge of *death*, with a fucking metal collar embedded in your neck!"

I winced at each addition and fought the reflex to curl in on myself when he reached shouting levels.

"Do you even remember how you got here?" he asked, his voice painfully tight, but at least he wasn't yelling anymore.

"Most of it's a blur. I vaguely recall them letting me go and running through the woods." I pointedly left out the part where they'd said they'd be hunting me.

Zahir spun on his heel and stalked back toward the bedroom, anger clearly lining his lean frame.

"Now, what are you doing?" I asked, following him.

"I'm calling Ezra."

I staggered to a stop. "Who's Ezra?"

He waved a dismissive hand as he plucked up his cell phone from the nightstand. "He's a local werewolf." Jealousy spiked through me so hard it was a wonder I didn't cry out. Zahir glanced at me when I didn't continue talking. Something must have shown on my face because he did a double take. "It's not like that, Aidan. When you stopped showing up at the bar, I tried to find you. I'd have called, but I didn't have your number. He's the only werewolf I could find for nearly a hundred miles."

"I don't have a phone," I said, my voice sounding hollow even to my ears.

"What?"

"The pack had a few, but they were communal. I couldn't risk giving you the number. Because..." They'd find him, and then they'd take him from me, just like they took everything else.

He studied my face as he waited for me to continue. When I didn't, he let out a heavy sigh. "I really think you should talk to Ezra. Please let me set something up."

I couldn't help but feel that my staying here was contingent upon talking to Ezra. After a stifling silence, I nodded. "Okay. But not here. Somewhere public. Neutral." Realistically, I knew that this mysterious Ezra character had likely already been in Zahir's house, but I was here now, and I didn't want any other wolf near him.

Chapter 18

Zahir

I still wanted to march out the door and murder every last son of a bitch that had the audacity to lay a hand on Aidan, starting with his so-called Alpha. A single night's sleep couldn't change that. They'd messed up Aidan in ways I couldn't even begin to comprehend. But worse than all of that, he thought it was *normal*. I might not know much of anything about were-wolves, but even I recognized that everything about his shitty pack was about as far from normal as it was conceivably possible to get. And to top it all off, Ezra was out of town for the next three weeks. I'd been banking on him to fill in the gaps and hopefully illuminate the overall wrongness of what Aidan had endured.

I let out a heavy sigh and raked my fingers through my hair. Aidan's body may have healed, but it didn't take a guru to know he had psychological scars that could give the Mariana Trench a run for its money. Yet he continued to act as if everything was fine. At least he'd stopped expecting me to turn him out, given the first opportunity.

"What's with the face?" Aidan asked from the bedroom doorway. I'd actually gotten him to sleep in the bed with me last night. What I hadn't expected was for him to shift into his wolf form to do it. I mentally shuddered as the image of his body gruesomely contorting filled my mind. "Hello? You still with me?" he pressed when I didn't respond to his initial question.

I shoved my phone into the back pocket of my trousers and met his gaze. "I need to go to the temple." Vishnu knew I'd shirked my duties beyond forgiveness. Truthfully, I was a little amazed that Guru Angira had tolerated it as much as she had. Maybe I wasn't giving the old serpent enough credit. She had been there for Aidan.

Confusion flashed across Aidan's beautiful face before understanding brightened his impossibly blue eyes. "That's right! You're a priest."

"Spiritual leader," I mumbled as I pushed past him, tacking on a belated, "in training."

He shrugged and followed me into the kitchen, where he'd made breakfast once again. "Same difference."

Rather than debate the nuances of faith and spirituality, I grabbed a plate and helped myself to some eggs. My heart squeezed painfully as I leaned against the counter to eat and watched Aidan wander aimlessly around. I didn't want to go to the temple. Didn't want to leave him here. It had nothing to do with not trusting him in my space on his own and everything to do with being terrified that if I let him out of my sight for even a minute that he'd vanish.

"So... how long will you be gone?" he asked casually, an undercurrent of tightness in his voice that I was probably imagining.

"Come with me," I blurted before I could think better of it.

He whipped around to face me, his surprise evident. "What?"

"Come with me," I repeated, my conviction strengthening. "To the temple. Guru Angira won't mind," I hoped, "and you can see where I study." Hell, if I knew why his approval of what I did mattered to me given I didn't want to be doing it in the first place. Except it did. A lot.

"I don't know," he dragged out, his gaze skirting over the floor. "Won't I be in the way? And I'm not exactly a naga."

I set aside my empty plate and stepped forward, suddenly determined to get him to agree. "That won't matter. While we cater to nagas, we offer spiritual guidance to all sorts."

"What makes you think I need spiritual guidance?" he asked. I floundered for a second at unintentionally implying that he did, then I noticed the playful smirk teasing his lips. My bout of anxiety evaporated, and I scoffed.

"Not from *me*. From someone who's actually competent and qualified to give it. So, what do you say? I'm sure you'd like to get out of here for a bit." I waved, taking in the small house.

He pulled his bottom lip between his teeth and worried it. After giving me a searching look, he finally nodded. "Okay."

Relief washed through me like drinking the coolest water after wandering the desert.

"But..."

And just like that, it dried up so fast it left cracks in the parched earth. "But what?" I asked, praying my voice didn't betray my nerves.

"First, tell me why you're not 'qualified' to give spiritual guidance."

My mouth opened and closed a few times before I convinced words to come out. "I'm just... not. I'm no good at it." He made a strange sound at the back of his throat. Disbelief? Agreement? Whatever it was, I wasn't touching it with a ten-foot pole. There was no use in digging. I simply wasn't cut out for the spiritual life and that was the end of it.

"When do we leave?"

"Now, if you're ready."

He nodded. "Let me just grab my shoes."

I followed him to the front door, where it didn't escape my notice that his shoes sat neatly beside mine on the rack. He passed me mine and slipped on the pair I'd lent him. His feet were smaller than mine and the shoes seemed to swallow him. Honestly, the clothes weren't much better. I'd have to make sure to get him things that suited him. And a phone. Fuck, I still needed to get him a phone.

The drive to the temple was quieter than I expected, but not strained. I periodically glanced at Aidan to find him staring out the window at the landscape zipping past.

"This place is really out there, huh?" he mused aloud.

I chuckled to myself as we rounded yet another bend in the road, bringing us that much closer to the hidden temple. *You have no idea.* By the time I pulled into my designated parking spot at Cumberland Falls, he was practically vibrating in his seat.

"You doing okay over there?" I teased as I put the car in park.

"Why didn't you tell me you work at a State Park?"

I didn't know whether to laugh at his wide-eyed look or grab his face and kiss the hell out of him. "What do you mean?"

He rolled his eyes like it was the most asinine question anyone had ever asked him. "Woods, trees, forest, werewolf." He gestured wildly at the landscape. "I'd have come to visit you."

Warmth flooded my chest at his simple proclamation and I had to fight to keep the smile off my face. "Let me show you the temple first and check in with Gurudevi, then you can run to your heart's content." The joy and excitement emanating off of him was almost enough to make me forget how despondent he seemed at the house. Now I felt like a real ass for not thinking to bring him here sooner. "It's, um, a bit of a walk to the temple from here, though there's a hidden trail we can use to cut through."

"Okay," he replied, abandoning his study of some foliage to follow me into the woods.

The journey at once felt too long and not long enough. I wanted to stay with Aidan and soak up more of his enthusiasm, but, then, it wasn't like I could run with him. Would he be okay running on his own? I didn't know how being exiled worked, just that it was bad. Worry slithered through my veins as we broke through the trees and Cumberland Falls came into view.

"Whoa." Aidan's wonder pulled me out of my spiral.

I glanced over at him, unable to suppress the grin pulling at my lips. "That's nothing. You should see it during the full moon cycle."

He turned wide eyes on me. "What happens during the full moon?"

"Ever heard of a moonbow?" I asked. He shook his head and my smile grew. I reached for his hand, automatically lacing our fingers. "Then I'll have to bring you back. Come on. Time to introduce you properly to my guru."

We were halfway to the hidden entrance that led behind the falls into the temple when I realized what I'd done. I flexed my fingers around his and tightened my hold. Even though I hadn't consciously done it, I couldn't shake how right it felt to have his hand in mine. And he hadn't pulled away. I regretfully relinquished my hold so we could traverse the somewhat narrow passage. His sharp intake of breath betrayed when he caught the first glimpse of the temple entrance.

"Anyone ever tell you this place is ridiculous?" he mumbled, his voice tinged with awe.

"I can't say anyone ever has," Guru Angira said, as she slithered into view. "Though I suspect my apprentice has been tempted a time or two." She spared me an indulgent smile before returning her focus to Aidan. He swallowed and took a half step back, placing him more firmly behind me. "It's nice to see you awake. You seem to be recovering well from your ordeal."

He shot me an anxious glance. I silently cursed at forgetting to tell him that Gurudevi had come with Ezra.

"Aidan, this is Guru Angira. I should have mentioned she also came to help while you were... indisposed. Please don't be angry," I added softly, for his ears only. It took an active effort not to reach out and cup his face, to smooth away the worry creasing his brow.

He wiped the hand I'd been holding on his pant leg and stepped forward. "Um, it's nice to meet you. I'm Aidan Stor—I'm Aidan. And, uh, thanks for helping, I guess." He paused, his gaze wandering around the ornate interior of the temple before returning to Gurudevi. "Sorry, I don't know what the proper greeting is. Do I shake your hand? Do I bow?"

She laughed her dry laugh. "Only if you want to." Her gaze slipped past him to rest on me. "Swami Zahir, are you prepared to resume your practice?"

I resisted the desire to look at Aidan and nodded. As I stepped forward, I shifted into my naga form, luxuriating in letting my scales breathe for the first time in too long. My resulting sigh of relief almost completely eclipsed Aidan's soft exclamation.

"Wow."

"What's wrong?" I asked, twisting to look at him over my shoulder.

He slowly dragged his gaze over me, from head to tail and back. I couldn't help but shiver beneath his heady scrutiny. His tongue flicked out to wet his lips. "You're beautiful. I don't think I've ever even seen that shade of blue." Abruptly his cheeks darkened, and he looked off to the side. "Um, I'll just go for a run while you... do whatever it is you do. I'll be back before sundown."

"Word of caution to stay out of sight of park goers. There haven't been wolves in Kentucky since the 1800s. Wouldn't want to start a panic." She offered him a wry smile.

"Thanks for the tip," he replied, walking backward back the way we came. His gaze darted over to me. "See you later."

I raised my hand, not sure what was going on and still reeling a bit from him calling me beautiful like he actually meant it.

"He is nice. I can see your draw."

My head snapped up at Gurudevi's interesting choice of words. "What do you mean by that?" I asked, moving toward her and trying to keep the scowl from my face.

She laughed. "He seems quite taken with you."

"He hasn't seen me in this form before. I suppose it was a nice thing to say... for a furball. Though he's clearly colorblind. My scales are green."

Gurudevi glanced over at me, much like she'd done countless times over the last few weeks. "Your scales are changing."

"I beg your pardon." I looked down at my torso, then twisted to take in my side. Okay, so some of my scales had a more bluish hue. That could easily be due to the way the light hit them. Not that it had ever been the case before. I frowned, returning my focus back to my meddling guru.

"I am happy for you. Though I'm sure you'll disagree, you're already more settled." Her knowing smile was almost the final straw. How could I have forgotten how irritating this place could be? Since when was my sense of obligation to this path so strong? "Oh, do not be so in your head. Come, you have studying to make up."

I groaned to myself and wondered if it was too late to escape to the woods with Aidan.

Chapter 19

Aidan

Nothing could beat running in a new forest, especially one as beautiful as Cumberland Falls State Park. I glanced back toward the living room where Zahir was occupying himself by cleaning up the remains of dinner. Well, almost nothing. I released a frustrated sigh as I stepped into the bathroom and turned the water on. While we'd managed a few heated kisses here and there, I'd have to be blind not to notice how he always pulled back.

I stepped beneath the scalding spray and tipped my head back. Unlike the thin layer of dust coating me, the tumble of doubt didn't wash away. At first I'd assumed it was because he wanted to make sure I was fully healed, but I'd been that for days. Fuck. A week now.

Grumbling to myself, I snatched up the fresh bottle of shampoo. It couldn't be that he was afraid I'd hurt him. And there was no way he was worried about hurting me. I snorted to myself at how absolutely ridiculous that would be. I was a werewolf, for fuck's sake. There wasn't much I couldn't come back from, my most recent brush with death being the perfect example. So why wouldn't he let things go further?

A sinking feeling made my stomach twist. Was it me? Had he tired of me already? I was taking up a lot of his personal space. And he was essentially footing the bill for everything. That was probably irritating. While Zahir seemed social enough, I didn't have a clue whether snakes in general could be considered "pack" creatures. Maybe he needed space.

The sinking feeling turned sharp, not unlike the onset of a change, at the thought of leaving. I didn't want to go, but was staying selfish? What was I really bringing to the table? I leaned against the tiled shower wall and pressed my thumbs against my brow. Sadly, it did nothing to ease the tension building there. I needed to find some way to contribute. Not easy without my own transportation, but I'd figure something out. I always did. Maybe once I wasn't such a damn freeloader, Zahir would want me again, because I sure as fuck wasn't done wanting him.

I was still running through ideas when I finally turned off the water and stepped out of the shower. I wrapped a towel around my waist and moved to stand in front of the mirror on autopilot. It wasn't until I cleared a section of mirror to see my reflection that I remembered I didn't have any dye. My jaw tightened as I flicked at the wretched blond strands. There was no point in trying to go back to dying it now, seeing as how the genie was already out of the bottle. Though I wasn't fully convinced that Zahir didn't mind the color.

I sneered at my reflection. He'd called it *nice*. Obviously a lie. Then it hit me. Maybe it was the stupid fucking hair that had cooled Zahir's interest in me. I could have smacked myself. It made so much sense. He hadn't started getting extra weird—he was a snake, so he was always *weird*—until he'd found out I wasn't actually a brunette. I eyed the razor chilling on the counter and contemplated for a hot second simply shaving all of it off. I gave an involuntary shudder as I recalled how badly that had gone the last time I'd tried it. Unlike my littermate, Jace, I could *not* pull off the bald look.

Not interested in staring at myself any longer than absolutely necessary, I spun around and opened the bathroom door. Two steps later, I realized I wasn't the only one in the room. I lifted my head to find Zahir standing just inside the bedroom. His gaze was nothing short of hungry as he took in my near naked body from head to toe. He took a deep breath and let it out slowly. I could practically *feel* him reining himself in.

"I was just coming to ask if you wanted dessert. I believe I have some mango sorbet in the freezer," he said, meeting my gaze. If it wasn't for the distinct smell of desire slowly curling through the room, I'd swear I imagined his heated look.

Maybe I was wrong. Maybe he did still want me. Still had no clue what was keeping him from acting on it, but that was a problem for another time. Right now, I had a snake to seduce. I gave him a lopsided smile and strolled toward him. "I could go for some dessert."

He swallowed hard and seemed to struggle to keep his eyes from wandering again. "Okay. I'll get the bowls out. How much would you like?" He shook his head. "Stupid question. I'll just give you a bowl and if you want more, you can get it. It's not like—"

I finished closing the distance between us and placed a finger on his lips to stop him talking. For all that he was always so put together, he was absolutely adorable when he rambled. "Not ice cream," I said, dropping my voice.

"It's sorbet," he corrected in a whisper when I moved my finger to trace his amazing lips.

"Whatever it is, it still won't taste as good as you." Okay, that was cheesy as fuck, but it had the desired result. Zahir's eyes dilated, and the muted desire wafting off of him tripled.

We held each other's gaze for a long moment. Electricity seemed to crackle between us as we pulled closer and closer together until there was barely any space separating us. I licked my lips in anticipation of tasting his while my heart hammered so loud it was a wonder he didn't comment on it. His gaze latched onto my mouth and whatever had been holding him back snapped.

I braced myself for an intense kiss, like when we'd first come back to his place ages ago. However, I was not prepared for the gentle brush of his lips over mine. Before I could get in my head again, he followed it up with another and another. Each one slow and methodical, until my lips were buzzing. I tried to take control and deepen the kiss, when he pulled back just enough to look me in the eye again.

"There's no rush." He cupped the side of my face and ran his thumb over my moist lips. "The only place either of us needs to be is right here." My heart gave a weird flutter at the promise in his words, then he leaned down to seal our mouths together once again.

Desperate to touch more of him, I mirrored his hold, cupping the back of his neck while he took his time exploring my mouth. I was hard pressed to decide if I liked the slow torture. Actually, I was just hard. Really fucking hard. I barely even registered when my towel gave up the ghost and fell to the floor.

Zahir moaned as his free hand settled on my bare hip and tugged me closer. "I wasn't entirely honest before. About your hair," he whispered, teasing my lips with his teeth.

I went rigid as I waited for his declaration of deficiency. If he preferred the brown, I'd happily go back to dying it. "Yeah?" I asked, my stupid voice cracking.

"Mmhmm." He removed his hand from the side of my face to run his fingers through the quickly drying locks. "The blond is more than nice. You were exceptionally handsome as a brunette.

But with the blond..." He sighed almost... wistfully? "You're absolutely gorgeous. It suits you in a way I couldn't have imagined."

Seriously, my heart needed to calm the fuck down. It swelled, filling my chest with a warmth I wasn't sure I'd ever experienced before. Unable to bear another second of not kissing him, I leaned forward to capture his mouth once more, though he refused to let me intensify the pace.

Cupping my neck, he tilted my head back to give him room to trail more of the unhurried kisses along the column of my throat. While I got lost in the sensuous tease of his lips, he trailed his other hand over the swell of my ass, lightly kneading the globe as he pressed me closer. His fingers trailed along my crease, and my swollen cock twitched with anticipation. There wasn't a doubt in my mind that my trapped erection was creating a wet spot on his shirt.

I tangled my fingers in the hair at the base of his skull and angled his head back so I could go back to kissing him. The light flicks of his tongue threatened to destroy what little patience I possessed. Then his finger brushed over my entrance. A needy sound I didn't even recognize slipped past my throat.

"Is this okay?" he whispered.

"Yes," I replied just as softly, already craving so much more.

"Are you sure?" he asked, rubbing my hole more firmly as if to underscore pressing the issue.

"Fuck yes," I gasped. "I haven't been able to stop thinking about you inside of me again."

Zahir made a choked sound and buried his face against my neck.

Those annoying doubts flared up with a vengeance. "Is that okay?"

"It's perfect," he mumbled, before nipping at the tender skin and raising his head to snare my mouth in a heated kiss that ended way too soon. "You're perfect."

I definitely wasn't, but it was hard to argue with his tongue in my mouth and his finger teasing my ass. At any rate, it was time I wasn't the only naked one. I moved my hands to his waist, eager to get his clothes off.

He hummed against my lips, then grabbed my hands. "Not yet." As if not getting to touch his bare skin wasn't bad enough, he stopped playing with my arguably eager hole to prevent me.

"But..." I suddenly wondered how good snake dark vision was and if he could see that I was pouting.

He brought my hands up and kissed my palms, making my heart do another one of those silly flutters. "Let me take care of you."

I swallowed thickly, my throat suddenly tight. When was the last time someone had put my needs over theirs? Not because they had to, but because they *wanted* to? "O-okay."

"Good. Lay on the bed and put a pillow under your hips." He stayed where he was as I scrambled to do exactly what he said.

I snorted as I angled my hips to add the pillow. "I feel stupid."

He chuckled and advanced on the bed, looking every inch like the predator he was and, fuck me, if that wasn't outrageously hot. "I promise you'll forget all about it."

Considering how awkward I felt, I seriously doubted that, but this was clearly his show now and I wasn't about to do anything to jeopardize where things were going. So, I propped myself on my elbows and watched as positioned himself between my thighs.

"Fuck, I've wanted to do this for way too long." Before I could ask why he hadn't, his tongue *literally* snaked out of his mouth to curl around the base of my dick. I damn near choked on air as a tongue that was definitely way longer than it had been a minute ago explored my shaft like we had all the time in the world. Except I wasn't going to make it, especially when he swallowed my dick down. Too soon, he pulled back off and went back to torturing me with his absurdly long and impressively agile tongue, using it to tug at my balls before wrapping it around my shaft once more.

I moaned deeply and fought the need to come so hard it was I wonder I didn't partially shift. Fuck, how good would that feel in my ass?

"Let's find out, shall we?"

Damn. I'd said that out loud.

He chuckled deep in his throat and moved lower, gently maneuvering my legs to give him more room to work. A jolt of pure ecstasy rocketed up my spine as the tip of his tongue fluttered over my clenching hole in the most snake-like move imaginable. I drove my head back into the pillow and lost myself in the intense sensation. When his narrow tongue easily slipped past the tight ring of muscle, I swore I saw the Goddess herself, quickly followed by a super moon as he pressed against my prostate. Nope. Still liked snake magic better, and it felt more accurate now than ever.

"Fuck. *Fuuuuck*," I moaned. "I'm gonna— Z!" I'd been aiming for his name, but only made it through the first letter when he stroked my pulsing dick and kept eating my ass. My orgasm hit me like an explosion and I spurted stream after stream until I was nothing more than a panting mess.

"That's a good start," he said appreciatively, before tasting my release with his sinuous tongue and placing a tender kiss on the inside of my quivering thigh. He slithered down the bed until he was standing once more. My greedy gaze tracked every movement as he took his time removing his clothes. He gave me a smug grin when he noticed my hungry gaze and that my dick was already rallying for another round. "I'm pleased to see the stories of werewolf stamina wasn't an exaggeration."

Mother of the moon, had he *looked it up*? My face heated as the things I'd looked up after our encounter came to my mind. Luckily, he didn't give me long to dwell on my embarrassing search history. He crawled up the bed again, this time his thick cock swaying slightly as he laid over me. I didn't think twice about dragging his mouth down to mine, only a little surprised to find his tongue its usual size.

He rolled his hips, causing our dicks to slide against each other. I moaned and thrust off the bed to meet the heady drag. He tugged at my swollen lips with his teeth, then pulled away from my mouth to pepper kisses along my jaw and throat.

"You're so damn perfect, Aidan," he murmured against my heated skin. I completely blamed my following shiver on the tickle of his tongue.

"Please," I whispered with what little breath I could catch.

He raised his head from where he'd been torturing the sensitive skin on my neck and stared down at me. His dark hair fanned over his forehead and I struggled to place his expression. "You don't ever have to beg, sweetheart."

My heart squeezed both at the sentiment and the endearment.

"Tell me what you want," he whispered, leaning down to kiss the corner of my mouth.

It took me a moment to find my voice, and I gripped him tighter, like he might vanish if I let him go for even a second. "I want to feel you inside me."

The smile he gave me as he shifted back made my heart flutter. "You really are perfect, sweetheart." He coasted his hands over my thighs, before slicking us both with lube, and positioned the swollen head of his cock at my entrance. Then, in the longest, slowest thrust ever, he buried himself in my ass.

I gasped and reflexively clenched around him. Fuck, he felt incredible, and he'd loosened me up so much there wasn't even the hint of a burn. My breath continued to catch as he used unhurried thrusts to drive me back to the brink.

Suddenly, he hooked one of my legs over his shoulder and slid a little deeper. Our mutual groans merged. Each of his following thrusts had his heavy cock dragging over that sweet spot and threatened to unravel whatever was left of my sanity.

"Yes. Oh Goddess, yes. Z," I moaned, rocking my hips up to meet his increasing speed.

"I've got you, sweetheart. Let go."

As if the husky command was all that was holding it back, my orgasm tore through me. I might have cried out, but I was soaring too high to care.

Zahir groaned, and he curled around me as he picked up his pace even more. "You feel so good, Aidan." He mashed our mouths together in a messy kiss that was more just us breathing into each other. His rhythm faltered and he thrust deep as his climax hit.

As he devolved into smaller, sporadic thrusts, something deep inside seemed to stitch back together. It was as if I hadn't finished healing and now I was finally whole again.

"Told you that you'd forget about the pillow," he mumbled into the side of my neck as he struggled to catch his breath.

I barked out a laugh.

He released a deep moan and settled more of his weight on me. "Ugh, don't do that," he grumbled, which of course just made me laugh again and hold him closer.

Chapter 20

Aidan

I dialed the shower back from face-melting to a light scalding and stepped into the tub. As the water drummed on my back, I couldn't help but smile to myself. Even sharing the single shower with one other person didn't compare to having to fight for space and *hot* water. And it certainly didn't hurt that Zahir's water pressure was killer.

I hummed contentedly as I reached for the shampoo and lathered up my hair. It was getting to the shaggy side of too long. I'd need a haircut sooner rather than later. Still, not having to dye the damn stuff at every turn was a relief I hadn't realized I needed. My grin widened as I rinsed the suds.

Zahir liked my hair. More than liked. And he took nearly every opportunity to tell me. If someone had told me a year ago—hell, a month ago—that I'd *like* being called pretty and beautiful and gorgeous and stunning, I'd have broken their jaw without a second thought. Now though? Now I kind of lived for the sweet words that fell from Zahir's lips anytime things got heated. Which was basically all the time since we'd finally crossed that invisible line.

I chuckled to myself as I took my time working in the conditioner that would make my once dreaded hair feel like silk. It had only been a week, and we'd fucked on damn near every surface in Zahir's small house. Except the cushy couch. But I was working on that.

"Mind some company?"

I poked my head past the shower curtain and nearly laughed again at seeing Zahir's rumpled state. A morning person, he was not. Not that I cared. He was cute as fuck, with his dark hair sticking up in odd directions and a crease from the sheets still lining his face.

"Well?" he pressed a tad grumpily, causing me to smile.

I pulled back the curtain the rest of the way and damn near wiggled with excitement as his gaze raked over me. "What are you waiting for?"

"For you to move the fuck over," he muttered, likely forgetting that I could hear him with my advanced hearing. He paused with one foot hovering over the rim of the tub and asked, "Is it bearable?"

I ripped my gaze away from his half hard cock that was already making me salivate. Man really did have a pretty dick. Again, not something I'd ever have thought I'd be thinking. But it was true. I smiled and moved back, shielding him from the intense spray. "Already turned it down."

A small smile curved his lips as he finished stepping in. "Careful, I might think you were *hoping* I'd join you."

"Maybe I was," I teased back, shuffling around him in the confined space so he could enjoy the water as well.

He hummed appreciatively as he tilted his head back and let the water run over his tight muscles. Gradually, his shoulders relaxed, and I took that as my cue to lean forward and place kisses along his collarbone. His hum turned into more of a groan as I coasted my hands over his defined pecs and trim waist. "Aidan," he said, the undercurrent of warning clear in his tone. A warning I promptly ignored.

"Yes?" I asked, playing dumb, then teasing his nipple with my teeth.

He sucked in a sharp breath and I didn't even need to look down to know he was fully hard. Before he could think of someway to deter me, I sank to my knees and licked his shaft from root to tip. The small bead of precum was my reward, and I savored the salty sweetness of him.

I wrapped my hand around the thick base and teased his slit with the tip of my tongue before sucking him deeper. His muffled curse was all the encouragement I needed. I hollowed my cheeks and took him deeper, abandoning my hold to lay both my hands on his thighs for support as I bobbed my head.

He let out a deep groan, the tension beneath my palms betraying how hard he was fighting not to buck into my mouth. "You're going to make me late."

I pulled off with a pop. "So you'll be a few minutes late. Tell me to stop," I challenged.

He chuckled and threaded his fingers through my hair. "Fucking furball."

I smirked and lapped at his tip, enjoying his gaze on me.

"So damn pretty, with my cock in your insanely hot mouth."

I nuzzled into his groin, still amazed that he didn't seem to have hair anywhere else on his body beside his head. Once his faint, musky scent fully saturated my senses, I returned to sucking him. If I was careful, I could shift just enough to bypass my gag reflex and take him down all the way. I just had to make sure not to sprout extra pointy teeth.

"Oh fuck!" he shouted when I swallowed around his length. His hold on my hair tightened and he finally let go of whatever was holding him back to fuck my mouth in earnest.

My tears blended with the water still pouring around us, but nothing on this green earth could get me to stop taking my snake apart. I reached for my aching cock, matching my strokes to the pace he'd set.

"That's it. Just like that, sweetheart."

I moaned around him. No one had ever called me anything like that before and actually *meant* it. Needless to say, I was quickly getting addicted to the tender endearment. My hand quickened, my release hovering just out of reach.

"Fuck. *Fuck.* I'm there. Fuck, sweetheart, you're so damn perfect." His nails dug into my scalp as he thrust with abandon, then released down my throat with a guttural cry.

I swallowed every last drop, then wiped my mouth with the back of my hand, more out of reflex than necessity. And apparently, somewhere through all of that, I'd come myself. With a smile I couldn't lose if I tried, I levered myself back up and planted a kiss on his lush mouth. "Better than chai?" I teased.

He released a full laugh that lit me up inside even more than the sex. I fucking loved it when he laughed. Loved it even more when I was the one that made him do it. "Better than chai," he said with another small laugh, and wrapped his arms around me. "But we really should get a move on."

"Yeah, yeah."

Truthfully, I didn't actually *want* to make Zahir late for his... job? Studies? Apprenticeship? I was still pretty fuzzy on what he actually did for money. He didn't steal it, that was for sure. Whatever it was, I didn't want to jeopardize it, so I dressed quickly and was ready to go when he plucked up his keys and made his way toward the door.

The drive was much the same as it had been every other time we'd made it. I tried hard not to focus too much on how useless I felt, having to be carted along to do nothing useful.

Zahir's hand settled over my thigh, and I glanced at him. "Everything alright? You're unusually quiet this morning."

There was probably something seriously wrong with me that I actually *enjoyed* his look of concern. I shook my head. "Nah, mind's just wandering."

"The full moon is coming up, right? Next week?"

I stiffened involuntarily. It wasn't like I'd forgotten. How could I? I was a werewolf, for fuck's sake. But I may have been trying not to think about it too much. I'd never gone through a full moon without my pack. Was that when the effects of my exile would start to really take effect? Because, if I was being honest, aside from being sad, and yeah, maybe a little depressed, the separation hadn't really lived up to my morbid expectations. I mean, I was fine. Or, at least, I thought I was.

He gave my thigh a light squeeze and flashed me a timid smile. "I was thinking, since you like running in Cumberland Falls so much, that it'd be the perfect place. And I, uh, could finally show you the moonbow?"

I frowned at him, not really sure why that was a question. Then what he was suggesting registered. "You want to come with me?"

His cheeks reddened, and he removed his hand to strangle the steering wheel. "It was just a thought. You can really only see the moonbow around the full moon and I've been wanting to show it to you for a while. But I totally understand if the whole full-moon-thing is something you'd prefer to do on your own. I mean, it's not like *I* could run with you, anyway. Right, yeah, totally stupid idea. Forget I said anything."

"No," I said quickly, prompting him to give me a curious look. "I... I'd really like for you to show me the moonbow. And... and it'd be nice not to be there on my own."

"Yeah? Okay, yeah. It'll be great. You're going to love it, Aidan," he said, noticeably brightening. "It's absolutely beautiful."

We pulled into his designated space at the Park, then made our way along the twisty path to get to the secret entrance of the cave that housed his temple. The walk through nature was always pleasant and already my paws itched to feel the press of dirt and fallen leaves beneath them. But I liked waiting to part ways with Zahir until he was within the fancy temple.

Per usual, Guru Angira was waiting at the entrance for us. The old snake gave me a grandmotherly smile before turning to Zahir, who'd already transitioned to his naga form. My breath caught at how unbelievably beautiful he was, exactly the same as it had every other day I'd seen his true form.

"Zahir, we have some visitors coming this morning for spiritual centering and guidance. Would you brew a fresh pot of tea so it is ready when they arrive?"

He lightly bowed his head. "Of course, Gurudevi. I'll await you and our visitors at the cushions." He glanced over at me with a smile in his eyes. "See you later, furball."

"You know it, scales," I replied cheekily, before waving absently at the guru and turning on my heel to head out the side entrance that let out into a deeper part of the woods.

A muted rumble gave me pause as I neared the exit, but I shook it off as nothing. Except when I opened the door to leave, it *wasn't* nothing. It was raining. No, not raining, pouring down so hard I could barely see three feet out.

"Well fuck," I said a little louder that I intended. Clearly, I'd been so wrapped up in Zahir and my stupid thoughts to *smell* the imminent fucking rain. It wasn't like it mattered if I got wet during a run, but if I didn't have to... Yeah, not getting soaked and smelling like wet dog was better.

"You're welcome to remain in the temple," Guru Angira said in her wispy voice that honestly sounded a lot like the way her scales rasped over the smooth stone floors. It also scared the living daylights out of me.

I whirled to face her, instinctively already starting to shift. The seams of my shirt strained and I could hear the threat of popping threads in my sensitive ears. It truly was unfair that Zahir's clothes shifted with him and mine didn't.

Her eyebrows arched in surprise, and I quickly dismissed the start of my change. "Well."

"Sorry," I replied abashedly, glancing behind her for Zahir, even though I knew he couldn't be there. "Are you sure it won't be any trouble? I don't want to be underfoot."

She waved a dismissive hand and turned on her tail, only pausing long enough for me to join at her side. "Of course not. The temple is open to all, though not all take advantage."

"Really?" I glanced sideways at her. "But isn't it, like, a religious thing?"

She nodded. "To an extent. But Hinduism is more about embracing the spirit and finding peace than it is about upholding a rigid standard of religious doctrine."

"Oh," I said, not sure what else to say. "Um, cool?"

She chuckled her weird papery laugh, which was comforting in its own weird way. "Oh, look. I believe our visitors have arrived."

I followed where she was pointing to see a cluster of nagas in various jewel tones speaking with Zahir in a hollow filled with cushions. He directed them to sit and began to look around at the same time Guru Angira pulled me back against the wall.

She held up a finger to her lips and smiled conspiratorially. That's when I realized two things: Zahir hadn't seen us and Guru Angira was a mischievous old bat.

"Um, aren't you supposed to be out there too?" I asked quietly.

She snorted softly. "He can handle this. Would you like some tea? I have some in the back."

I darted a glance out to where Zahir had clearly given up looking for the Guru. "Sure?"

Chapter 21

Zahir

Living with Aidan was, in a word, easy. Not that I'd ever given any consideration to what it might be like living with a werewolf. Some things I knew to expect, like the substantial appetite and regular need to shift. What I hadn't anticipated was how positively *domestic* it all was. Sometimes I worried that the reason behind Aidan's need to do things around the house was because he worried he wasn't earning his keep. Which was something I couldn't get him to grasp that he didn't need to do. He had a place here for as long as he wanted it, no strings attached. Selfishly, I hoped he wanted it for a long time to come.

Then there were moments like this where I could see how much joy a simple domestic task brought him. Me? I hated to cook. It was an evil necessity at the best of times. Aidan, however, clearly loved it. Didn't hurt that he was a damn good cook, either. I walked up behind where he was stirring something on the stove, intending to wrap my arms around him and nuzzle his neck. Before I got the chance, though, he twisted and offered me a spoonful of what he was making.

"Taste this," he ordered.

I held his intense blue gaze as I sampled the offering. Flavor exploded on my tongue. It was a miracle I didn't moan in ecstasy like some kind of porn star. Sweet, merciful Annapurna had seriously blessed this man with a gift.

"Is this spice right?" he asked when I failed to say anything, too caught up in the simple taste.

I released the spoon and bypassed it to savor his lips just as much as I had the small offering. "It's divine," I murmured before pulling away.

"Are you sure?" he pressed, the uncertainty in his voice as unmistakable as it was in his eyes.

I maneuvered to wrap my arms around his middle, pressing his back to my chest. "Very sure. You've hit the perfect balance of heat and flavor." He noticeably relaxed in my hold and I gave into the desire to press my nose into the hollow of his shoulder. "I still can't believe you just *taught* yourself how to make tikka masala. I haven't had any that good outside of India since my daadee—grandmother—came to visit years ago."

"I told you, I like cooking and finding new recipes. Plus, I... I wanted to make something you would like."

It was probably for the best that he couldn't see my face, since I was probably sporting a teeth-rottingly schmoopy expression. "For the record, I love everything you make. And if you were trying to impress me, you already have." He fidgeted as if the praise made him uncomfortable, and I tightened my hold. "You are amazing and quite talented. I consider it a great privilege and honor when you grace me with your talents."

"Z... it's really not that big of a deal." He rolled his shoulders, betraying that I'd pushed his discomfort as far as he could stand.

I placed a kiss on the side of his neck before releasing him and putting a small amount of space between us. "Perhaps to you it's not. But I don't intend to take it for granted."

"You're just glad you don't have to keep ordering takeout," he teased, brandishing the spoon at me with a playful smile that made my heart flip.

"That too," I replied, just as cheekily.

He snorted and resumed stirring. "Get down the plates?"

I smiled to myself as I did as he asked, marveling once again at the easy domesticity of it all. Three years ago, I'd been bitter and angry about being uprooted from what I viewed as a life of reckless freedom to apprentice with the oldest guru of our time. I didn't have a say in it then and I didn't now, but for some reason, that didn't bother me as much as it once had.

I finished helping Aidan plate the food, and we settled at the table together in a pattern that was becoming more familiar by the day. He was all set, with fork in hand, to devour the delectable meal, when I reached over and plucked the utensil free of his grasp.

He made an indignant sound that I fought hard not to laugh at. "I know you're not trying to get between a werewolf and dinner. *Especially* on a night with a full moon," he said, giving me a glower that was more of a pout.

"Relax, furball. I wouldn't dream of it. I just figured if we're going to eat a traditional Indian meal, then we should eat it in the traditional way." He watched me with a decidedly suspicious expression as I reached over the table to secure a piece of naan. Fuck me, he'd even made the naan from scratch. It was still warm. I cleared my throat in a futile attempt to ease the sudden lump, and illustrated tearing off a piece of the bread and using it to gather rice and masala, then popped the perfect bite in my mouth. I didn't bother to hold back my groan of appreciation this time.

"Okay..." he dragged out, eying the torn naan on my plate. Finally, he reached for a piece of his own and replicated the process.

"With your right hand," I gently corrected before he could get too far.

He gave me a look, but didn't question the distinction. It took a few tries before he really got the hang of it, but my heart swelled at seeing him stick with it.

"If it's too much, you can use the fork," I suggested, refilling our plates with another helping.

He shook his head and secured another piece of naan. "This is fine. I maybe even kind of like it?"

I ducked my head so he couldn't see me grinning like an absolute fool. "When we're finished, I'll clean so you can do anything you need to in preparation for tonight."

"Not really much to prepare for, but I won't say no to not having to do the dishes." He gave me a feral grin with far too many pointy teeth.

More than a little suspicious of his response, I glanced past him into the kitchen. That's when I realized he'd used damn near every pot and pan I had. While that wasn't saying much, it still made a hell of a mess. I groaned far less enthusiastically, and he chuckled.

"How about we tackle it together? Now that I have got a bit of a knack for it, I won't use so many dishes next time."

I smiled and nodded my appreciation while I fought the urge to launch across the table and smother him with kisses at the implication that he planned to stick around. Once the kitchen was back in order, we slipped on our shoes and headed out to the car.

"What's this?" Aidan asked, holding up a nylon bag I'd put in the backseat. "Pretty sure it wasn't here yesterday. I'd have noticed something highlighter orange."

"Oh, I, uh, thought it could come in handy when you shifted. You know, so your things don't get messed up and they're easy to find," I said awkwardly, ducking my head to twist the key in the ignition. Now that I said it out loud, the idea sounded a special kind of daft. Seriously? Help find his stuff? Like he wasn't a werewolf and could probably fucking *smell* it? When Aidan didn't respond to my babbling, I risked a glance at him. To my surprise, he looked touched by the gesture.

"You really brought this for me?" he asked, his fingers creating a soft whisk sound as he absently brushed them along the material.

"Yes?"

"Wow, that's..." He ran his free hand through his hair and blew out a breath.

I cringed. "It was stupid, right? Just forget you saw anything." I twisted around to toss the damn duffel through to the trunk. Aidan's fingers clawed into the bag and I looked back at him.

"No. It's not stupid. It might be one of the nicest things anyone's ever done for me." He gently pulled the bag from my grasp and moved it to his lap. "You just *saw* this and thought of me? I didn't have to ask or do anything. You just thought it would be useful and brought it along," he said wistfully.

Vishnu, preserve me. This man was breaking my damn heart. On an impulse, I wrapped my hand around the back of his neck. When he turned to look at me, a hint of mist shone in his eyes. "Sweetheart, if you like the idea of having a bag for your things when you change, I will get you the best damn bag I can find."

His lips twitched with the makings of a smile. I thought for sure he'd be slinging some sass, but instead, he sank his teeth into his bottom lip and looked back down, though it failed to hide his blush.

I cleared my throat, released him, and threw the vehicle in reverse. "Right, we've got a date with a full moon."

"And a moonbow," he added, flashing me a smile that about near stopped my heart.

The drive to the park was quiet without being awkward. I was tempted to reach over and thread our fingers together, but wasn't sure where he stood on handholding. Did he think it was sweet? Juvenile? Was it something he would ever initiate? By the time we parked by the falls, I was well and truly in my head.

"Moonrise should be in about an hour," Aidan said as he got out, nylon bag in hand.

The statement brought my attention to the fact that I'd just been sitting in the driver's seat while the car idled. I turned it off and got out as well. "That gives you plenty of time, right?"

He gave me a cheeky grin. "More than. And you're sure we have the place to ourselves?" he asked, glancing around. The falls were a little farther on, but that didn't change my answer.

"We should. I made sure that the park notified people that this area is closed for maintenance."

He let out a low whistle. "That's freaking cool. So... where will you be while I'm running?" He glanced at the dark vehicle.

"I'll wait for you at the falls. They're that way." I gestured toward the worn path opposite the small gravel parking lot.

"I'm sure I'll find it." He tapped the side of his nose and winked at me. I was still chuckling when he set the empty bag on the hood of the car and started to strip. He finished shoving his things inside and zipped it closed before stepping close. I was always down for a naked Aidan and happily wrapped my arms around him. He tilted his head back and teased me with the promise of a kiss. "I won't be long."

"You better not," I replied, my voice coming out rough, then stole the kiss he was withholding.

His smile stretched practically ear-to-ear when he stepped back. He rolled his shoulders, flashed me another wink, then began his shift. It'd be nice to say that after a few weeks of watching him shift like it was nothing, I'd be used to it. Alas, nothing about the sight of his body breaking and reshaping was ever going to feel *normal*. He finished and shook out his stunning golden fur, then loped away.

I waited until he'd vanished into the trees, then slung the bag across my body and began the walk to the waterfall of Cumberland Falls. When I arrived at the viewing platform, I was relieved not to see anyone around. I slowly made my way down to the water's edge, where I stripped down like Aidan had in the parking lot. Then had a laugh at myself for forgetting to bring a bag for *my* clothes.

Shrugging, I stuffed mine beside his, situating our shoes beside it. Satisfied that the probably waterproof bag was well out of reach of the water, I transitioned to my naga form. I scratched at a spot on my arm where it seemed my scales had become uncharacteristically dry and slithered into the slightly cool water. I shivered violently, silently cursing my cold-blooded nature, and swam deeper into the pool.

I lost myself amidst the soft ripples and thundering falls. Periodically, I glanced up at the sky, waiting for the moon to get high enough to create the moonbow. Not that I was worried about missing it, more just eager to share it with Aidan. Once the moon was nearly at the optimal viewing angle, I swam closer toward the shore. I was about to transition back to human form when a gasp stole my attention.

"Full moon at midnight," Aidan cursed softly, eyes wide, bare toes digging into the sandy ground.

I smiled and finished getting out of the water to go stand behind him, wrapping my arms around his middle once more. My heart gave a happy flutter when he placed his arms over mine and leaned against me. "What do you think?" I whispered in his ear, resting my chin on his shoulder to take in the remarkable sight with him.

"It's absolutely beautiful," he replied just as softly, voice tinged with awe.

I took another moment to appreciate the majesty of the muted rainbow colors arching over the pool, then nuzzled into his neck. "Swim with me?"

"I'd love to," he said, twisting to look at me. "But..."

I pressed a kiss to the side of his neck. "But what, sweetheart?"

"Don't get me wrong," he said quickly, "I absolutely love water, but I'm, uh, not a very good swimmer." If he didn't already sound so embarrassed, I'd have teased him.

"Then I guess it's a good thing I'm here." I took his hand like I'd wanted to do in the car, letting the thrill of him tangling our fingers wash over me as I led us into the mostly still water. It was a little slow going, but eventually I got us positioned just shy of right beneath the moonbow.

Wonder continued to shine in Aidan's eyes as he looped his arms around my neck and looked up at the simple magic of nature. "It really is amazing. Thank you." His shy smile when he looked at me was going to get us both drowned when I forgot how to breathe, let alone swim.

I slashed my tail in the water to make sure we stayed afloat and tried to get a handle on how hard I was falling for this wonderfully sweet wolf. Aidan might have been the purest soul I'd ever encountered. He deserved every soft thing the world had failed to give him. To be cherished like the treasure he was. As I leaned forward to press our lips together, I silently vowed to make sure he would never have to fight for the right to exist again, to make sure that he knew every single day what a precious gift he was.

Chapter 22

Zahir

I awoke and immediately let out a sigh. Carefully, so as not to disturb Aidan, I rolled to lie on my side, propping my head up with one hand while reaching to brush my fingers over his golden locks with the other. He snuffled into the comforter and shimmied closer. After several weeks of living together, I was finally getting used to waking up beside a literal wolf half of the time. If I was being honest with myself, though, I couldn't shake the feeling that it was... odd. Even for a werewolf.

Giving into the temptation of his warmth, I curled around him and stroked his soft fur. He made a muffled rumbly noise, that I at least *thought* sounded pleased. Leaning close so I was by his ear, I whispered, "Come on, sweetheart, time to get up."

He made another, far less happy noise, and bodily scooted into me. I let out an undignified "Oof" and flicked him on the ear, prompting him to lift his head and shoot me a disgruntled glare.

"Don't give me that look. We don't want to be late for our meeting with Ezra." Hopefully *he* would have answers to the questions that had plagued me about Aidan's peculiar mannerisms. I swiveled around and got out of the bed. A glance back showed that Aidan had burrowed deeper into the sheets. I huffed in frustration. While I knew he wasn't exactly eager to chat with another werewolf—especially after what had happened to him—I also knew he needed it. Even if he couldn't see it. "Let's go, furball. Unless, of course, you'd rather I call and tell him to just come here?"

In the blink of an eye, Aidan was scrambling to be free of the now very tangled sheets, then promptly began shifting back to his human form.

"I figured that'd get your attention," I commented, crossing my arms over my chest.

He glowered at me as he straightened and rubbed at his ear, even though I knew for a fact there was absolutely no way it still hurt. "We're meeting him at the Daniel Boone National Forest, right?" he asked as he reached for his jeans from the day before.

"Yes," I reassured him for the thousandth time. He'd been adamant about meeting Ezra somewhere public with lots of people that were nowhere near the house *or* the temple. Pointing out that Ezra had been to both places before had done absolutely nothing to dissuade him. I glanced at him out of the corner of my eye, picking up on his obvious anxiety. "It's going to be fine. He just wants to get to know you better and make sure you're okay."

Aidan let out a massive huff. "I know. I *know*. It's just..." He trailed off, dragging both of his hands through his hair. Suddenly, I had a thought that might help ease his nerves. I dug through the bottom of the closet until I found what I was looking for.

"Why don't you wear this?" I held out a white and blue University of Kentucky Wildcats ball cap.

He gave me the same soft expression he'd given me over the nylon duffel bag. "Yeah?"

I shrugged, forcing myself not to make a big deal of nothing. It wasn't like *I* thought he needed to hide his hair. "It goes with what you're wearing."

He plucked at the simple white t-shirt he'd put on while I'd been rummaging. "It does kind of match, huh?" he said with a crooked grin as he pulled it on.

"And you still look gorgeous," I said, stepping into his personal space and tugging the rim straight. I caught a faint hint of pink coloring his fair cheeks before I brushed my lips over his. "We really do need to get going. It's quite a drive."

He snorted. "Until you've been riding for several hours completely exposed to the elements, you don't *know* what a drive is."

Rather than play into what would inevitably turn into stalling tactics, I began shoving him out of the bedroom and toward the front door. "We'll grab something to eat along the way."

"But Zahir," he whined, poking out his bottom lip for good measure.

"Don't you even with me, furball. We both know you love junk food every bit as much as you love home-cooked meals." He flashed me a cheeky grin, then bounded over to the car, leaving me to grumble to myself as I locked up.

The drive was even longer than I anticipated, mostly due to the obscene number of people on the road and the lack of anywhere to park once we arrived. Apparently, of all the days we could have met up, we picked the one that had every children's summer program within fifty miles there on a field trip. Oddly, Aidan seemed more buoyed by the crowd than put off.

Resigned to having to wade through clusters of shouting kids, I searched the picnic area for Ezra. At last I spotted him at a table on the far side, set back a way from the covered pavilion in the center. As an added bonus, either through some wolfy charisma or just damn good luck, none of the abundance of children were anywhere near the table he'd secured.

"There he is," I said, pointing him out to Aidan. Instantly, all of Aidan's anxiety returned. I reached for his hand and gave it a light squeeze. "Hey, I'm right here. If you feel like things are taking a turn, just say the word and we'll leave. All I ask is that you give him an honest chance. He really helped me when I didn't have anyone else to turn to."

Aidan took a deep breath, then slowly released it. "Okay, let's see what he has to say."

That sounded suspiciously like "Let's get this over with," but I let it stand. We remained hand in hand as we skirted around rowdy children and made our way to where Ezra was waiting.

"I was beginning to worry you'd gotten lost," Ezra said with a wide smile, standing to greet us.

"We're not that late, are we?" I shot Aidan a look, but he just tugged his cap down more firmly and kept his gaze downcast. "Uh... yeah, so Aidan, this is Ezra Thatcher. Ezra, this is Aidan," I said awkwardly.

"Nice to meet you. Properly," Ezra said with what I was sure was a charming smile, but he could cut that shit right out.

Reflexively, I tightened my hold on Aidan's hand, tugging him slightly closer to me. I frowned at the sudden possessiveness clawing at my chest. "We should sit."

Ezra glanced at me, undoubtedly picking up on my strained tone and who the fuck knew what else. Fortunately, he didn't press, and gestured for us to take a seat. "I can't say what a relief it is to see you all healed up," Ezra continued like the two of us weren't acting all kinds of strange. He gave me a sheepish smile. "To be honest, I wasn't nearly as confident as I made it seem that he'd come around."

"I'm sitting right here," Aidan snarled unexpectedly.

Ezra's gaze flicked to him, briefly darting to me, then back again. "Um, so you are. Sorry. This whole thing has been pretty weird. That's a big reason I wanted to meet with you. I was hoping you could fill in some of the blanks for me and my pack. I'm sure you can understand why we would want to know about a threat that could do that to a *were* in his prime."

Aidan fidgeted in his seat and mumbled something that might have been an agreement.

I rested my hand on Aidan's thigh and gave it a light squeeze of encouragement. "I think you should tell Ezra who did this to you and why."

"Any details you could share would be really helpful," Ezra prompted. "Though I understand if you can't remember too much, considering how drugged you were. Pri told us what she could, but she was pretty shaken up."

Aidan's head shot up, his blue eyes wide as he leaned forward eagerly. "You know Pri? Is she okay? Did she make it home okay?"

"Uh, yeah, she did. I think maybe you saved her life," Ezra said, his gaze once again flicking between us.

"Thank fuck." Aidan released a heavy sigh, like he'd been holding his breath since we'd arrived. "It would have really sucked if I went through all of that and they caught up to her, anyway. So, she's part of your pack?"

Ezra's brow pinched in a frown. "She is. But, I'm sorry, I'm confused. It sounds like you're suggesting the *weres* you were with did that to you."

"They did." Aidan shrugged as if it was nothing, but I could feel his tension beneath my palm.

"But... weren't they part of *your* pack?" Ezra looked especially confused now. I bit my tongue to keep from blurting the truth and braced myself for his reaction.

"They are. Well, they were. I'm not part of the pack anymore," Aidan replied, shrinking in on himself.

The emotions that flickered over Ezra's face ranged from disbelief to denial to outrage. "Your pack did that to you?! Why?!"

Thank Vishnu the children were also shouting and Ezra's raised voice barely even cracked the din surrounding us. "Maybe keep it down?" I suggested, while massaging the increasing tension in Aidan's leg beneath the table. "Tell him, sweetheart. He needs to know."

Aidan gave me a pained look, then swallowed thickly. "Because I helped Pri get away. They did... what you saw. Instead of killing me outright, though, they wanted me to suffer a little more for defying the pack and exiled me."

The grimace instantly followed by sympathy on Ezra's face, told me everything I needed to know. Exile for a werewolf was *bad*. "Fuck," he muttered. "That's just plain cruel." Abruptly, determination replaced his horrified expression, and he straightened. "I'm talking to Alpha about bringing you into the North Carolina pack. No one deserves to die like that, especially for *saving* someone."

"Can you... can you really do that?" Aidan asked. The hope in his voice damn near broke me. Had he been suffering some wolfy affliction, and I'd been completely unaware?

"I don't see why not. Lee—our Alpha—has done it before. Pria actually was one of the rogue *weres* he incorporated into the pack. Granted, it's not the norm, but it feels like the least we could do. Can I ask what your pack was doing in the area?" Ezra asked cautiously.

"I don't see why not. Besides, it's not like I'm part of the Stormfire pack anymore, anyway. Though, I'm not sure what insight there really is to provide. We've always moved around a lot. Most we've ever stayed in one place was a year."

Judging by the confused shock on Ezra's face, that was every bit as abnormal as I'd expected it was. "The Stormfire pack doesn't have territory?"

"No?" Aidan glanced at me askance, but whatever answer he was looking for, I didn't have it.

"Why?" Ezra pushed.

"How should I know?" Aidan replied defensively. "It's been like that since before the pack took me in."

Ezra held up his hand. "Hold up, you lost me again. You weren't born into the pack?"

"Of course not. None of us were. That's part of why we don't feel the need to have territory. Or, at least, that's why I always assumed. They saved me after my birth pack was attacked. Only me and a few others survived." Sadness overtook Aidan's face, and he dropped his head. "Well, just me, in the end."

"Aidan, you're going to have to really break this down for me. Who attacked your original pack? Are there *no* children in the Stormfire pack?"

I felt as much as saw Aidan bristle. "Of course there are kids. They're just kept separate from the adults until they've had their first shift. I was, along with the other two from my birth pack."

"And what happened to them?" Ezra asked without an ounce of mercy.

"Not everyone survives the change, you know," Aidan snapped. Ezra was undoubtedly about to press for more answers that I wasn't sure Aidan was capable of providing and they were working each other into a frenzy, so I quickly stepped in.

"Aidan, will you shift just your hand for Ezra? Nothing too drastic. I just want him to see something."

"Why?" Aidan asked at the same time Ezra snorted.

"Really, Zahir? Even a snake should know better than..." Ezra trailed off as Aidan placed his hand on the table. Within seconds, his fingers lengthened and sprouted deadly claws. "What the fuck?" Ezra gasped, lurching up from his seat.

"How long does it take you to fully shift, Aidan?" I asked, without looking away from Ezra's face.

Aidan shrugged and let the claws recede back into human hands. "I don't know. Couple minutes tops."

"Can your whole pack do that?" I added, taking a stab in the dark.

"Of course. All werewolves can," he scoffed.

Ezra was still shaking his head as he resumed his seat. "That's not possible. It takes at least ten minutes to complete a shift, and... and we definitely can't isolate a shift like you just did."

"What do you mean? Of course you can." Aidan twisted to look at me, his confusion stamped plain as day on his face. "Can't they?"

"I don't think they can, sweetheart. I think your pack is... special."

"But... But..." Aidan stammered, looking between me and Ezra. "No! That's not right. It's not supposed to take that long. It means something is wrong. Letting a *were* suffer like that is... No, it's not true." He vehemently shook his head. Ezra and I seemed to reach the same horrible conclusion in the face of Aidan's adamant denial.

Mercifully, Ezra was the one to ask, "What happened to the children who didn't survive the shift?"

Tears welled in Aidan's eyes and I wanted nothing more than to hold him close and tell him everything would be alright. But it wasn't. "They... their change... they were *suffering*," he croaked out. "Alpha said it was a mercy."

My stomach twisted at hearing Aidan confirm our worst fears, while Ezra looked as though someone had sucker punched him.

Abruptly, Aidan pushed up from the table and snarled, "Fuck you. You don't know what you're talking about." Then he stomped toward the parking lot.

Ezra dropped his head in his hands and let out a haggard breath. "Fuck. *Fuck*. That's so messed up. I don't even have words. His *whole* pack can shift like that? And anyone who can't..."

"Believe it or not, I think it gets worse than that," I said, watching Aidan stalk across the field, heedless of the children running around him.

"How can it get worse?"

"From what I've been able to gather from our time together, the pack was very controlling. Aidan doesn't seem to remember anything from his childhood before he was taken in and not much at all before he was integrated with the mature wolves. I don't think that was the first time Aidan was exposed to the drug, either. He... remembered it."

"Mother of the moon," Ezra gasped. "What the hell is wrong with this pack?"

"I honestly don't know." I glanced at where Aidan had finally reached the car and was now circling a motorcycle parked nearby. "There was something I wanted to ask, but didn't want to do it in front of Aidan."

Ezra gave me a wary look. Not that I could blame him after all the bombs we'd dropped on him today. "What?"

"Do werewolves typically shift to sleep or, better yet, in front of people?"

"No. The sleep I guess is a preference, but most of the *weres* I know don't. As for the other, absolutely not. It's when we're at our most vulnerable and incredibly private." He paused, then asked the obvious next question. "I take it Aidan does both?"

I nodded, sorrow filling my heart. "I think it was compulsory."

"Fuck. I get every pack is going to do things their own way, but that's seriously twisted. Let me guess, he thinks it's normal."

"He does. As well as believing his hair makes him some kind of freak," I added without really thinking.

Ezra glanced toward where Aidan was now crouched down by the motorcycle. "What's wrong with his hair?"

"Nothing, if you ask me. But apparently he's been dying it brown to avoid being treated like a second class werewolf—like a dog. It's actually blond."

The growl that rolled out of Ezra threatened to have my cobra hood flaring. "Someone seriously needs to put an end to these psychos." Still grumbling to himself in agitation, he stood and nodded for me to join him as we made our way to the car park. We were about halfway there when he glanced at me with a curious gleam in his eye. "Why didn't you tell me you two were bonded?"

I lurched to a stop and stared at him. "What?"

"When he was MIA, and you were blowing up my phone. I get it now—not that I appreciated it—but it makes sense why you'd be desperate to get him back."

I shook my head. "I don't understand what you're talking about."

"Seeing you together, it's obvious you two are bonded. *Anyone* who's seen a bonded pair before wouldn't be able to miss it," he continued, like he still wasn't speaking another language.

"For fuck's sake, Ezra. Speak plainly. Let's assume I'm *not* a werewolf for a second and try using words the rest of us might grasp."

"Uh... right. Sorry." He rubbed the back of his neck and huffed out a breath. "It's kind of like the werewolf equivalent of soul mates, except *way* more. Like if something were to happen to you, he'd die too."

I thought back to all the less than subtle remarks Gurudevi had made about me being more settled, how it would take a *mate* to bring my soul that kind of peace. "A true mate," I whispered. I wasn't sure how much I believed it, but there was a certain rightness to hearing the words.

"Guess you could look at it that way," Ezra said with a shrug as he resumed eating up the space between us and Aidan.

"But... how could we not know? How does it happen? For werewolves," I clarified.

Ezra gave me a sidelong look. "Have you had sex?" He immediately rolled his eyes. "Obviously you've had sex. I can smell you all over each other, and you're definitely bonded. What I mean is, have you had *unprotected* sex?"

"That's none of your damn business."

He held up his hands defensively. "And I'm not saying it is, but that's how it happens for werewolves. I'm sure someone somewhere knows the nitty gritty of why and how, but that's the gist of it. And if you *had* before he went missing, it explains how he could find you that night." He glanced at where Aidan was now appreciatively stroking the vibrant green paint on the motorcycle and lowered his voice to where I could barely hear. "Given everything else I've learned about his shitshow of a pack, I'm gonna go out on a limb and say he's just as in the dark about that as he is about everything else."

"Fucking hell," I hissed under my breath and massaged my temple. While I'd expected this meeting to bring a number of revelations where Aidan was concerned, I was past my breaking point. We were mates? And already sealed together from the sound of it. I absently scratched at my arm and joined Ezra where he'd already reached Aidan while I struggled to wrap my head around things.

"Yeah, so sorry again about coming at you like that," Ezra was saying.

Aidan glowered at the gravel and stuffed his hands in his pockets. "It's fine."

"It's really not," Ezra said with a sigh. "I'm still going to talk to Alpha about bringing you into the pack." Aidan merely nodded, but I could feel the hope and relief radiating off of him. "You like bikes?" Ezra asked, pointedly shifting the focus of the tense conversation.

Aidan noticeably brightened and one of his adorable half-smiles tilted his lips. "Fucking love 'em. Spent a lot of my time with the pack working on them and fixing up any other engines that had issues."

"No shit?" Ezra crossed his arms and considered Aidan.

"Yeah. It was one of the few things I was good at and the others didn't give me grief about." Aidan winced at what was undoubtedly a slip. "Anyway, this one's a real beaut'." He gave the machine a wistful look.

"Thanks. She's mine," Ezra said with a smirk.

"*Nice.*" Aidan held out his fist for them to bump.

"So, really good with machines, huh? How'd you like to come work for me at my garage?" Ezra asked. Aidan's face beamed with excitement, his eyes comically wide as he stared at Ezra. I'd have laughed at the sight if it also wasn't so damn endearing.

"For real? You'd trust me to do that?"

Ezra shrugged. "I could always use another pair of hands that have a knack with motorcycles. Ever work with Harleys?" he asked, patting the tank of the bike.

"Pretty exclusively, actually. No certification, though," Aidan admitted, his exuberance dimming.

"Pft. We can get you *that*. But there's no piece of paper that can replace honest talent. Think it over. You can let me know what you decide when I get back to you after talking with Lee," Ezra said, moving closer to the bike and swinging his leg over.

"Yeah. I will. Thanks, you know, for everything."

Ezra might not have been able to detect the sudden thickness in Aidan's voice, but I sure as hell did. I wrapped an arm around Aidan's waist, tugging him into my side, and placed a firm kiss on his temple.

Ezra gave me a knowing look before cranking the engine. "I'll be in touch." With those parting words, the engine roared, and he drove away.

Aidan leaned into me once he'd gone. "Fuck, I can't believe he just offered me a job." He'd offered him a hell of a lot more than that, but it was clear Aidan still needed time to process the ramifications of everything else.

"We really need to get you a phone now," I said, squeezing his side. "What do you say we check out the Natural Arch Scenic Area?"

He glanced up at me, a broad smile on his lips and his eyes perfectly reflecting the clear sky above. "I'd really like that."

Chapter 23

Aidan

If I was going to have a job, I couldn't rely on Zahir to drive me everywhere. He had his own shit to take care of, his own responsibilities. And, despite how adamant he was that he was total shit at the whole guru-thing, from what I'd seen, he was doing a damn good job. Yeah, I wasn't about to fuck up his studies so I could enjoy a little independence. Which was why I was currently crouched in a thick cluster of bushes, staring at the house the Stormfire pack had taken over.

I'd told Zahir that morning, I wanted to stay behind, maybe wander around town or something. He'd smelled skeptical, but had smiled and encouraged me to have a good time. And I would totally do all of that... right after I got my bike back.

I plucked at my already sweat-soaked shirt and huffed a breath. It had to be fucking ninety degrees, and the breeze was nonexistent, leaving the heavy air feeling stale and dead. While uncomfortable, it was definitely working in my favor. Maneuvering around the house without being seen *and* staying down wind was damn near impossible.

After a few nonstarters, I finally found a vantage that gave me a perfect view of the bikes parked behind the house and immediately cursed. There were way too many bikes around for me to sneak up without being noticed. I sat back on my haunches and reconsidered my plan of attack. At least my ride was still there, though it would have been handy if it had been parked at the end of the line rather than dead fucking center.

It was possible Garett had given the bike to someone else, though admittedly, I was a little surprised they hadn't simply cannibalized it for parts. I peeked back through the thick foliage hiding me from view, noting the few pack members wandering around the backyard.

"Shit, shit, shit," I muttered. The smart thing to do would be to try again another day or, better yet, give up the endeavor altogether. But I'd always been a stubborn shit, and I wasn't leaving without *my* Harley.

"Maybe I could just make a break for it," I mused aloud. Wasn't like anyone would expect an exiled wolf to show up out of the blue and try to rob them. Then again, exiled wolves were also usually *dead* wolves. Still, it was the only course of action that had even a sliver of success.

Stealing myself, I leaned forward, mentally debating whether it would be better or worse to shift my legs for the mad dash. I took a deep breath and decided against it. If I really had to run, there was no way I could ride the bike with my legs bent the other way.

"Here goes nothing." I moved the largest limb blocking my path and came face to face with Jace. I let out a yelp and fell back on my ass, automatically scrambling backward.

A deep frown creased Jace's features as he dipped through the foliage to come closer. "Aidan? What the fuck are you *doing* here?" he asked, his voice deep and ominous.

Unfortunately, that's also when it occurred to me that this scheme had been a really *really* bad idea. I knew what happened when a pack came across banished *weres* that were somehow still alive. They didn't stay that way. Now the ultimate goody-two-shoes of the Stormfire Pack was glaring down at me like I'd lost my damn mind. Which, okay, fair.

"Dude, seriously. The *fuck*? Are you *trying* to get dead? While we're at it, how are you even still alive?" he demanded in rapid fire.

"I came for my ride," I said. It sounded even stupider when I said it out loud. Damn, maybe I did have some kind of death wish. Maybe it was part of being exiled. Doing stupid shit that would end with me in pieces.

He ran a hand over his shaved head and let out a sigh that sounded strained. "Mother of the moon, you've never exactly been the brightest crayon in the box, but this is dim, even for you."

"Who are you calling an idiot?" I snarled. "I was kicked out for *saving* someone. And, you know, fuck it. I'd rather face death as an exile than be part of a pack that kills children and calls it mercy." I didn't know why I said that last bit besides that it had been bouncing around my head since the meeting with Ezra. I wasn't even sure it was true. Or I wasn't until a strange darkness clouded Jace's face and he looked like he'd been gut punched. "Holy fuck! It's true?!"

"Would you keep your damn voice down? Or are you trying to get us *both* killed?" he hissed. I snapped my mouth shut so fast it sounded like I swallowed a bubble. Jace glanced toward the house. "Fuck, Aidan, why'd you have to come back? You know anyone that sees you is compelled to turn you in. You *know* that, right?"

I swallowed thickly. "How long?"

"How long, what?" he grumbled irritably.

"How long have you known?" I demanded.

He gave me a dark look that made me feel like a rabbit in a snare. After a minute that felt like a damn month, his shoulders sagged. "Too long. Haven't you ever wondered why we moved around so much? Didn't have territory of our own?"

Now I really felt as dim as he accused me of being, because I hadn't, not really. "I just thought... I don't know what I thought. And I don't see why it matters, anyway," I added defensively.

"The pack has been filling its ranks by taking *weres* from other packs for years. Doesn't make much sense to stick around where survivors might come looking for revenge."

I stared at him while his words tumbled around in my brain, refusing to settle. *Survivors.* "What... What are you saying? Is that..." The question stuck in my throat, threatening to choke me.

"Yeah," Jace said softly, his brown eyes sad. "It's how we came into the pack. I'm originally from somewhere in the Midwest—Utah or something—and I think your batch was grabbed along the West Coast."

That was... a lot. A hell of a lot more than I was prepared to deal with right now. I stuffed down the twisted sense of betrayal along with the dozen other questions that bubbled up and pushed myself to my feet. "Are you gonna turn me in, or what?" I asked, dusting the dirt and leaves from my ass. "Because if not, I have a bike to get." I took a step forward, and Jace's large hand landed squarely on my chest.

"No."

I puffed up. I didn't really want to go at it with one of the few pack members I'd gotten along with, one I'd viewed as a littermate, a brother. And I definitely didn't want to do that within howling distance of the rest of the pack.

"I'll get it. Go to the dinky gas station two roads over. Wait for me there."

I studied his face. Far as I could tell, he was serious. He was really going to not only let me go, but get my ride. "Okay. I'll wait."

He gave a sharp nod. "Good. Now get the fuck out of here before someone like fucking Eliott or Scott sees you." I'd already begun to withdraw when he tacked on, "And Aidan? Don't ever fucking come back."

I made my way to the meeting spot with his dire warning ringing in my ears. In hindsight, coming here really had been one of my dumber ideas, but I hadn't wanted to resort to my usual methods of getting what I needed. Zahir knew I wasn't a saint by any stretch of the imagination, but I didn't want to steal anymore if I didn't have to. Didn't want to be a disappointment in his eyes. Thankfully, Jace didn't let me sit with my thoughts for too long.

The familiar rumble of a Harley had my ears twitching only an hour after I left the house. I was already smiling as I exited the gas station with my impulse purchases in a small plastic bag. Maybe I should have been more worried that Jace had set me up and the entire pack would be rolling up to finish what they'd started. But if that had been Jace's end game, why bother letting me go in the first place?

Gravel crunched beneath the tires as Jace pulled into a nearby parking space. "Sorry it took me so long," he said, kicking out the stand and cutting the engine. "Had to deal with some nosy fucks wanting to know what I was doing with your ride."

"No big." I undid the buckle on the right saddlebag and dropped my purchases inside. "What'd you tell them?" I asked as he finished dismounting.

He smirked. "That I was taking it to a local scrap yard to see what I could get for the parts."

I let out an indignant squawk and caressed the not-so-shiny gas tank. "Don't listen to him. You're better than some second-rate scrap yard."

Jace chuckled and stepped back so I could take his place. "I did a quick once over to make sure no one had gotten any bright ideas. Everything looked okay, but you've always had a better hand with the bikes than just about everyone."

"Yeah, yeah. I'll be sure to give her a full body check and tune up." I cranked the engine and took a moment to let the soothing sound and vibrations roll over me. Eventually, I peered over at Jace, who was standing awkwardly off to the side. "Uh, thanks again. You know, for everything."

He shrugged his excessively broad shoulders. "Don't mention it. And I meant what I said before. Don't come anywhere near this shit show. It's not safe."

It was on the tip of my tongue to ask if he knew just how different we were from others of our kind, that our ability to shift like we did was not only unusual, but rare as fuck. Part of me suspected that he already knew. Ultimately, it didn't matter. So I revved the throttle, gave him a nod, and ripped out of the lot.

One thing I'd always loved about riding was how quiet my mind went. There was more than enough to keep my brain in a constant tailspin, but the only thing that occupied my thoughts was how the wind felt and the turns in the road. It was already getting late by the time I wound my way back to Zahir's place. A warm, fuzzy feeling spread through my chest when I realized he was already home.

I pulled up to the front of the house, but didn't bother cutting the engine. I was swinging my leg over the seat to go get him, when he stepped outside, with a rolling pin, of all things. "What are you planning to do with that?" I asked, laughing.

He glanced at the wooden pin, then scowled at me. "You gave me a fucking heart attack. I didn't like the idea of you being alone, so I cut out early. Imagine my surprise when you were nowhere to be found, *and* you left your new phone on the damn counter."

"Oops. That's gonna take some getting used to. I've never had to carry one all the time. Also," I said, walking toward him, "I told you I planned to wander around town." Despite his scowl deepening, my heart still fluttered at the idea that he'd been worried about me.

"Yeah, well..." He fizzled out and set the pin aside. He huffed and glanced at the bike idling in the drive. "Where'd you get that?"

"Don't worry, I didn't steal it. Well, technically I did. But is it really stealing if it's already mine?" Zahir narrowed his eyes in suspicion. Before he could dive deeper into *where* I'd gone to retrieve the bike, I stepped fully into his personal space. "Go for a ride with me."

A hint of wariness edged his scent as he looked past me to the rumbling bike. "I've never ridden on one before."

"And I hadn't done a lot of things before I met you," I replied with a wicked smile. I stepped closer to better judge the nuances in his scent and to rub my hands along his arms. "I'll keep you safe. Please come with me. Let me share this with you." I stared into his deep brown eyes and willed him to say yes.

He cast another furtive glance at the bike. The wariness was still there, but it couldn't mask the surge of excitement, giving his normally light scent an intoxicating tang, like green apples. "I don't have a helmet."

"Good thing Kentucky is a no-helmet state, then. But if you'd feel better with one, mine is in the saddlebags."

A smile bloomed on his face, and I forgot to breathe for a hot minute. Zahir was a stunning man, and it still broke my brain a bit that he directed those smiles at *me*. "You sure it'll fit? I mean, you do have a big head."

I threw my head back and cackled. "It'll fit fine, scales. Now come on." I fished out the helmet from the opposite saddlebag I'd stowed my gas station loot, then swung my leg over the saddle and held it out to him.

He took a deep breath, but didn't hesitate to clip on the half-skull cap. His mount was a little awkward, and it took a few moments of him wiggling around in a way that wasn't doing my dick any favors before he settled. "Okay. Now what?"

"Now? You hang on tight." I caught his scoff as he looped his arms around my waist. Chuckling to myself, I knocked back the kickstand, revved the engine, and took off with practiced ease. Zahir let out a squeak and immediately tightened his hold. It had been a while since I'd ridden with anyone else, so I took my time getting comfortable with the change in weight distribution. Once I was confident I could handle the curves and Zahir wouldn't fall off, I opened her up.

I wasn't sure how long we'd been riding beyond the sun setting. Eventually, Zahir relaxed enough to loosen his death grip on my middle. Then he relaxed enough to let his hands roam. Which, yeah, that was creating a growing problem. It became harder and harder to focus on the winding road, especially when he slipped his chilly hands beneath my shirt and trailed his long fingers over my abdomen.

I caught sight of a turnoff and prayed to the Goddess that it led somewhere isolated. The asphalt turned to gravel, then to dirt as we climbed higher. Finally, the "road", if it could still be called that, leveled out into a vista that offered a stunning view of the Appalachian foothills we'd ridden through. Best of all, there wasn't another soul in sight.

No sooner did I kill the engine than Zahir swung his leg off and stumbled a few steps. "Whoa," he said, clinging to the seat he'd just vacated.

"Easy there, scales. Give your legs a chance to adjust." I neglected to point out that I had no such issues. Where I expected him to fire back with a witty remark, he beamed at me.

"That was magnificent! Why haven't I ever done that before?" He chuckled at his blatant enthusiasm and shook his head, slowly straightening up. "Seriously incredible. Thank you."

The want I'd been diligently ignoring surged. I closed the distance between us, simultaneously capturing his mouth and popping the helmet free. It tumbled to the ground, but neither of us paid it any mind.

"Need you," I gasped against his lips, dropping my hands to his fly.

He grunted and attacked my mouth with ferocity. "Fuck yes," he growled, then tapped the brakes. "Wait. Here?"

"Yes, here." I nipped at his lips and palmed his erection.

He snickered. "Alright, furball, and what did you plan to use for lube?"

"Way ahead of you." I flashed him a cheeky grin before pulling out the new bottle I'd purchased at the gas station earlier.

"Aren't you a regular boy scout?" he teased, but the heat in his words gave him away. He grabbed the bottle from me when I closed the distance once again to kiss him. The groan he let out when I squeezed his dick through his briefs had my balls tightening. "Where do you want me?"

"Inside me," I replied with as much *duh* as the question deserved.

"Fuck, Aidan, you're killing me," he gasped when I slipped my hand past the elastic to caress the warm skin beneath. "Seriously, where?"

Oh. Right. "On the bike." My next kiss landed on his cheek when he turned to look skeptically at the bike. I finished freeing his glorious cock and nibbled at his jaw. "Sit on the back like before."

As awkward as he looked attempting to straddle the bike with his pants undone, he was downright graceful compared to my floundering attempt to get into position in front of him. A task made that much more difficult when he kissed along the back of my neck the second I was within range. I grumbled in frustration as I fought to push my jeans down enough and not topple off the back. I'd just gotten my dick and half of my ass free when he stopped me.

"Let me, sweetheart," he said, his husky voice wreaking havoc on my control and making me that much more desperate.

"Z," I whined.

"Hands on the handlebars," he ordered. No sooner did I lean forward than he shimmied my pants down a few more inches. I was on the verge of calling this what it was—a really dumb idea—when he planted a hand on my back and pressed my chest onto the gas tank. "Such a pretty hole. Already clenching for me."

Between the awkward maneuvering and the strain of denim right beneath my balls, the position was far from comfortable. Then he slipped a finger inside and comfort was the last thing on my mind. "*Yesss*," I moaned when he added another digit.

"You're so fucking beautiful, laid out like this for me. So ready, so perfect."

The sweet praise went straight to my head, making me lightheaded, and had me squirming. "More," I panted.

On cue, Zahir replaced his fingers with the fat head of his dick. I hissed at the burn, worried my impatience had got the best of me, but soon enough it relaxed into the stretch I'd come to crave. I attempted to drive back to take more of him, then let out another frustrated whine when nothing happened. Before I could get too upset, he grabbed my ass, his thumbs sliding along my crease, and spread my cheeks wide. My breath caught as he plunged deep in one smooth stroke.

My position didn't really allow for much beyond rocking back to meet him, leaving me at his complete mercy. And I'd be lying if I said I didn't fucking love it. Our heavy grunts filled the air as he fucked into me again and again, just the way I needed. Every stroke pushed me closer to the precipice, but it continued to hover out of reach. Aching for release, I shifted my legs enough to gain some height and adjust the angle, ensuring he hit that perfect spot. The second his next thrust struck home, I could have howled in ecstasy if I could have caught enough breath. *That*, that right there.

"I'm close, sweetheart. You're so damn tight," he grunted, between flexes of his hips that pegged my prostate without an ounce of mercy.

I mumbled an incoherent reply that might have been "Me too," but my brain was scrambled. There was only the intense pleasure singing in my veins with the waning moon overhead providing the perfect backdrop. Despite chasing it, my orgasm took me by surprise. I cried out, barely checking the reflexive tightening of my hands from wrecking the handlebars.

Zahir dug his fingers into my sides, forcing my ass back to meet his increasingly frantic thrusts. "Aidan!" he shouted, burying his length one last time. Contentment washed over me as he spilled his release inside. The moment was earth-shatteringly perfect, and I wanted it to go on forever. But deep down I knew the itch, the *need*, would return. It always did.

We took our time catching our breath before finally beginning the even more awkward process of getting off of the bike. I stared down at where my release had painted the gas tank and couldn't help but think how good it would look permanently painted like that. But that was for another time. For now, I grabbed some leaves and wiped it clean.

I finished putting all of my clothes back where they were supposed to be and grinned at Zahir. "I've always kinda wanted to do that," I admitted with a laugh.

"Oh yeah?" he teased, arching an eyebrow at me, a smile playing on his lips. "Which part?"

"All of it." I laughed again and shook my head. "Fucking on my ride beneath the moon. Though I can honestly say that me being the one bent over wasn't exactly part of the original fantasy. Not that I'm complaining *at all*," I added with a throaty rumble. I fucking loved having Zahir's dick inside me. A chuckle slipped out. Maybe one of these days that fact would stop surprising me.

Zahir hooked his fingers in my belt loops and tugged me into him so our chests pressed together. "And what other fantasies can I help turn into reality?" he asked playfully.

I gave into the temptation of his lips so near to claim a languid kiss as I considered the question. Did I have any other "fantasies?" I had a warm bed to curl up in at night. The prospect of a job I was guaranteed to love. I got to cook whatever and whenever I liked. Had the most beautiful forest to run in without the danger of ever being thrown in a doghouse. But more than any of that, I had Zahir. Someone who liked me exactly as I was, who didn't make me feel ashamed to be myself. In a way, I already had all of my other fantasies.

Smiling to myself at that interesting revelation, I moved my kisses away from his mouth to trail my lips along the long column of his throat. A feeling of unbelievable peace wrapped around me and I hummed contentedly, "I love you."

Zahir stiffened and whatever air was in my lungs froze despite the warm, humid night. He slowly leaned back to meet my gaze while I stood there with my mouth hanging open like I was waiting for a rabbit to hop in. "Say that again," he said, his voice uncharacteristically raw.

"I..." My words trailed off, and I struggled to get my brain to work again. I wanted to take it back or say it had to do with the moment, but somewhere between my brain and my mouth, there was a definite disconnect. Probably because I *didn't* want to take it back.

He cupped my face, staring intently into my eyes, and I started to shake. "Aidan, say it again." This time, it sounded more like a plea.

I coughed to clear my throat, but still nothing. I couldn't swallow, let alone string two words together.

"I need you to hear me. I will never be okay with what your pack did to you. *Never*. But I also have to acknowledge that they shaped the wolf I love. Shaped *you*. I love you, Aidan." He pressed his forehead to mine and let out a shaky breath. "Fuck. I love you so much I don't even know what to do with myself."

My breath hitched, and my eyes suddenly stung. I'd have shaken my head to dispel the threatening tears if Zahir wasn't holding my face captive. As a result, the traitorous things spilled free to slide unhindered down my cheeks. This was ridiculous. It wasn't like no one had ever told me they loved me before. But not like this. Never like this. "Z," I managed, my voice cracking and nearly turning into a broken sob.

He pressed a tender kiss to my salty lips, and I realized he was shaking as much as I was. "I love you, Aidan. And no matter what it takes, I won't ever let anyone hurt you again."

Pride had me wanting to push back. I was a fully grown werewolf. I didn't need anyone to protect me. That fact didn't stop the ache in my heart. I *wanted* that. Wanted someone to put me first instead of treating me like an afterthought or inconvenience. Someone who actually *cared* about whether I was safe and happy. I sniffled, unable to do much else.

Zahir gently wiped my cheeks clear with his thumbs. "Please say it again."

"I love you," I whispered. The band of fear that had tightened around my chest when I first uttered the words eased slightly. I stepped closer to him, eliminating whatever space could exist between us, all but cocooning myself in his arms. "I love you, Zahir," I repeated, looking into his deep brown eyes. The remaining tightness disappeared at seeing the joy shimmering in them.

Chapter 24

Zahir

I nuzzled into the back of Aidan's neck, enjoying his warm human form pressed against me in the bed.

"It's too early to be awake," he grumbled, burrowing deeper under the covers.

I chuckled and placed a kiss at the nape of his neck. "And here I thought you were a morning person."

"Yuck it up, scales. *Someone* wore me out last night."

I was tempted to scoff. Wearing out a werewolf was like trying to extinguish the sun by lighting too many candles. Besides, if anyone was going to be worn out after our marathon of love-making once we returned from the amazing motorcycle ride, it was me. Rather than say any of that, I tightened my hold around him, dragging his back flush against my chest. I wasn't sure how long we floated in that cocoon of bliss when I noticed Aidan had tensed.

"Z?"

"Is everything okay, sweetheart?" I whispered, concerned by his plaintive tone.

"Why am I not dying?"

I stiffened and fought to relax again. "What do you mean?"

"It's been nearly two months since I was exiled and I'm not wasting away."

"Do you..." I paused to clear the sudden tightness in my throat. "Do you feel like you are?"

"No? I mean, I miss my pack. Or, at least, the feeling of pack. It makes me sad, but I don't feel like I'm losing my mind or will to live or anything."

I bit back a relieved sigh. I couldn't bear the thought of losing Aidan after having found him. Especially not when it was possible that he could be so much more than simply a man I fell in love with. "I'm sorry you're sad. Hopefully, you'll like the North Carolina pack."

"Yeah, maybe."

"What is it, sweetheart? What are you thinking?"

He seemed to shrink in on himself and was quiet for a minute. Finally, he asked, "Do you think my pack lied about that too?"

His voice was so small, it broke my heart. Unsure of what to do, I held him tighter. "I don't know. Ezra seemed to think you were doing remarkably well, given the circumstances. So, maybe not?"

"Then why am I... okay?" he asked with a huff.

The other things Ezra said, specifically about Aidan and myself came to mind. "What do you know about bonded pairs?" I asked. "Was that something that ever came up in your pack?"

He wiggled around until he was facing me and his expression told me everything I needed to know. "Bonded what?"

"Ezra said—" An unfamiliar ringing sliced through the air. It wasn't until Aidan rolled over that I realized it was his new phone.

"Speak of the devil," he said with a chuckle. He swiveled to a sitting position and swiped to answer the call. "Sup?"

Sadly, I did *not* have superior werewolf hearing and couldn't make out what was being said on the other end. I did, however, see Aidan's face brighten with surprise and what I'd peg as tentative excitement.

"Really? Wow. That's... Fuck I don't even know what to say. Oh. Uh..." Aidan glanced back at me and the softest smile curled his lips. "Moonbow." Ezra said something else and Aidan nodded. "Yeah, okay. I'll keep an eye out for it. And, you know, thanks again. For all of this." He hung up and placed the phone back on the nightstand.

I sat up, causing the sheets to pool around my waist. "What was that about?"

"Good news on the pack front. Ezra's Alpha wants to meet me, but Ez seems pretty confident it's a done deal. He called the meeting a formality." He shrugged and stood, offering me a stunning view of his perky ass. Try as he might to look and sound casual, I could tell this was huge for him.

"And what was the moonbow thing?"

"Oh. Uh, apparently his Alpha thinks it'd be a good idea to get me a new identity. Well, sort of anyway. And he needed a last name. It was the first thing that came to mind. Is that okay?" he asked sheepishly, and it might have been the most adorable thing I'd ever seen.

I tugged him back into the bed and was rewarded with a chorus of sweet laughter. "I think it suits you perfectly."

"Yeah?" he asked, his eyes shining.

"Absolutely. You're both rare and stunningly beautiful."

His cheeks turned bright red, and he shoved me back. "Ugh, so sappy."

"And what are you going to do about it?" I challenged.

He snorted and rolled his eyes.

"That's what I thought. You love it when I'm 'sappy'," I said with a wide grin and air quotes.

He took me off guard by getting up close and crooning, "Maybe I do." The following sweet kiss had my breath faltering. His hand drifted up my torso, brushed along my clavicle, then caressed my arm.

I winced, pulling back at an unexpectedly sharp sting on my left bicep. "What in Vishnu's name..." I stared at the piece of literal fucking skin hanging off of my arm.

"I swear I didn't do that," Aidan said, his hand hovering above the wound.

I met his anxious gaze. "No, of course not. I know you didn't, sweetheart."

"I think I know what may have caused it, though."

"Oh?"

"Um, please don't take this the wrong way, but your skin has been getting drier and drier. Almost... scaley." He grimaced.

"Fuck me," I hissed, quickly vacating the bed and dashing into the bathroom with my phone. Once I securely locked the door, I brought up the phone's camera and used it to get a closer look at the peeled back skin. Oh, it was scaley, all right. "Motherfucker," I muttered, closing the camera app and opening my contacts. I selected *Guru Warden* without a second thought.

"Let me guess, you're calling to say that you will not make it in today," Gurudevi said upon answering instead of a traditional greeting.

"Yes," I growled in a fair imitation of the one Aidan had given Ezra at the park.

"What is it this time?" If it wasn't for her teasing tone, I might be concerned about recrimination. While apprenticing to become a guru wasn't a "job" exactly, it also wasn't to be treated lightly.

"I'm fucking shedding."

"Oh! Well, honestly, Zahir, I don't see why you're acting so surly about it. It's a perfectly natural process. Take the time you need. I'll see you next week?" The hint of a question was fair, given every naga shed at a different rate. I was fortunate that a week was sufficient. Except there was one glaring problem with all of it.

"Don't you dare hang up! You're going to tell me what in Vishnu's name is going on."

She scoffed. "We both know this is not your first shedding cycle, Zahir, but if you really need me to explain the mechanics of it—"

"I know how shedding cycles work," I cut her off with a snarl. "What I *don't* know is why I'm shedding so far outside my normal cycle. I'm not due for at least another three months," I added, dropping my voice to a whisper. As angry as I was, I was more freaked out.

"Sweet, sweet Zahir. I tried to tell you your scales were changing. It makes perfect sense that you'd have to undergo a full shed to fully incorporate the evolution."

"No disrespect, but if you don't tell me exactly what you mean in the next minute, old woman, I am never setting foot in that temple again. You can find a new damn apprentice to boss about."

She huffed. "That seems a tad dramatic, especially since I *did* try telling you. Several times. Let me be direct. Your scales are evolving because you found your true mate."

"For fuck's sake. Not this again," I grumbled, rubbing my forehead to ease the headache building there. I was finally coming around to the possibility, but wasn't prepared for this.

"Believe me or don't. You know the truth in your heart. Either way, you're shedding now and your scales will be markedly different afterward. Take the week, Zahir. Spend time with your adorable werewolf. You can deny it all you like, but you two are inextricably linked. Your scales changing is just the first step. We can discuss the others once you've had a chance to embrace the reality."

"But—" The dial tone filled my ear. I pulled the device away to confirm that she'd in fact hung up on me. "Miserable old cow," I muttered to myself. "Some help you are." I yanked open the bathroom door and stopped short at finding Aidan just outside, looking absolutely devastated.

"I'm sorry. Really. I shouldn't have said anything. It's none of my fucking business. I'll be more careful, I swear." He crossed his arms over his chest, tucking his hands into his armpits like they were responsible for this whole mess.

My heart squeezed at how upset he'd gotten in the few minutes I'd been gone. I immediately held open my arms, and he stepped into them. "This isn't your fault, sweetheart. You didn't do anything wrong."

He lifted his head from where he'd buried it against my chest. "What *is* wrong?"

"At the risk of grossing you out," I began, brushing his hair back from his face, "I'm entering a shedding cycle. It's likely been ramping up for a while now. That's why my skin has been so dry."

"Why would that gross me out? I sprout fur all over my body and damn near break every bone when I shift. Shedding sounds downright normal," he added with one of his cheeky grins.

"Suppose when you put it that way." I chuckled. "It just took me off guard, is all. It's not..." I hesitated to get into the graphic details, not the least of which because I didn't fully understand them myself. "It's just early."

"So... what does that mean? How does a shedding cycle work?" He asked, his blue eyes bright with curiosity.

"It's a little different for every naga. The long and short of it is we shed periodically to accommodate growth. The cycles get farther apart as we get older. Mine averages about once every six months. I generally spend the week lounging around in my naga form and trying not to go insane from the itching."

I swear his ears perked up. "You mean I get to cuddle with you in your naga form?"

My mouth hung open as I processed his question. "Do you *want* to snuggle with my naga form?"

A light pink infused his cheeks, and he dropped his gaze to where his fingers were gently stroking my chest. "Kinda. But I wasn't sure how to ask. I mean, I curl up with you in my wolf form all the time. Is it really so different? Aside from the not being able to really talk part."

"I guess it's not." I smiled and cupped his face. "You, my love, are an absolute fucking treasure." His cheeks got so hot they burned against my palms, but that didn't stop me from leaning down to press our lips together. "Full warning, I probably won't be much for company. I tend to get pretty irritable. Please don't feel you need to stay with me while I go through this insufferable process."

"Do you not want me here for it?" he asked.

I smiled encouragingly at him. "I'm not saying that at all."

"Okay."

Five days later and I was on the verge of climbing the walls, my scales itched so badly. I couldn't think of a time it had been this bad since my first major growth spurt. But no matter how cranky I got or how much I snapped, Aidan had yet to leave my side. I'd reiterated countless times that he didn't have to put up with this shit, to which he'd reply with his usual grin, "I know."

Not even the extra squishy couch or binge watching older seasons of our favorite baking show could distract me from the extreme discomfort. With each day that passed, I became increasingly convinced that I would die from the incessant itching. I grumbled to myself and struggled yet again to find a comfortable position.

"Do you need more snake oil?" Aidan asked over his shoulder. He was lying on his side in front of me. At first, his warmth had helped soothe the burning itch of dehydrating and separating skin, but now it wasn't really cutting it.

Tempting as it was to remind him—again—that it was basic hemp oil with absolutely nothing "snakey" about it, I was trying hard not to take my frustrations out on him. "No," I muttered, unable to contrive additional platitudes.

He carefully rolled over to face me, a smile threatening to emerge. It didn't take a genius to know that he was probably trying not to laugh at how I was pouting. "Come here," he ordered gently. He curled his hand around the back of my neck and I let out a sigh at the sweet—albeit fleeting—relief his touch provided. Before I realized what was happening, he'd tugged me down and pressed a kiss to my lips.

"But I'm gross," I whined.

"I don't think so." As if to punctuate his point, he kissed me again, teasing the seam of my lips with his tongue. I opened for him without a second thought and got lost in the sensuous glide.

"You'll miss the show," I stated when I pulled up for air.

He flashed me a smile that managed to be both sweet and wicked. "It's on demand."

"Right." The word was barely out before his mouth was back on mine. I hummed appreciatively at the very welcome distraction from my misery. It still baffled me he wasn't remotely phased about kissing or touching me while I was completely covered in scales. Then again, another naga wouldn't have minded. Why should I?

His warm hand, still slick from the last round of oil application, coasted over my side and I rolled into his touch. He continued to captivate my mouth with languid kisses while he adjusted his trajectory to run his palm down my chest.

I moaned at just how good it felt. He'd been gentle when applying the oil, but nothing like this. I slipped my hand beneath his cotton t-shirt to caress his warm skin, lightly scratching with my claws.

"You sure you don't need any more snake oil?" he teased, his hand continuing to venture down the full length of my torso and beyond. His roving faltered, and he looked down. "What the fuck?"

It took a half second too long to drag myself out of the fog he'd put me in. "Aidan, wait. Don't." Too late. He pressed more firmly on the bulge where my ventral scales transitioned to caudal scales. I gasped and covered my eyes. Mortified didn't come close.

"Do you have... *two* dicks?"

"They're weird, I know. It's a snake thing," I said, back to being miserable, with a hefty side of embarrassment. This never would have happened if I could exercise some of my sexual frustration like we normally would. I chanced a peek between my fingers and found him staring back at me with wide eyes.

"Why didn't you *tell* me?"

"Beg your pardon?" I asked, thrown for a loop at his decidedly *not* freaked out attitude.

"Oh, this is fucking happening." He twisted around, plucked the hemp oil from where it was sitting on the floor, then maneuvered so we were facing each other once more. "Anything I should know?" he asked, shoving his sweats down until his swollen cock sprang free.

I nearly swallowed my tongue at the realization of what he had in mind. Then he wrapped a tentative hand around one of my hemipenis. "Sensitive!" I hissed, my brain nearly whiting out from the sensation.

He gentled his touch and leaned forward to capture my mouth in a brief kiss. "I can work with that."

All I could do was lie there in disbelief as he wriggled into a better position, lining up my hemipenes with his cock. They bumped against each other, and a ripple of ecstasy made me shudder. After another small adjustment, he squirted the hemp oil onto his palm then wrapped his hand around all three, perfectly sandwiching his cock between mine. I gasped and clung to him as he gave an experimental stroke.

"They're so different," he panted. "If your human dick is basically both of these put together, no wonder you're so big."

I'd never really thought about it before and, in all fairness, thought wasn't coming too easily for me right now. "Haven't... haven't done this... like... this."

"New things for both of us, then."

A moan stuck in my throat as I writhed beneath his touch, my body reflexively undulating to meet his strokes. I pressed our lips together in a sloppy kiss, still clinging to him for dear life while he unraveled me one stroke at a time. "Aidan."

"Feels so good," he crooned, sounding just as wrecked as I felt.

"Nngh," I responded, coherent speech abandoning me. I laid a trail of what could only generously be called open-mouthed kisses along his jaw and down the side of his neck. In an alarming twist, my fangs threatened to drop. It took every ounce of control I had to fight off the impulse to sink them into his smooth flesh. Desperate to keep them to myself, I buried my face against his shoulder, using the pressure to keep my lips firmly closed. I even went so far as to try to use my tongue to push them back against the roof of my mouth.

Through it all, Aidan never faltered. Not even when my claws sank into the meat of his hip to force him closer. "I'm gonna come. Fuck, Z. I'm so close. I'm right there. Come with me?"

The breathy plea propelled me over the edge, and my orgasm crashed into me. I threw my head back as far as I could, my fangs dropping despite all my efforts, as I came so hard I lost feeling in my fingers and the tip of my tail. It wasn't until I could finally catch my breath that my fangs withdrew.

Aidan released a breathless laugh and sagged into the couch. "I guess more dicks equals more mess."

I glanced at our collective spend and groaned.

"I knew it was just a matter of time before we fucked on the couch," he said, a playful lilt to his voice.

"It's a good thing I love you."

His eyes twinkled with his exuberant smile. "More than the couch?"

I chuckled. "Don't push it. Now help me clean this up before my favorite piece of furniture is ruined forever." I was already mentally preparing the cleaning supplies we'd need, so was wholly unprepared for him to press a quick kiss to my lips. "What was that for?" I asked, startled.

"Took your mind off of things, didn't it?"

I stared at Aidan and his soft, pleased smile in wonder. "I really do love you, furball."

"Love you too, scales."

Chapter 25

Aidan

I blew out a raspberry and paced the small living room for the billionth time. I still didn't see what the big deal was. So he thought shedding his entire body was gross. So what? I'd seen *way* worse things over the years. I mean, that whole incident with Carver and that gator in Tallahassee. *No* reptile had any right to be that big with that many damn teeth.

I shook off the gruesome memory and checked the time again. Seriously, how long did it take to peel off some dead skin? Zahir had even said nagas, like most snakes, shed their whole body in one fell swoop. The waiting probably would have been more bearable if I was actually *with* him right now. But he'd put his foot down. Tail down? Whatever. He'd made it really fucking clear that as much as he appreciated my support, he'd be doing this last bit on his own.

The screen on the back door snapped shut. I slid across the room to see through the passage that divided the kitchen and breakfast table from the front of the house. A tension I didn't even know had been riding me instantly relaxed at seeing Zahir.

To my surprise, he was in his human form. Though I guessed that made sense if he didn't want to draw attention from unsuspecting human-humans. What I didn't like one bit was how ragged he looked.

"What's wrong?" I asked, already frowning as I walked closer. "I thought finally completing your shed was supposed to make you feel better, not worse."

He gave me a haunted look that stopped me dead in my tracks. "I need..." He took a deep breath, and I scented a wary sadness coming off of him. Sour notes of vinegar tainted his normal spring shower to the point I couldn't even detect it. "I need to talk to you about something."

"W-what is it?" The anxiety I'd just ditched returned with teeth. "Were you not able to shed? It's okay if you need more time. I'll get the oil." I rocked back on my heel, ready to race into the other room.

"No," he said firmly, holding up a hand. "No, it's not that," he added more gently. "The shed... went fine." His hesitation said otherwise.

"You're freaking me out, Z."

He scoffed. "Yeah, well, you're about to be a hell of a lot more freaked."

"What the fuck is that supposed to mean?"

He let out a resigned sigh and walked around the table to stand in the open kitchen. It didn't escape my notice that he was still keeping distance between us. I was tempted to close it for that reason, but truthfully, I was scared. What was going on? Why was he being so cagey? *Finally*, he looked me in the eye.

"Like I said, I completed the shedding cycle like I normally do. Except..."

Sweet mother of the moon, he was killing me with all the suspense.

"I, um, I'm different now." He dropped his gaze and my heart lurched into my throat.

"What? How? Not that it matters to me. I love you no matter what." But did he still love me? Was that what had changed?

He almost smiled, but the sadness was still in his eyes and the vinegar clouding his scent hadn't dissipated. "I really hope that's true. It's my scales. You remember how when you first saw my naga form you thought they were blue?"

I frowned. There was no "thought" about it. Unlike our canine cousins, werewolves weren't colorblind. If anything, we saw a wider range of color than most creatures.

"At the time I thought it was really odd, since my scales have always been a deep sea green."

"So... are they blue now?" I hazarded a guess. I suppose if I emerged from a shift and my fur was a completely different color, I'd be pretty freaked. Then again, I probably would have jumped for the moon just not to be fucking blond anymore.

"Sort of." He rolled his shoulders and shifted to his naga form.

My legs gave out. I barely grabbed a kitchen chair in time not to crash to the floor and sat. *Hard.* I could barely wrap my head around what I was seeing. It was definitely Zahir, of that I had no doubts. But he was... was...

He groaned and stared down at his scaled hands. "I know. I *know.* It's—"

"Beautiful. *You're* beautiful," I said, though breathing was proving to be a challenge.

"Really?" The surge of hope in his scent nearly obliterated the vinegar.

"You look like the water at the Florida beach. I wasn't supposed to go, but I went anyway. Figured, if I couldn't see the ocean, the Gulf was the next best thing. I... I... I don't know what to say. You're just... stunning. Can I?" My hand shook as I held it out.

He nodded and slithered toward me as I stood. "Be careful. I'm still a little slippery."

"Uh-huh," I replied absently. "Is that why you're so shiny?"

He chuckled. "Only partly. Our scales are typically pretty shiny after a shed."

"So not sensitive?" I asked, carefully reaching for his hand.

He shook his head, and a wide smile stretched across his face. "You won't hurt me." The scent of vinegar was completely gone now, swallowed up entirely by the smell of a summer storm.

I actually fucking whimpered when I finally touched him. It was hard to reconcile how dry his scales had been before with how unbelievably smooth they were now.

"So... you don't mind?" he asked with the slightest lilt of teasing.

"Mind? Why the fuck would I mind? Zahir, you were gorgeous before, but this is on another level. Does this happen to all nagas?" I asked, still mindlessly trailing the tips of my fingers over the nearly glowing scales. They were almost turquoise, they were so bright.

"No, Aidan. It doesn't."

I looked at his face and tried to place his tone. It was almost excited, with a hint of mischief. "Do *you* like your new scales?"

His grin returned as he twisted his arm to catch the light. "They'll take some getting used to, but I think I do. Now, more important question." He paused, but I was at a loss. "Are you just going to stand there holding my hand, or are you going to kiss me?"

There was absolutely nothing remotely bad ass about the sound I made or the way I literally jumped into his arms. He shifted to his human form to catch me, returning my eager kiss with just as much enthusiasm. I didn't even notice when he moved so he could sit me on the kitchen counter.

"Let's go out tonight. To celebrate," I said excitedly once I could be bothered to come up for air.

"Like... a date?" The twinkle in his rich brown eyes gave away the tease, but I still melted.

"Yeah, like a date."

He cupped my face and brushed my lips with a sweet kiss. "Where did you have in mind?"

"How about *The Oasis*?"

He stole another kiss and grinned. "I think that sounds perfect."

Now that we had a plan in hand, there was no containing my excitement. It wasn't like I *hadn't* been out of the house, but this was different. This was a *date*. I rushed Zahir through taking a shower and getting ready, only realizing that I didn't have anything "date-nice" to wear after discarding nearly all of my shirts. I'd have to fix that later. Right now, the soft blue shirt would have to do.

By the time we pulled up to *The Oasis*, I felt like I needed to take a hard look at myself. Seriously, why the hell was I so amped for this? It wasn't even anything major. We'd drank together here plenty of times before the shit show with my pack. A glance around the parking lot showed the bar was as packed as ever for a Friday night.

"Hey," Zahir said.

I stopped trying to figure out if those were motorcycles parked behind a jacked pickup truck and swivelled to face him. "What's up?"

He reached over the center console and laced his fingers through mine. Then he brought my captured hand up and placed a kiss on the back. "I love you."

Suddenly, I knew why I was so over the moon to be here tonight. Sure, we'd bumped into each other here, but this was the first time we were here *together*. Everyone would know that the sexy ass snake sitting beside me was *mine*.

I awkwardly surged across the console to claim a kiss. "I love you, too," I said, unable to contain my wide smile. "Now, let's get inside before everyone else drinks all the moonshine."

Zahir threw his head back in a laugh and I watched, transfixed, as his Adam's apple bobbed. "I doubt there's any danger of that. But I wouldn't mind a drink." Outside his SUV, he bypassed my hand to slide his arm around my waist and I damn near melted.

"I'm gonna hit the head. Grab the drinks?" I asked, separating from Zahir once we'd walked inside the noisy bar.

"Meet at our usual table?" he replied, already angling for the bar.

I grinned at him, walking backward a few steps toward the restrooms. "You know it."

A couple minutes later, I was shocked to find that not only did I *not* have to boot someone out of our table, but Zahir wasn't there. It didn't take long to find him hovering at the bar, along with a few other irritated patrons.

"What's going on?" I asked, stepping up beside him.

"Some assholes are giving the bartender a hard time."

I glanced around. "Where the fuck is Arnie? He should have kicked these guys out on their asses already."

"Fuck if I know," he grumbled, crossing his arms. "I think he's out back having a 'chat' with another uppity patron. We'll likely be waiting until he's done."

"To hell with that. We came here to drink and have a good time. I'm not about to let these jerks spoil that."

"Aidan," he hissed when I stepped toward the three assholes hassling the busty witch behind the bar. "You know how strict Arnie is about people starting shit in his bar."

I rolled my eyes at him. "I'm not starting anything. I'm just helping these bozos move along." I finished pushing through the mini crowd clustered at the bar top waiting for drinks and tapped the guy who appeared to be their ringleader. "Hey, grab your drink and fuck off already."

As one, the three turned around and it felt like every major organ I had dropped into my stomach.

"Well, well, well. Look what we have here. And I thought this dive was gonna be a bust," Elliot said with a toothy grin that was all malice.

I staggered a step back, bumping into a bitchy patron who shoved me to the side. I stumbled, but mercifully kept my footing. "Wh-what are you doing here? How did you find me?"

"Dumb-fucking-luck," who I finally recognized as Leon said.

"Mother of the moon, how are you even still alive?" Barb tacked on.

Elliot advanced toward me, forcing those around him to move. "Not to worry, he won't be for long." Elliot cracked his neck and began to shift. The other two cackled and followed suit, gaining nearly a head over everyone as they embraced their partial shifts. The surrounding people gasped in shock and a few even screamed as they scrambled to get away.

My brain screamed at me to meet the obvious threat by shifting, but fear kept me human, barely able to keep stumbling backward. I couldn't even bring myself to look away long enough to find Zahir. Not while Elliot and the others were bearing down all teeth and claws, ready to finish what Garrett had started months ago.

"I was really hoping I'd get to do this myself. This is for Valerie," he snarled.

The image of a smiling girl that looked remarkably like me, right down to the blonde hair spilling around her face and bright blue eyes, flashed through my mind. But that didn't make any sense. No one in the Stormfire Pack was named Valerie, little kid or adult. And I certainly would have fucking noticed if someone else had the same cursed hair.

Suddenly Zahir was there. "Clearly you're new around here. There's no fighting at *The Oasis*. Take your drinks and go." I flashed him a panicked look before quickly returning my attention to the three.

Barb snatched a drink from someone standing too close. "Yeah, I don't think we will," she said, smashing it to the floor and crushing the glass beneath her boot.

"We're not going fucking anywhere until this piece of dog shit is good and dead," Eliott snarled, his eyes burning with barely contained glee.

My fear was probably stinking up the place, but I couldn't be bothered to care. I wasn't even sure what I was more afraid of, Eliott killing me in the most gruesome way he could imagine or him laying so much as a claw on Zahir. Bad ass as Zahir was in his naga form, no way could he take all three of them, not without getting seriously hurt at least.

"Is that all?" Zahir asked, his voice unnervingly calm.

Before I could ask him what the hell he was playing at or tell him to get out while he still could, he moved lightning fast to stand behind me. I yelped in surprise and a trickle of fear made the hairs on the back of my neck stand up when he trapped my arms and wrapped his hand around my throat.

Eliott barked out a laugh. "Much as I'd enjoy watching you tear the mongrel's throat out, you're no match for werewolves like us."

His distinction of "like us" slipped past my fear, and I realized Eliott knew we were different. He'd probably always known. He was also right.

"Clearly you've never met a naga before." Scales covered Zahir's hands and arms as he shifted to his true form. "Fun fact, naga venom is lethal to everything on the planet." He released a violent hiss, baring his fangs.

It took everything I had to convince my instincts to calm down and stand perfectly still when everything in me screamed "dangerous predator". On the upside, Zahir's show of aggression seemed to make the others think twice.

"How about I take care of your little problem for you, and you fuck off and leave the rest of us in peace?" He tightened his hold around my throat and I wheezed. "Better yet, fuck off and never come back. Or next time, it'll be you."

Eliott snickered, slowly reversing his change. "Sure, that'll work." Barb and Leon shifted back as well with a laugh. Obviously, my idiot former packmates were not buying the "most venomous creature on the damn planet" bit.

"Don't believe me?" Zahir threatened, lowering his impressive fangs down to brush the exposed skin at my collar. I fought the impulse to lurch away from the imminent danger, but kept the panic on my face. Then, in a whisper so low it was a wonder I could hear it over my racing heart, Zahir said, "I need you to trust me."

Peace washed over me. Of course, I trusted him. He was my everything. I winced at a sharp tug on my neck. I had a moment to register a strange coldness seeping into me, then everything went dark.

Chapter 26

Zahir

I let out a relieved breath when the door swung shut behind the three troublemakers from Aidan's former pack. A moment later, the roar of motorcycles permeated the bar and everyone relaxed as the sound gradually faded into the distance. I glanced toward Arnie, who'd finally made a reappearance, and he gave me an appreciative nod before replacing his nail studded bat to its place beneath the bar top.

"Phew, I am *really* glad that bluff worked," I said aloud, smoothing down my hood as I shifted back to my human form. "Guess even twisted furballs know better than to fuck with brightly colored serpents. Wouldn't you say, Aidan?" I frowned when he didn't respond with a quip or even so much as a laugh. "Aidan?" I looked down to find him still prone on the ground, deathly pale, with dark lines extending from the two large punctures my fangs had caused.

"Aidan!" I screamed, dropping to my knees beside him. I gently shook him. "Stop fucking around. They're gone now. You're safe. You're safe," I repeated, my voice breaking when he didn't stir. "Please, sweetheart, wake up. You have to wake up. Aidan!" I shouted again, shaking him more violently as I became desperate to rouse him.

"What's going on?" Arnie asked, stepping close. "Oh shit, you *actually* bit him. What the fuck, dude? I thought y'all were together now or some shit."

In the blink of an eye, I shifted back to my naga form and hissed a fierce warning. Just as quickly, my anger dissolved back into fear. "This wasn't supposed to happen. He's supposed to be okay! Gurudevi was so sure. Gurudevi." I switched back to my human form so I could free my phone.

"Zahir—" Arnie began, but I cut him off, already dialing Guru Angira.

"Help me get him to my car," I demanded. When he didn't move fast enough, I snapped, "Now!" The line picked up, and I sandwiched the phone between my ear and shoulder as I helped Arnie pickup Aidan. "Gurudevi, I need you to meet me at the temple. I'm headed there now. It's Aidan." I glanced at his drawn features. If his color wasn't so bad, he could have been asleep. "Something's wrong."

There was no telling how many laws I broke speeding to the temple. I didn't care. They could mail me a damn ticket. I glanced at Aidan in the rearview mirror, still lying in the exact position Arnie had set him down. His colour remained atrocious, but at least he was breathing. If only just.

"Fuck, let him still be breathing," I muttered to myself, taking the turn into the State Park a little too hard. I got the vehicle back under control and careened haphazardly into the usual parking lot. The SUV was still rocking from the abrupt stop when I killed the engine and hopped out. I carefully opened the rear door, mindful of Aidan possibly falling out.

"Come on, sweetheart. I've got you. Everything's going to be okay," I reassured him, though I was more attempting to reassure myself. I gently wedged my hands beneath his shoulders and began the arduous process of getting him out of the back seat. "Wow, you're heavy," I grunted when I took on the full weight of his top half. Nagas were strong, but we weren't exactly werewolf-strong unless we really set our minds to it.

"I'll get his legs," Gurudevi declared as she emerged from the hidden forest path that led to the temple.

I could have cried with relief. Truthfully, I hadn't thought much about *how* I would get him into the temple, just that I *had* to get him there. "Thanks," I panted, now at liberty to reposition Aidan without fearing I'd drop him. I didn't bother questioning whether she could handle his weight, just trusted that she knew what she was about. Once we had him more or less cradled between us, we set off for the path.

"Can you tell me what happened?" Gurudevi asked, her gaze flicking to Aidan's neck. I wasn't sure if I should be relieved or worried that the angry lines emanating from the wound had diminished.

We had to stop repeatedly to re-situate Aidan and take breathers, but I eventually conveyed the sordid tale that had led to this moment. "We wanted to go out to celebrate the end of my shedding cycle. It had been ages since we'd been to *The Oasis* and we thought it would be fun. But it seems that in our absence, some of his former pack found the place.

"There were three of them and they could all shift like Aidan does. They changed right there in the bar. They looked like creatures straight out of a nightmare. Apparently, it wasn't enough to torture and exile Aidan," I snarled. "They took one look at him and decided he needed to die. I couldn't stand there and do *nothing*. So, I shifted and threatened to kill them with naga venom."

Gurudevi shot me a sharp look as we squeezed into the narrow entrance at the rear of the temple.

"I wasn't actually going to. It was a bluff. But they weren't buying it, so I... I..." Words failed me and I directed my focus to positioning Aidan on the nest of throw pillows we kept in one of the back rooms. Once he was lying comfortably—I hoped—I stood there staring at him. "I don't understand. True mates are immune to each other's venom. And he is. My scales changed and even Ezra said something. He *is my* true mate. He has to be." It wasn't until my voice broke on a sob that I realized I was crying.

"Come here," Gurudevi said softly and enveloped me in her thin arms that seemed to be the only things holding me up. "Sh, sh, all will be well." She continued to make comforting noises while she rubbed my back and let me cry all over her.

"Why won't he wake up?"

"He will. You must have faith," she said, but it felt like an empty platitude, given how I could barely tell Aidan was even breathing.

A pained cry caught in my throat, and I held the guru tighter. "I never should have bitten him. What was I thinking?"

"Oh, my young pupil, it was always going to come to this. I only wish I'd had a chance to prepare you."

I pushed away from the smaller woman to stare at her in horror. "What?"

She sighed and leaned down to straighten a pillow that had fallen to the side. "How do you think nagas gain that immunity from their mate's venom? To all toxins? They must endure the bite. Traditionally, they'll undertake a private ritual, exchanging venom, then once they've recovered from the initial shock, there's a celebration to rejoice in their union."

"Is that what this is? Shock? And how do you know so much about fated mates?" Perhaps that last was a cruel question, as Guru Angira hadn't had a mate in over a century and never a fated mate as far as I knew.

She gave me one of her usual mischievous smiles. "I've assisted in my fair share of rituals. As for the other, I suppose it would be safe to say that what Aidan is going through is similar to shock. You must have faith, Zahir. He will recover, though I do not know how long that may take. Werewolves don't have venom, and his body is trying to determine whether it should accept the gift you have given him or reject it."

"He could reject it?!"

"Easy, young one. You see the dark veins stemming from where your fangs pierced flesh?" I nodded. How the fuck could I miss them? "Have you noticed how they are fading and getting farther from the wound?"

"Yeah," I replied shakily, not at all confident with where she was headed.

"I take this as a good sign. The venom is wending its way to his heart—"

"Last time I checked, that was a *bad* thing," I interjected.

She gave me a stern look, and I dutifully shut my mouth and bowed my head. "Let me rephrase. The magic of the venom is working towards his heart to imbue him with your gifts and protection. Were it simply going to kill him, the veins would have continued to darken and spread. They have not."

I swallowed hard, scrubbing the tears from my face. "What can I do?"

"Have faith," Gurudevi repeated, cradling my cheek. "Stay here tonight. I will make you some chai. I suspect you will not be doing much sleeping."

I mumbled a thanks as she left. Then I shifted to my naga form, coiled beside Aidan, and prayed to any deity that might listen. Vishnu had answered my prayers once. Perhaps he could be moved to do so again.

"Excellent work with the Pandan family today," Gurudevi said, slithering up beside me. "Your advice about finding common ground to facilitate communication ought to help them find more peaceful ways to understand each other that don't hinge on shouting and misconstruing meaning."

"Hmm," I responded noncommittally, unable to appreciate her praise. "How is he?" I chanced a glance at her, but wasn't surprised to see the sympathy on her aged face. We were going on two weeks and Aidan was still exactly the same as when I'd brought him to the temple.

"No change yet, I'm afraid." She placed a wrinkled hand on my arm that I could barely feel past the numbness that had overtaken me. "Have faith, Zahir. He *will* wake. I can feel it in these old bones. Whenever you doubt, look at the evidence you wear. Never in all my years have I seen or heard of a naga's venom harming their true mate."

I took a deep breath and tried to internalize her words, to will myself to believe them. The alternative was too dire to entertain. My moment of calm resolution proved to be fleeting when a small light flashing on the far wall accompanied by a faint beep intruded. I released a heavy sigh and rubbed my forehead. Of course, *now* my parents would choose to call.

"Would you like me to tell them you're unavailable? I can say that you're providing spiritual guidance and regale them with how well your studies have been coming along," Gurudevi offered, her voice kind.

"That won't be necessary, though I appreciate the offer. I've put them off long enough. Besides... I think it's time I told them."

She gave my arm a reassuring squeeze. "Don't feel pressured."

I nodded and slithered down the hall that led to the video-conference room to accept the call. Truthfully, it had less to do with pressure and more to do with there being no way to hide from my parents that something was horribly wrong or that my scales were a completely different color than they had been the last time we'd spoken.

Wanting to save that particular revelation until I'd broken the news, I shifted to my human form and clicked to accept the call. Instantly, my parents appeared on the screen.

"No, I will *not* try again later," Maa snapped at my father. "This will be the third check-in he's missed. I am his mother and I have a right to see my son and know he is well."

"Meri jaan..."

"I love you dearly, Montu, but no. I will not—"

I cleared my throat and my mother's head whipped around to face the screen, causing her long dark braid to swing into my father. "Hello, Maa. Pati." I pressed my palms together and bowed my head. "I implore your forgiveness for my repeated absence. I assure you, I am in good health."

"Ah, Beta," my father said with a warm smile. "It is good to see you. I was just telling your maa how you must be absorbed in your studies." He shot her a scolding look before his features softened once more.

"Thank you for your faith in me, Pati. Studies... have been going well. Guru Angira has me meeting with those seeking spiritual guidance now and has commended my performance." Even relating such good news left a hollow within me. No amount of success could ever replace Aidan's sweet smiles. Or his bright eyes. Or his joyous laughter.

My mother continued to examine me with a shrewd eye, before finally smacking the table they sat at in India. "You lie."

"Uma—" my father began, but she held up a hand to cut him off.

"Your studies may be exemplary, but you are *not* well. What is wrong, Beta?" The worry that infused her soft question broke me. I let out a cracked sob and buried my face in my hands.

"Zahir, what is it? Has something happened?" she pressed, her worry mounting.

I scrounged up what remained of my composure and met her concerned gaze. Both of them were now leaning close to the camera as if they could somehow come through the screen in order to comfort me. For the first time since I was a child, I wanted that more than I had the words to express. "It's... complicated."

"Beta," my father said in his deep voice, "there is nothing in this world or the next that is so complicated you cannot speak to us."

I tilted my head back to stem the threatening tide of tears and took a deep, shaky breath. "I found my true mate." It was the first time I'd owned the truth out loud. A part of me thrilled at hearing the words, but another, larger part despaired.

"Oh, Beta," Maa said in a gentling tone. "But this is joyous news. Why are you so sad? You must know that whoever they are, we would accept them with open arms and open hearts."

"Is it that you are uncertain? Perhaps you doubt the depth of their affection?" Pati asked tentatively.

I shook my head and shifted to my naga form before willing myself to meet their collective gaze. "I'm very certain."

My mother gasped and my father appeared to have forgotten how to blink. "Beta, your scales..." Pati trailed off.

"You are more stunning than ever," Maa said with a touch of awe that I'd never heard from her before. "What is this color?" She looked askance at my father.

He tilted his head to the side and finally blinked as he considered her question. I hadn't given it much thought beyond them being several shades lighter than my original Sea Green. "I have it! He is like the stone amazonite. Yes, that's the one," he said excitedly. Well, at least I had a name for it now.

Maa's smile slid from her face. "But, Beta, you have not yet told us why you are filled with such sorrow."

"I gave him the mating bite. But... but..." My voice caught, and I had to pause. "It's been over a week now, and he hasn't woken up. I don't know if it has something to do with him being a werewolf or... or... maybe I am wrong," I finished in a whisper. I expected one or both of them to have something to say about my slip that my true mate was a werewolf, but neither of them so much as batted an eye.

"My sweet son, I am so, *so* happy for you. I have every confidence that your mate will awaken when the time comes," Maa said passionately.

"That is what Gurudevi keeps telling me. That his current stasis is temporary and to have faith." I sniffled and sent up my millionth prayer that Aidan would awaken soon.

"Would you tell us about him?" Pati implored.

"Any pictures?" Maa added.

"His name is Aidan Moonbow," I said, my lips twitching with the ghost of a smile as I pulled out my cell phone. "Here we are in front of the Natural Arch at David Boone National Forest." I queued up the image and held it close to the camera.

"Oh. He's..." My mother faltered. "He's..." she tried again, but didn't get any farther. There it was. I'd known the criticism would come, eventually. "Forgive me, Beta, but I do not know how to say this without causing offense."

I covered my eyes with my free hand and let out an exasperated sigh. "Just say it, Maa. You cannot hurt my heart more than it already does."

She sniffed imperiously. "You always assume the worst of me. Perhaps I should tell Guru Angira to endeavor to teach you more grace."

"Apologies, Maa. What is it you would like to say?"

There was a long pause in which I dared not peek past my fingers for fear of seeing her disapproval. At last she said, almost wistfully, "He's absolutely adorable."

I dropped my hand from my face and nearly dropped my phone as well. A smile I hadn't expected stretched my lips, and the tension coiled inside relaxed. "He really is. But don't let him hear you say that. I doubt big, bad werewolves appreciate being called adorable." My mother's gentle laugh soothed my soul in ways I didn't know I needed.

"Tell us more about him?" my father encouraged as my mother rested her head on his shoulder.

"He is incredibly sweet. And thoughtful. I don't know if I've ever met another soul as pure as his. He's a talented cook and enjoys discovering new recipes. We even like the same cooking shows. Oh! And he made a tikka masala that rivals Daadee's." I paused and ran my finger over his smiling face on my phone. "I think you would really like him."

"He feeds my son. What's there not to like?" Pati teased.

Maa smacked him on the arm. "Hush," she scolded before turning back to me with a dreamy look in her eyes. "Tell us more. How did you meet?"

I wasn't sure how long we spent discussing all things Aidan beyond it was significantly longer than we'd normally chat. I told them virtually everything there was to know about the light of my heart. When we finally bid farewell, the sun had set, and I felt more hopeful than I had in days. Aidan *would* wake up and I couldn't wait to introduce him to my family properly.

Chapter 27

Aidan

A girl's laughter surrounds me, making me laugh as well. I turn to look at her and my smile grows to mirror hers. Everything about us mirrors each other. From our soft yellow hair, flying around our faces, to our dancing blue eyes and the mischief shining in them.

As one, we take off up the hill, racing to see who can get to the top first. We catch at each other's shirts to slow the other down, still laughing and stumbling our way up.

When we get to the top, we twirl around, soaking up the sunshine, the ocean mist already sticking to our skin. It's a big day, the best day. Today we go to the secluded cove for our first change.

Excitement buzzes beneath my skin. I can already change, but she's the only one who knows that. We've been keeping it secret, because we want to do it together, just like we do everything else.

A shout drifts to our high perch, followed by a howl. I seriously think I might explode with excitement, and I know she feels the same.

"Ready, Aidan?" she asks, holding out her hand.

I roll my eyes at her before smirking. "Duh," I say, but that doesn't stop me from taking her hand and squeezing it. We share one more wide grin, then throw ourselves down the hillside we just climbed. Almost immediately, our hands fall apart as we roll faster and faster.

A scream tears through the night. I shake my head. It hurts so bad. I feel like I need to do something to stop the screaming. Something is wrong. But I'm so disoriented, it's all I can do to stumble through the dark toward the sound.

"I'm coming," I mumble, shuffling as fast as my aching body will go. This wasn't what our first change was supposed to be like. "Where's my sister?" I ask groggily of the adults surrounding me. That feels off, but I can't put my finger on why. I look around for a familiar face and find none.

The scream comes again. Then the ear-splitting sound becomes garbled.

Fear moves my feet faster. A firm grip on my shoulder causes me to lurch backward. As I'm squirming to get away, to get to the sound, one of the adults in front of me moves just in time to see a ten-year-old girl half-shifted and covered with yellow hair fall to the ground with her throat torn out.

"No!"

The scream ricocheted inside my skull until it became a pain that encompassed my whole body. My eyes flew open, but the only thing I could see was the fat white moon dominating the sky. It wasn't until the back of my head cracked against the ground that I realized what was happening. I was shifting.

But that didn't make a damn bit of sense. I couldn't remember a time I didn't have complete control over the werewolf transformation. Even now, as I tried to fight the change, it barreled forward. Panic squeezed my heart as the shift crawled along at a snail's pace. Why was it taking so long?

I tried to shout, but the sound was lost as my mouth became a long muzzle. I rolled to my side, desperate to get a handle on this. Fire like the bites of a thousand ants raced over my body as blond fur sprouted. I heaved a sigh of relief despite the agony. Thank fuck, the change was almost through.

When I could stand without crashing on my face, I shook out my ruff and looked around to get my bearings. First things first. I needed to know where the fuck I was. My gaze glided over water shining with moonlight and I realized that the roaring in my ears was from the waterfall. Then I saw the moonbow. My tail wagged as I finally recognized where I was—Cumberland Falls.

Zahir.

I needed to find him. Why did it feel like forever since I'd last kissed him? The remnants of a dream started to surface. I shook it off. He had to be nearby. I danced around in a circle, searching the tree line along the banks. Then the heady scent of a summer thunderstorm with a faint undercurrent of sandalwood filled my nose. At last, I spotted him just a few yards away. Joy surged so hard in my chest that it was a wonder I didn't explode from it.

I'd only gone a couple of steps when his broken sob pierced my ears. I stumbled as worry eclipsed my happy. I grunted as I shifted back to my human form faster than I ever had in my life. Considering I averaged about a minute and a half, that was saying something. My body shook from the strain, and it took everything I had to keep moving. Two complete shifts back to back took their toll.

"Z? What's wrong?" I called, still working to close the distance between us. Now that I was focusing on him, it was no wonder I hadn't seen him initially. He was kneeling on the ground, hunched over with his face in his hands.

I forced my feet to go faster. Once I was close enough, my worry multiplied. He wasn't just crying, Zahir was full on breaking down with heaving sobs.

"Z? Talk to me." I tentatively reached out to touch his shoulder. He didn't respond. If anything, he cried harder. "Hey. Are you hurt?" I shook him gently, fear skittering up my spine.

"It worked. I... can't... believe... it... worked," he gasped out between soul wracking sobs.

"What worked? Z, you're freaking me out."

His hand closed over where I was gripping his arm. He took a shuddering breath and finally met my worried gaze. "You woke up. I'd almost given up hope. But Ezra was right."

I didn't have the first clue what he was talking about. All I knew was that my snake looked fucking *wrecked* and tears were still streaming down his face. His very human face.

"Why aren't you in your naga form? Has something happened? Is Guru Angira okay?" I asked, my mind going a thousand different directions as I kneeled in front of him. The memory of a gurgled scream nearly resurfaced again, but I forced it back down. "Zahir, please talk to me. What's going on? Why are you so upset?"

He sniffled and used the heels of his palms to scrub away the tears, but it didn't stop fresh ones from spilling out. "I'm n-not ups-set," he stuttered. "I'm *relieved.*"

"Okay..." I released my death grip on his arm and rubbed the back of my neck.

His gaze caught on something and I froze as he leaned forward to brush the tips of his fingers along my chest, right over my heart. "I wondered if you'd still have one," he whispered.

"Have one what?" I asked, still just as lost.

"There's a lot we need to talk about, but first..." Whip fast, he grabbed the back of my neck and hauled my mouth down to his. He swallowed my surprise with an intense kiss that had me wrapping my arms around him and pulling us flush in a heartbeat. We both knew I was all for sex in the wild, but for once, I wanted answers first.

I gasped for air when he released me. "Zahir, *what* is going on?" I loosened my grip around him and brushed away the latest stream of tears.

"I'm sorry. This is probably a lot for you. Actually, I don't know what it is for you." He peered at me curiously. "Do you feel any different?"

"No? Should I?"

He shook his head. "I'm honestly not sure. This is new for me, too." He took a deep, shuddering breath and maneuvered to sit on the shore. "Fuck, I don't even know where to start," he said, scrubbing his face.

I sat uncertainly beside him, tempted to ask yet again what was wrong. The mix of pebbly sand beneath my ass made me acutely aware of how naked I was. Normally, it didn't faze me, but I also felt increasingly out of my depth.

"Okay," he said, his voice stronger, and dropped his hands from his face. "Do you remember when I asked you if you'd ever heard of bonded pairs?"

I snorted. "I mean, yeah, it was like a week ago. Right before you started your shedding cycle."

He blinked. "Uh, let me backup. What's the last thing you remember?"

I frowned. "You'd just finished your shed, and we were going out to celebrate. Your new scales are so pretty," I added wistful-ly.

"What else?"

"We went to *The Oasis*. On a date." I smiled lopsidedly, then frowned again. "But... something happened. The pack!" I near-ly fell over in my haste to stand, but Zahir's hand on my arm had me sitting back down.

"Yes, some of your old pack was there, causing trouble."

"That fucker Eliott," I snarled, then cut my eyes back to Zahir, searching for any signs of harm. If that asshole touched so much as one scale on my snake, I'd tear his motherfucking throat out with my bare hands.

"I'm guessing that was the *extra* mean one," Zahir said with a small, sad smile. "They wanted to hurt you." He paused, and I watched his Adam's apple bob as he swallowed. "Kill you. They wanted to kill you. As lethal as nagas are, I'm not a fighter and I didn't want to gamble with your life." He let out a dry laugh without an ounce of humor. "Turns out I did that, anyway."

"Z, what are you saying? Did they attack us?" I couldn't remember fighting, but it wouldn't be the first time I'd had a weird blackout. I rubbed at my ear to dispel the echo of a scream.

"Yes... and no. Long story short, I pretended like *I* wanted to hurt you and I... I bit you."

"Um, say what now? Isn't naga venom like the most deadly on the planet?"

He met my gaze with steady eyes. "Not to their mate."

I blinked and rubbed my ear again. "Sorry, I've got this weird ringing going on in my ears. I don't think I heard you right."

Zahir smiled softly, but it didn't hide the anxiety darkening his eyes... or his scent. "You heard me right. I said 'mate'." He closed his eyes, took a deep breath, and let it out slowly before continuing. "Because that's what you are. My *true* mate. The one person in this entire universe that fits perfectly with my spirit. And I fit yours. And *this* is proof." He rested his hand on my chest in the same place he'd trailed his fingers.

I glanced down, my face scrunched in confusion, as he slowly moved his hand aside to reveal a patch of skin stained an interesting shade of blue. Not even blue, really. It was a lot more like the color of Zahir's new scales.

"Guru Angira had been trying to convince me for weeks—months, even, ever since I met you—what you really were to me. But I didn't—couldn't—believe it until my shedding cycle happened off schedule and I emerged with completely different scales. Even before that..." He trailed off, looking off to the side.

"What happened before that?" I whispered, my heart practically in my throat.

"Ezra. When we met him in the park, after you'd gone back to the parking lot, he asked me why I didn't just tell him we were bonded to begin with."

I frowned, a little embarrassed that I *still* didn't know what the fuck that was. "That's why you asked me if I'd ever heard of it." He nodded. "Except I haven't. What even does that mean? Bonded?"

He shrugged. "From what I gather, it's the werewolf equivalent of nagas exchanging venom."

"O-kay," I said, dragging out the word. "And how does that happen? Why didn't I know?"

He huffed a laugh without humor. "It seems werewolves complete—" He paused and shook his head. "No, that's not what he said. They *cement* the bond by having sex." He stared at me a long moment before adding, "*Unprotected* sex."

The air punched out of me like someone had buried their fist in my gut. "But we... That would mean... This whole time? Really?"

Zahir nodded, and it wasn't until he took my hand that I realized I was shaking. "While you were... asleep, I talked with him about it. *A lot.* He said werewolves instinctively know and will be compelled to finish the connection with their mate. He also said that, once the bond is cemented, being apart for extended periods becomes physically painful for werewolves, and they can find each other virtually anywhere."

I flashed to running through the woods, drugged out of my mind, my body just barely on the right side of death, and being unable to change. Yet, despite all of that, I couldn't recall wandering aimlessly. I'd run in a near perfect line straight to Zahir. Almost like I knew exactly where to find him.

"Are you okay? I know this is... *a lot* to take in. I didn't believe it myself for way too long." He cupped the side of my face and I looked at him, surprised to find my eyes watery. "I need you to know that is the *only* reason I would ever bite you."

"Because naga venom can't hurt their true mate," I parroted, my voice thick.

Sadness welled in his eyes, and his face crumpled. "But then you didn't wake up," he said, his lip trembling.

I immediately wrapped my arms around him, burying my face in his soft hair and pulling him close. "Sh, sh. It's okay. *I'm* okay." It took a few minutes before his quivering relented and he softened his clawed grip on my back to a more relaxed hold. "So, um, just curious, but how long *was* I out?"

He sniffled and pulled back to meet my gaze. "Two weeks."

"Two weeks?!" I glanced up at the full moon and realized why that seemed so off. "But I was supposed to meet with North Carolina Pack Alpha."

"Don't stress about it. They already know something came up. I filled Ezra in on the situation when he called about when to pick you up. That's when he told me about moving you to be beneath the full moon."

I snorted. "It's basically the werewolf equivalent of 'just put some Windex on it'. A catch all."

His smile was much more genuine as he lightly trailed the back of his fingers along my cheek. I leaned into the caress, choosing to focus on what I could feel rather than the heavy revelations. "I definitely got that, which was why I was so surprised when it worked. You have no idea how glad I am to see you awake."

"Why was I asleep? What exactly does the naga venom do to their," my throat threatened to close up, but I pushed the words out, "their true mate?"

"In theory, it makes the recipient immune to all poisons, venoms, toxins—you name it. So, yeah, now you've got that going for you. But in order to do that, it burns away any that are already in your system, which is usually—"

I barked a bitter laugh, interrupting him. I held up a hand as I fought to get the surge of hysteria under control. "It's no wonder I was out for so long."

"What do you mean?"

"Zahir, the shit that was in my system when I showed up half-dead at your place—the serum—it's a poison. I've been exposed to it for as long as I can remember." As I continued, pieces clicked into place. My spotty memory, the pain, times I felt unusually weak. Things I'd all but forgotten. Things buried so deep, they'd never be found. "They used a version of it to train us when we first started shifting. To better control our shifts. They only stopped using it when you could control every aspect of the change at will."

"That... that's fucking *barbaric*," he hissed, fury rolling off of him and edging his scent with something akin to the burnt ozone of a lightning strike.

I shrugged. "It was my normal. I never knew anything else. Or at least, didn't remember anything else... until now."

A crease formed between his brows and I wanted more than anything to smooth it away. "But you do now? Remember things?"

"It's coming back in pieces. But yeah." I let out a heavy sigh. "I think... I think I had a sister. A twin." Shock exploded across Zahir's face, but I didn't let that stop me. "I think the pack killed her when she couldn't shift like the rest of us." I closed my eyes and felt a cool tear run down my cheek. After a shaky breath, I opened them again. "Her name was Valerie."

Chapter 28

Zahir

Aidan had a twin and his ass-backward pack had fucking *murdered* her. I cupped his face with both of my hands as silent tears streamed down his cheeks.

"Oh, sweetheart, I am *so* sorry." It didn't nearly encompass how much my heart ached for him or his tragic loss, but it was all I could think to say.

Wetness clung to his lashes as he looked at me with shimmering blue eyes. "I'm pretty sure I saw them do it. But it's all so fuzzy. I don't know if I forgot because they used so much of the serum on me in the early days or because I needed to. So much of what I *can* remember is spotted with black holes. A weird coldness and then... nothing."

Fuck. How could his own people have done this to him? Why didn't anyone stop them? Abruptly, I realized I was staring at him and hadn't said anything for a while. I cleared my throat and gently wiped his cheeks with my thumbs. "Probably a little of both, I'd imagine."

"Yeah." He dropped his gaze and took a shuddering breath before raising his head again to give me a wobbly smile. "We're kind of a mess," he said, huffing a laugh and standing with me.

"That we are. Well," I glanced past him toward the pool, "we could go for a swim." His face screwed up at the suggestion, though he quickly softened his expression. "*Or* we could go back to the temple. I have to grab some of my things anyway, before we head home."

"Home," he sighed dreamily, lacing our fingers as he moved to walk beside me.

I gave his hand a gentle squeeze and guided us towards the woods. We'd gone a decent ways beneath the canopy when he glanced at me. "What?" I asked, carefully stepping over an up-turned tree.

"Why do you have things at the temple? I've never noticed you bringing anything extra before."

"Oh, uh..." I ducked my head, suddenly hating how good werewolf night vision was. No way he couldn't see the blush burning my cheeks. "I've been staying there since... I've been staying there."

He tilted his head to the side, his gaze filled with a mild confusion. "You stayed by my side? The whole time?"

"Of course," I replied quickly, my earlier embarrassment at being unreasonably clingy forgotten. "I mean, I did leave. Once. To get things so I wouldn't have to again."

He made a pleased sound in his throat and bumped me with his shoulder. We continued in relative silence to the primary entrance of the temple. Our clasped hands were a grounding presence that I desperately needed.

It wasn't until we stepped inside that something occurred to me and I lurched to a halt. "Shit, I didn't even think. It's the full moon. Don't you need to, you know?" I mimed running with my fingers.

A rich laugh that was an absolute balm to my weary soul rolled out of Aidan. "Sorry," he said, when he sobered up. Then he smoothed the line between my eyebrows. I hadn't even realized I was scowling.

"You're so cute. While werewolves are compelled to change during the full moon, running isn't technically a requirement. It's just nice." He shrugged and stretched his arms over his head, highlighting his fit body. When he dropped them back to his sides, he let out a deep sigh. "Besides, after two full shifts, I'm beat. I'll take a hard pass on shifting again. Only thing I'm interested in is food and lots of it." He grinned, and I rolled my eyes.

"You and your stomach, furball." I gestured to the hallway at the back of the main temple that led to the tech room and other areas not intended for visitors. "My stuff is back this way."

The enchanted sconces placed along the walls provided a pleasant ambient glow as we travelled deeper into the cavern. Unfortunately, not even the relaxing lights could diminish the anxiety coiling around my chest as we neared the room where I'd stayed with him. It didn't matter that he was awake and well now, fear and despair lingered there. I knew there was no logic in the feelings, but they persisted just the same.

I released a heavy sigh as I pushed open the door, prompting the sconces within to glow brighter. It damn near killed me to release Aidan's hand, but I couldn't very well gather things one-handed while dragging him across the room.

"Wow, that's *a lot* of pillows. Is this where you slept?"

I paused mid-stuffing the sack I'd used to bring things from the house. It was generous to say that I'd slept. I mostly cried or stared at his prone form until I passed out from exhaustion. "Yeah, this is where we stayed."

"Zahir."

I turned at the soft entreaty, surprised to find that he'd crossed the room and was now right behind me. "Yes?" I replied, my throat suddenly tight with the emotions—the despondence—that had plagued me in this room.

He searched my face for a moment, then said just as softly, "I will always come back to you. Do you hear me? No matter what this life throws at us, I will *always* find my way back to you."

My heart seized painfully at his words, then it relented, leaving peace in its wake. "I fucking love you, Aidan Moonbow," I said, wrapping a hand behind his neck and smashing our mouths together hard enough to bruise.

He groaned, his fingers digging sharply into my sides as he met my tongue stroke for stroke. "Love you too, scales," he murmured with what little air I let him have.

Finally, I pulled away with a gasp, needing so much more than just his mouth. I needed to remind myself he was alive. That we both were. "No more nearly dying. My heart can't take it."

"No promises, but I'll do my best." He gave me a cheeky grin and I couldn't stop the laugh that burst forward.

"Fuck you, furball," I snickered.

He stepped close and dropped his voice to a heated purr. "Pretty sure that's your job."

I went from half hard to being hard enough to pound copper in an instant. "Fuck, Aidan, you have no idea what you do to me," I groaned, capturing his mouth in another scorching kiss.

"I think I have a pretty good idea." He squeezed the now prominent bulge in my pants and I nearly choked on my tongue. Then it became a mad scramble to get me out of my clothes.

We tumbled onto the nest of pillows. Aidan's joyous laughter filled the room, pushing away the suffocating darkness that had once filled it.

"What do you want?" I asked, running my hands along his sides, appreciating the definition and power beneath my fingertips.

"Your dick in my ass would be a good start," he quipped, chuckling.

"That so? What if I have a better idea?"

He snorted, his bright smile flipping into an almost scowl. Before he could find his retort, I flipped him over so that he was on his stomach. Then I maneuvered to a better position and pulled his hips back. "I'm liking where this is going," he teased.

"Good, because I plan on claiming every centimeter of your gorgeous body." I cupped the perfect globes of his ass and placed a kiss on each cheek before spreading them to reveal his tight hole. I licked a stripe along his crease, ignoring his clenching hole for the moment, as I continued to lick and nibble at the sensitive skin.

Aidan's whimper was all the encouragement I needed. I teased his quivering rim with the blunt tip of my tongue. As I finally pierced the tight ring, I elongated my tongue to its serpentine version. I felt like I'd barely begun when I realized he was rocking back to meet each thrust of my tongue and babbling incoherently.

I'd never have guessed I'd be so into eating ass, but reducing Aidan to blissed-out putty made it addictive. His shout filled the room and likely drifted down the empty hallway as I pressed against his prostate. *How's that for snake magic?* Rather pleased with myself, I did it again and again until he was shaking beneath my ministrations.

"Z! Please! Fuck. Tell me you have lube or oil or *something* in here," he said, his voice rough. That his eagerness matched my own had me squeezing the base of my dick so I wouldn't combust prematurely.

"There's oil," I said, coming up for air. "Just past the cushions. It's either anointing oil or scale oil. Either way, it'll do."

Aidan scrabbled over the pillows to get to the elusive bottle. Cursing in frustration when it apparently rolled out of reach and he had to shimmy further. I'd have laughed if I wasn't also so desperate to be inside him.

"Got you!" he exclaimed, twisting around and brandishing the small bottle of clear liquid victoriously.

I didn't give him a chance to re-situate, just grabbed his ankle and yanked him back closer to me. The silk pillows made a soft whisk as he passed over them, finally settling on his back in front of me. "I'll take that." I plucked the oil from his slack grip and smirked at his wide-eyed expression. When he remained mute, I arched an eyebrow and added, "Unless you prefer a different position?"

"No," he replied quickly, his already flushed cheeks darkening. "I, um, like being able to see you."

"And I like being able to kiss you." I leaned over his body and sealed our mouths together. While I savored his sweet kisses, I pressed an oiled finger against his hole, slipping deep with next to no resistance.

He gasped and arched into me, practically levitating off the pillows, which were totally going to be ruined after our debauchery.

"That's it, sweetheart. I love hearing how good I make you feel." I added another finger, not because he needed it, but to see the ecstasy wash over his face. Any other time, I'd gladly tease and edge him until he couldn't take anymore. But tonight, neither of us had that level of patience.

I removed my fingers and slicked up my cock, rocking back on my heels so I could line up with his clenching hole. A bead of precum pearled at the top of his swollen dick captivated my attention. I momentarily abandoned my trajectory to lean down and lap it up, sucking on his head for good measure.

A string of sounds that I was pretty sure were supposed to be expletives poured out of him. Unable to pull myself away from my delicious prize, I sucked him down to the root. His curses devolved into pants and whimpers. His fingers tangled in my hair briefly before he began pushing me away.

"Too much," he gasped.

I relented, rocking back once more and placing the blunt head of my aching cock against his hole. In one smooth stroke, I slipped past the tight ring into pure fucking nirvana. We groaned in unison as his insane heat squeezed around me. My hips took on a life of their own as I thrust into him over and over.

I grabbed one of his ankles and raised it to rest on my shoulder before leaning down to hover over him. His resulting moan as I slipped deeper pushed me dangerously close to the edge. I staved off the pending orgasm through sheer force of will and continued rocking into him.

Sweat beaded his forehead as he clawed at my arms and shoulders like he couldn't decide where to grab me. I closed the small distance between us so I could taste his moans, resting my weight on my forearms. His foot slipped from my shoulder and he locked his ankles behind my back, adjusting his angle just enough so that the following thrusts pegged his prostate.

"Yes. Fuck. Yes. I love you so fucking much," he gasped with the meager air he acquired between kisses.

I tilted my weight onto one arm and placed my hand over the blue scale that now guarded his heart. "I love you too, scale-heart."

Without warning, Aidan's ass became a vice, and he threw his head back into the cushions. His release pulsed between us while he clung to me with a death grip. The borderline painful squeezes sent me over the edge with just as much warning. My thrusts turned haphazard as he milked me for all I was worth until all I could do was collapse on top of him.

Our breathing gradually regained a normal rhythm, and I rolled to the side, both to stop crushing him and to get cooler air on my torso. "Seriously, though, no more almost dying," I said, turning my head to look at Aidan. The golden halo of his hair framed his face, and his cheeks were still rosy from exertion.

"I don't know... If the sex is going to be this epic every time I come back from the dead..." he teased.

"That's not even remotely funny," I replied, grabbing a near-by pillow and smacking him with it.

He chuckled as he shoved it aside and stood.

Alarm shot through me, and I bolted upright. "Where are you going?"

"Easy, scales," he said, leaning down to grace my lips with a light kiss. "I'm just gonna grab something to clean us up. You lay down and rest. You've earned it." He placed his fingers on my chest and gave a gentle push, then with a wink and a smirk, he sauntered his sexy ass over to the table still covered in my half-assed attempt at packing.

He returned with what I hoped was a cloth or small towel and *not* one of my shirts. Not that he gave me a chance to determine what it was as he tenderly cleaned us up, stealing sweet kisses throughout. When he finished, he tossed the fabric aside and slid down to nestle beside me.

We lay like that for a while, our legs tangled, exchanging soft nothings, and just... existing. I was on the verge of slipping into slumber, my responses getting farther apart and less coherent, when the last voice I wanted to hear popped our bubble.

"It's so good to see you awake, Aidan," Guru Angira said from the open doorway. "Did I not tell you to have faith, Swami Zahir?"

I yelped and covered my crotch with one of the abundant pillows. Was she really standing there casually saying "I told you so" while we were clearly naked?

"Hey, Gurudevi," Aidan said, popping up without a care in the world for his nudity. Fucking werewolves. "Thank you for watching over him when I could not," he said as he approached her. Then, to my absolute amazement, he pressed his palms together in prayer hands and lightly bowed. Just like that, I fell even more impossibly in love with the man. Not just a man. My *true* mate.

Chapter 29

Aidan

By the time we got dressed, finished gathering Zahir's things, and loaded into his SUV, I was positive he was going to combust from the mortification of being found naked by his guru. So I did what any loving boyfriend—*mate*, yeah that was going to get some getting used to—would do. I badgered the shit out of him to tell me everything that had happened while I'd been flirting with death... again.

"I really don't know how many ways I can tell you that nothing happened," Zahir huffed, his irritability getting the better of him.

"You said I was out for two weeks. I find it hard to believe that *nothing* happened," I pushed.

His knuckles whitened as he gripped the steering wheel even tighter and his lips thinned.

Truthfully, I felt a little bad for pressing him so hard. Even if Gurudevi hadn't pulled me aside before we left, I could smell it in the room we'd been in—Despair. Zahir had not been in a good way while I'd been out of commission. Unfortunately, I also agreed with Gurudevi that he needed to work through that before he'd be anything close to okay.

"Is there like a therapist or something for supernaturals?" I asked, abruptly changing the topic. Zahir looked at me so sharply that the vehicle swerved into the other lane before he got it back under control. "I mean, it's not like a regular human therapist could help, since humans aren't exactly supposed to know about us. Besides, how would they even relate?"

He gave me a cautious look, this time careful to keep the SUV squarely in our lane. "I don't know. Why do you ask?"

I shrugged and glanced out the window, already resigning myself that whatever I said would come out wrong. "Seems like there'd be a lot of call for one."

"How so?"

I snorted and glanced back at him, mentally noting how close we were to his place. "Seriously? I'm not so stubborn that I can't recognize I have a fuckton of trauma. Especially now that I'm getting back snippets of memories from when I was brought into the pack." I waited a beat as I watched the pain wash across his face on my behalf, then added, "And so do you."

For possibly the first time in my life, I actually got the timing right. So when Zahir suddenly slammed on the brakes and we screeched to a halt, it was in his driveway. "Beg your pardon?" he asked, sounding every bit as affronted as he looked.

"Z." I reached over the console and carefully removed his death grip on the wheel so I could take his hand in mind. "Face it. Things have been one clusterfuck after another since we met."

"Yeah, but we're here now. We're fine. We're together."

"And..." I trailed off, and he narrowed his eyes as he scowled harder. "And I think there's still some stuff you need to work through about becoming a guru's apprentice." There. I said the things. And... yep, he did *not* look happy.

His mouth opened and closed a few times. Then he ripped his hand out of mine. "That's preposterous!" He flung open the car door and got out, shooting me a scathing look before slamming it shut.

"Zahir," I called, scrambling to get out of the SUV. "Don't be like that. You know I'm right."

He snorted as he stomped up to the front door. "I do *not* need therapy."

I closed the distance until I was hovering behind his back. I tentatively placed a hand on his shoulder and was a little surprised to feel just how tense he'd become. "And what about me?" I asked softly.

He stiffened a moment, and I felt the fight go out of him. He glanced at me, then released a heavy sigh and turned around to cup my face. I leaned into the touch, hating that I'd put the sorrow that now swam in his deep brown eyes. "I love you so much, Aidan. *So* much. You're my one true mate and nothing will ever change that. But..."

"But what?" I asked, my voice barely above a whisper.

"But you've already endured so much. I worry that trauma therapy—reliving all of those horrors... I can't lose you." He rested his forehead against mine.

"You won't lose me. I would never let that happen." He leaned back enough to give me a nasty look. "Again," I amended with a cheeky grin. "Yes, I've endured a lot, but I also survived all of it. Trust me to be strong enough to heal."

His next sigh sounded a hell of a lot like resignation. "I know you're strong and I do trust you, *believe* in you. I just..." He squeezed his eyes shut and leaned against the panelling by the door. When he finally reopened his eyes, my heart squeezed at the pain shining in them. "While I was... waiting for you to wake up, I wasn't okay, Aidan. Each day that passed with no sign of improvement, I gave up a little more. If you hadn't changed during the full moon... I don't think I could have gone on without you."

"Z," I breathed, my chest tightening at what he was suggesting.

He shook his head. "There was no way I could continue to exist in a world you weren't in. Especially..." He took a shuddering breath. "Especially when I was the one responsible for removing you from it."

"Zahir, no." I wrapped my arms around him, squeezing him tight before loosening my hold enough to lay soft kisses along his jaw and finally on his lips. "I have *always* known that you would never hurt me."

He scoffed. "Yeah? Is that why you were such a shit when we first met?"

I gave him a playful smile. "Maybe. Also, getting under your scales is stupid fun."

He chuckled and searched my face. "I know you're right. It will take more than pushing on and ignoring the past. I just don't know if *I'm* strong enough."

"I'm going to avoid howling about how you said I'm right and focus on this super serious moment."

He chuckled again. "Oh, is that what you're doing?"

"Absolutely," I replied with a wide grin. "But for the record, I would like to have that in writing. Maybe we could frame it and hang it on the wall."

"We'll see about that." His laugh was fuller this time, but doubt still shone in his eyes.

"You don't have to be strong by yourself. We have each other. I mean, that's what this whole mate business thing is. Right? You're stuck with me."

He cupped my face once more and looked at me like he was seeing straight through to my soul. "Sweetheart, there's no 'stuck' about it. I wouldn't want to get rid of you even if I could."

I pressed our lips together. "Does that mean we'll keep an ear open for someone that would qualify as a supernatural therapist? For each other."

"I feel very handled right now. But yes. For each other."

My smile grew as my heart filled with light. "Oh, I've got some thoughts about handling you," I said, reaching between us to squeeze his cock through his pants.

"Yeah?" he asked breathily, his eyelids fluttering as he tilted his head back to rest against the wall.

"Mhmm," I hummed, nuzzling his exposed neck while I continued to stroke him over his clothes. Fuck, the things I wanted to do with this snake. "But I doubt your neighbors would appreciate having to watch all the ways I'd like to 'handle' you," I whispered before lightly taking his earlobe between my teeth.

Zahir released a guttural groan and thrust his hardening dick into my hand. "Probably not."

I chuckled into the crook of his neck, not in any hurry to get inside as I worked him up. The pheromones coming off of him were light, but no less potent. I buried my face against his smooth skin and inhaled deeply.

"Would it be weird if I asked what I smell like to you?" he asked suddenly.

I had to bite my lip to keep from laughing outright. "It might be. But pretty much everything about our relationship is weird. What's one more thing? Besides, I *love* the way you smell."

"Really?"

"Definitely. Always have. Though it's changed a bit."

"How so?" he asked, worry spiking briefly through his scent.

"Well, before your scales changed, you smelled like the air right before a spring shower. Full of promise with a hint of sweetness that lingered on the tongue."

"And after?"

I groaned and buried my face against him once more, nipping the sensitive skin. "Now you smell like a full-blown summer thunderstorm. I can practically taste the lightning," I said, running my tongue up the side of his neck and causing him to shiver. "It's addictive. Strong. Powerful. As much devastating as it is essential."

"Wow. That's, um..." He cleared his throat, clearly embarrassed, but it didn't change how hard he'd become against my hand.

I nipped at his neck again. "Inside. Now," I growled, giving him a firm squeeze before letting him go, so he could turn back to unlock the door. No sooner did I hear the click of the latch drawing back, then a thought occurred to me. "Be right back," I said, stepping off the stoop and making my way toward my bike, which was mercifully still parked by the house despite our lengthy absence.

"Where are you going?" Zahir asked, turning to look at me while the front door swung open behind him.

"You remember that shirt I was wearing the night we first hooked up?" I asked as I worked the buckles on my saddlebag free.

"Of course. I remember thinking how uncannily similar it was to my scales."

I paused, straightening. "Huh, I suppose it did. Funny, I never made that connection. Anyway," I said, resuming my task, "I kept the shirt so I could have some of your scent. But now—" I flung open the saddlebag and pulled out the shirt. On a whim, I inhaled the lingering scent, then laughed to myself. "It doesn't compare." With a goofy grin, I turned to make my way back to the front door.

"Wait. Something fell out." He took a step forward as I reached down to grab a folded scrap of paper that had clearly been torn from something else.

I wracked my brain for what else I might have stored in the bag while I unfolded it. But once it was open, there was no doubt that I hadn't put it there. I stared down at Jace's distinctive handwriting and tried to make sense of the words.

NC Pack. 2 mo. <u>*Warn them*</u>*.*

"What is it?" Zahir asked, suddenly by my side. "Is it something to do with your former pack?"

All at once, the pieces clicked into place. "Fuck!" I dropped the shirt and made a beeline for the open door.

"Aidan, what is it?" Zahir asked, hot on my heels.

"When's the last time you talked to Ezra?"

"I don't know. Couple days before the full moon, I think. He said he was headed to the Pack House for the run. What's going on?"

"Fuck, fuck, fuck. Where the hell is my phone?"

"It's on the charger in the kitchen. Aidan, talk to me. What's going on?" He followed me into the kitchen and I thrust the crumpled piece of paper at him. He scanned the note several times while I picked up the cell and dialed Ezra. "I don't... this is just gibberish."

"Pick up, pick up, pick up," I pleaded as the phone continued to ring without a response. "Fuck, please don't let me be too late." I squeezed my eyes shut when I got his voicemail. I immediately ended the call and tried again.

Zahir held out the scribbled warning. "Aidan, what does this mean?"

Before I could answer, the line finally picked up and a very cranky Ezra answered. "What the fuck, Aidan? First the snake and now you?" I heard the distinct sound of rustling sheets. "Do you have any idea what time it is?"

"Ezra, I need you to listen to me."

"Wait. Aidan! You're awake!"

"We can talk about that later. First, I need to know where you are," I said quickly.

"I'm at the House. Remember? We were supposed to go together so you could meet the Alpha and formally welcomed into the pack."

"Yeah, I know. Sorry about that. But more importantly, is everyone okay?" I shot Zahir a panicked look when Ezra took too long to respond. "Ezra?"

"Yeah, yeah, I'm here," he grumbled. "Everyone is fine. I don't know what you're going on about."

"The Stormfire Pack is planning to attack."

Chapter 30

Zahir

I glanced over at Aidan in the passenger seat and fought to keep my nerves in check, though I was pretty sure I was doing a shit job of it. We were already halfway through the drive to reach the North Carolina Pack House. So far, he'd spent most of the time looking out the window and soaking up the lush scenery. But surely I wasn't the only one who was anxious about this meeting. Right?

A succession of small dings eclipsed the music playing faintly in the background. I smothered a groan as I glanced down to see that the low fuel light had popped on. Dammit, I knew I'd forgotten something. Maybe if I hadn't been so distracted by this monumental meeting for Aidan and yet *another* promise of death on the horizon, I'd have remembered to do something as simple as top off the tank before we left.

Aidan leaned over the console to peer at the dash. "Already?"

"The SUV is an older model. It doesn't exactly get great mileage," I grumped.

A teasing smile brightened his face. "You forgot to fill up, didn't you?" he snickered.

"Shut up."

His playful snicker turned into full-blown laughter.

"Ugh, are you going to be this insufferable the whole way there?" I asked, raising an eyebrow at him before returning my attention to the road. Fortunately, we were coming up on an exit that boasted no fewer than four gas stations.

"Hey, I offered to drive, scales."

"Well, you may be used to sitting for four hours straight, but I could do without the windburn and sore ass." He snickered again, and I felt a responding smile tug at my lips. How someone could be so obnoxious and still put me at ease when I needed it most, I'd never know. Then again, I supposed I did. True mates and all that.

"If it makes you feel better, I'm almost positive my ride gets even worse gas mileage," he said as we finished refueling and slid back into the vehicle to resume the long drive. We hadn't even made it back onto the interstate when he suddenly demanded, "Pull over."

"What? Aidan, we literally just stopped."

"Pull over," he insisted. "There at that little shopping center." I slowed, but didn't flick on the blinker. He paused from pressing his face against the glass to look at me fully. "Please, Zahir? I... I think I've been here before."

I wasn't about to argue with his soft entreaty, so I pulled into the gravel parking lot. Once the car was in park, I looked around, noting the small collection of cars. Despite its off-the-beaten-path location, the store seemed to have a steady flow of business and appeared well maintained. I was still peering at the front entrance when I heard the click of a seatbelt releasing.

"Where are you going?" I asked, as Aidan's door swung shut behind him. I muttered a curse and scrambled out of the vehicle to stand beside him. "Did you need to pick up something?"

He shook his head while his gaze scanned the immediate area. "I thought so."

"Thought what?" I asked, my exasperation getting the better of me. We'd left obscenely early for the drive. I hadn't even had my morning chai. Of course, if Aidan had had his way, we'd have left the second he hung up with Ezra.

"This is where it happened," he said softly. There was no missing the sadness that suddenly weighed him down. "This is where I saved that girl."

It was a wonder my jaw didn't fall. This was where his fate had been sealed. Where one selfless act had cost him his pack and led to his gruesome torture. I swallowed down the well of emotion threatening to undo me and stepped close enough to wrap an arm around his shoulders. "And now you're going to do it again," I said, pressing a kiss to the side of his head.

"If we're not too late."

"Ezra would have called. We might not have a lot of time, but we're definitely not too late. Come on, let's get back on the road so we can make sure they're as prepared as they can be." I ran my fingers through his brilliant blond hair and gave him a reassuring smile. He nodded, and we resumed our drive.

This time, I refused to let the fear of what awaited us—awaited Aidan—consume us. I cranked the radio, enjoying teasing Aidan by finding the absolute worst songs and stations. We weren't talented singers by any stretch, but we had fun anyway. Best of all, we stopped focusing on what *might* happen and embraced the moment together. Then we turned onto a long dirt drive.

I wasn't sure which of us turned the music down, but the tense hush of anticipation slowly filled the vehicle as we passed through a veritable forest. Abruptly, the trees gave way to reveal an open landscape and an apple orchard of all things. Still ahead, an enormous white house with pillars reaching up at least two stories shone in the early morning light.

I cleared my throat and gripped the steering wheel tighter. "I guess this is it." Aidan didn't respond. I was a little afraid he was holding his breath.

Gravel crunched under the tires as we followed the drive to where it made a "U" in front of the mansion. Because, really, what else could you call it? To my surprise, lines of cars filled the driveway and cluttered on the grass, forcing us to park several car lengths back from the main entrance.

"There are a lot more people here than I expected. Do they all come here for the full moon?" he asked. I really hoped the question wasn't directed at me. Fuck if I knew. Being mated to a werewolf didn't magically clue me in on all of their idiosyncrasies.

I released my hold on the wheel and swivelled to face him. "You ready?"

His breath hitched, and he paled. "Fuck. There are so many."

I glanced back through the windshield and marvelled at finding that the front porch had filled with people. A small consortium separated itself from the mass of bodies, walking down the front steps to stand in the open. When I looked back at Aidan, I saw all the anxiety I'd wondered if he was experiencing.

He spun to look at me, his eyes wide with barely contained panic. "What if they don't like me? What if they blame me for the Stormfire Pack coming here? What if they decide I can't join their pack?" The shimmer of unshed tears welling in his eyes tore at my heart.

I cupped his cheek and made soothing sounds. "Hey, everything is going to be okay." He tilted his head back, likely to stem the threat of tears, and I moved my hand to hold his chin.

"Sweetheart, look at me." He took a shaky breath before finally lowering his head back down. "No matter what happens, you are *not* alone. You don't have to face this on your own. I'll always be with you. Even when we're apart," I added with a small smile and lowered my hand to rest on his chest. "My beautiful scaleheart."

Ignoring the gathered crowd clearly waiting for us, I leaned forward to capture his mouth. It would have been tempting to leave it at a simple peck, but that wasn't what Aidan needed. He needed to know that he was loved and cherished, and that, come what may, I would always be there for him. He sank into the kiss, lazily tangling his tongue with mine, and I couldn't help but marvel again at this amazing man who'd found his way into my life.

"Thank you," he whispered when we finally pulled apart.

"I love you." I squeezed his hand and gave him the most optimistic smile I'd ever worn. "Now, what do you say we go meet your new pack and figure out how we're going to make your old pack suffer for their arrogance?"

He chuckled, but the wet shimmer had gone from his bright blue eyes. He let out a big breath and smacked his hands on his thighs. "Okay. Let's do this."

No one in front of the house moved as we exited the vehicle and walked up. We stopped in front of who I assumed must be the Alpha by virtue of the fact that he was standing in front of the gathered crowd. He had deeply tan skin, bright hazel eyes, light brown hair, and a face that conveyed both authority and a sense of familiarity.

To my relief, Ezra was right beside him. On his other side stood a large Black man that looked like he could give Arnie a run for his money. Just behind them, two women rounded out the welcome committee. One with fair, freckled skin and light red hair. The other with brown hair and tan skin.

My gaze swung back to Ezra. He subtly inclined his head in a nod, and I nearly let out a relieved breath. He'd filled them—or at least the Alpha—in on some of Aidan's more *interesting* quirks. The last thing I wanted was for Aidan to be treated like an outcast by yet another pack. Hopefully, if they anticipated any odd behavior, they could better manage their reactions.

Next to me, Aidan shifted his weight from foot to foot, his anxiety coming off of him in waves. Before I could make any move to comfort him, the man at the forefront stepped forward and extended his hand.

"Aidan Moonbow, it's a pleasure to finally meet you. I'm Liam Heldman."

There was a tense pause before Aidan took the proffered hand. His fingers curled around what appeared to be a firm grip. Then the most remarkable thing happened. An almost imperceptible wave of energy rippled over him, starting at his crown and running the full length of his body.

A warm smile spread across Liam's face. "Welcome to the North Carolina Pack, Aidan," he said. Although he'd spoken at an even volume, the gathered crowd still clustered on the wraparound porch sent up a cheer.

The people immediately before us were a little more subdued. Ezra wore a wide, goofy grin and winked at Aidan. The red-haired woman's grin was nearly as broad. The remaining two's smiles were significantly smaller, though no less welcoming.

Aidan's smile was slower in coming, but when it emerged, it shone so brightly my breath caught. Abruptly, he huffed an awkward laugh and released Liam's hand. "I'm sure it won't come as a surprise when I say that I'm thrilled to be here. I only wish it could have been under better circumstances."

"Agreed," Liam said with a nod. "Why don't we go inside? Then we can be comfortable while we talk." He gestured toward the front of the house and the crowd parted as if by magic. Ezra and the slim brunette stepped to the side, while the tall Black man and the redhead moved to lead the way inside.

I waited until the group was halfway up the stairs before turning to Ezra. "Thank you again for putting this together so quickly. And for filling them in on Aidan's... quirks," I whispered as quietly as I could.

"No problem. He's a great guy and doesn't deserve any of what has happened to him. Plus, he's kind of saving our hides."

"I just want him to be happy and to finally experience the acceptance he's been fighting for his whole life."

Ezra nodded, his face drooping with sadness. "And he—"

"Are you not joining us, Zahir Khatri?" Liam asked from the porch, his voice carrying over the buzz of voices.

I glanced at Ezra, who shrugged. "Uh..." Frankly, I didn't expect to be permitted inside the house, let alone invited to join in a sensitive conversation.

"We don't believe in separating bonded pairs here. You're as much a part of this pack as Aidan, now." Liam smiled, and I prayed I didn't look as dumbfounded as I felt. "Please join us."

I made my way nervously to where they'd stopped just at the top of the stairs. When my gaze fell on Aidan and his beaming smile, though, my nerves evaporated. The smaller group spun back to go inside once I caught up.

As we passed the rest of the pack lingering on the porch, soft words of "Congratulations" and "So glad you found us" and "Welcome to the pack" assailed us. All the positivity had me tearing up. I couldn't imagine how Aidan felt to be surrounded by a pack that was actually happy to have him.

Liam led the way down a long hallway, past a grand staircase that dominated the front room. For as old as the house—mansion—clearly was, it had been well maintained over the years.

We stopped about halfway down the hall and turned into a large study.

Books lined the room in dark-stained shelves built into the walls, ranging in size, color, and age. An equally dark desk dominated the right side of the room, with a padded desk chair on the far side and two office chairs on the other. Completing the image was a cluster of four comfortable looking chairs arranged casually on a plush green carpet. I nearly laughed aloud at the blatant recreation of the forest we'd passed through earlier.

The four of us followed Liam's direction to sit in the comfy chairs while he retrieved one of the office chairs. He maneuvered the chair to sit across from Aidan and me between the other two. Once we were all settled and the door shut, Liam took a minute to take us all in, then nodded as if he'd found what he was looking for.

"I apologize for ushering you in here so quickly, without introducing everyone. Normally, I'd have let you ease into things here and take your time getting to know everyone. Well, everyone that's here."

Out of the corner of my eye, I saw Aidan's jaw drop. "You mean there's *more*?"

The Black man chuckled, a deep sound that reverberated through his chest and filled the room with a warmth like that of a crackling fire. "Many more. Not everyone can make it to the House for the full moon. I'm Dakarai, the Beta of the pack. But please, call me Daka." His grin was just as warm as his rumbling voice. He leaned forward to shake first Aidan's and then my hand.

Liam winced. "Like I said before, not the way I usually do things. Call me Lee. Only my mother calls me Liam." He gestured to the red-haired woman. "This is Charlie. She's filling in since my mate is out of state at the moment. Sylvia should return in the next couple of days. Though, I confess, in light of what's headed our way, I'm half-tempted to tell her to stay away," he added, running a hand over his face.

Charlie shot him a scathing look. "And how well do you think that would go over?"

"I said 'half'," Lee defended himself.

I shared a look with Aidan. Judging by his expression, he was equally surprised at how informal and relaxed the interaction was. "It is a shame we won't get to meet her," I said cautiously.

"Huh?" Lee responded, swiveling to face us once more. "Oh, I'm sure you'll get the chance." He gave himself a good shake while Charlie rolled her eyes and a small smirk played on Daka's lips. "Right, down to why we're all here under less than ideal circumstances."

Aidan stiffened beside me and his earlier anxiety returned with a vengeance. "I'm sorry that I've brought this to your door."

"What are you talking about?" Lee asked with a frown. "Ezra filled me in on everything you two have shared with him so far, and absolutely *none* of this is on you. What I still don't understand is *why* the Stormfire Pack is coming here at all."

Aidan glanced at me. His memories had slowly been returning, though there were still as many holes as not. Truthfully, given how truly horrific some of them were, part of me wished they'd remain in the dark. At the very least, between our illuminating conversation with Ezra and some of Aidan's earliest memories surfacing, he had a working theory what the Stormfire Pack had really been up to all these years. And why they were here now.

"Go ahead," I encouraged him with a slight nod.

"So, I'm sure Ezra told you I can control my shift, that everyone in the Stormfire Pack can control their shift," Aidan began, his voice wary. Lee nodded, but didn't interrupt. "It wasn't until recently that I learned that wasn't the norm, that *we* were the odd ones. Anyway, once I knew that, I started putting the pieces together. Everywhere we went, we always managed to pick up—*save*," he amended with a growl that made my scales rustle. "*Weres* without a pack. We were always told something horrible had happened, like a moonstruck wolf or hunters."

Lee flinched, though I couldn't be sure if it was the reference to whatever a "moonstruck" wolf was or the hunters that caused the reaction. Daka cleared his throat and leaned forward intently. "You said 'we were told'. Does that mean there are others who are equally in the dark?"

"I think so," Aidan said. "I'm just guessing, but I can't believe I was the only one not in the loop."

Daka nodded and leaned back. "Sorry to interrupt. I may have experience with 'selective sharing' of information." Lee gave him a sympathetic look before returning his focus to Aidan.

"Anyway, now I know the truth about why those *weres* didn't have a pack... and why the children that are 'rescued' are always kept separate. The only *weres* they ever brought into the pack had complete and total control over their shift. Any who didn't..."

Thankfully, the implication was clear judging by Charlie's gasp and the storm clouds rolling across Daka's dark features. A hardness entered Lee's eyes, but he otherwise didn't react.

"How much control over your shift are we talking? Ezra tried to tell me, but I still find it hard to believe," Lee said with an undercurrent of doubt.

"I could change right here in less time than it would take you to get a cup of water. But, um, apparently shifting in front of an audience is... wrong?" He glanced at me askance. Aside from the horrors he'd endured, this was the thing that Aidan struggled with the most. How every aspect—his entire life—of being a werewolf wasn't quite right, and in many cases, outright taboo.

I wanted so much to reach out to him, provide what little comfort I could. But I didn't know the first thing about pack politics and didn't want to risk jeopardizing his status in his new pack.

"So, um, I'll just show you by doing this." Aidan held out his arm, and I watched the now familiar bubbling of skin as the appendage morphed into a hairy arm, ending in viscous claws.

"Moon blind me," Daka whispered. "I've never seen such a thing." He looked at Lee, who appeared equally unsettled.

"But why here? Why *us*?" Lee finally asked.

Aidan blinked at him, and confusion slowly eclipsed his face as he glanced between the three of them. "Because you have people who can do it too. They wouldn't come otherwise."

Lee shook his head. "I don't know of anyone in our pack who can do what you just did or complete a full shift in under two minutes."

"She can," Aidan said, pointing at Charlie with a now fully human hand.

Charlie snorted. "Believe me, I can*not* do that."

Aidan tilted his head to the side and considered her a moment before saying, "Maybe not now, but with the right training, you could. It might be too late to have as much control over it as I do, but I'd bet my life you shift faster than damn near anyone else in the pack."

Lee and Charlie shared a look. Then, with a nod, Lee faced Aidan once more. "So you *can* tell without seeing it firsthand. And all children are taken because they don't know yet."

Where Aidan appeared shocked that they'd set him up to test him, I struggled to control my mounting anger. We were here to help. Aidan had been through more than enough and did not deserve to be tricked like this.

A warm hand slid into mine. I glanced down to find Aidan's fingers curled around mine. Like that, my anger diffused...

mostly. I maneuvered my hand to lace our fingers, and he squeezed so tight I was a little afraid of losing circulation.

"I am sorry to lead you into it like that, but we needed to know if it was something you could tell without being guided," Lee apologized, his features soft and empathetic. "Time is precious and running out faster than we chase it. If it's alright with you, I'd like to have some food and drinks brought in as well as a few others so we can plan our next move. Any information you can share could be the thing that keeps this pack alive."

"I suggest we also take the time to relieve ourselves if need be. This promises to be a long day," Daka said, lending weight to his words by standing.

Lee chuckled and slapped Daka on the shoulder. "You, my friend, always have the best ideas." Daka snorted and he and Lee walked out of the room with Aidan not far behind.

I had exactly half a second to act. I snagged Aidan's wrist with my hand and faced Charlie. "Could I ask you a question?"

She blinked, clearly startled. "If this is about me not being forthcoming about my ability to shift, I truly am sorry. We didn't mean any offense. We just needed to know how the Stormfire Pack could have singled us out."

"No, it's not about that, but I appreciate the apology, nonetheless. No, this is about..." I glanced at Aidan, who was looking at me askance. I took a deep breath, grounding myself, and releasing my anxiety. "Does the pack know or have access to a therapist? A supernatural therapist," I clarified.

Charlie stared at me in obvious surprise at the random question, and I could practically feel Aidan's shock that *I* had been the one to ask. Abruptly, Charlie barked out a laugh. "Full moon at midnight. You're never going to believe this. My brother-in-law. He founded a clinic for supernaturals. Apparently, a lot of us are pretty messed up."

"You're right, I don't believe that," I replied, shaking my head.

She shrugged. "I'll give him a call tonight and see when he's free. Remind me to give you his number later." She gave us a bright smile, then left as well.

I looked at Aidan when he tugged on my arm. His soft smile made my heart flutter. Suddenly, I was worried I'd overstepped. Then he wrapped me in a hug.

"I'm really proud of you," he whispered. "We're going to get through this together."

I hugged him back, sinking into the comfort and reassurance. "Yes, we will."

Chapter 31

Aidan

I squeezed my eyes tighter and prayed for my brain to shut up enough for me to fall asleep. Unsurprisingly, it did nothing except make me even *more* hyper aware of my surroundings. Not that anything was wrong with them. The room Lee had let us use during our stay at the house was more than comfortable. The bed was like a damn cloud. The desk was neat. Even the walls were a nice color. Though I did wonder about the baseball gathering dust in the corner. It seemed an odd thing, given how clearly everything had been updated recently. Nope, no amount of willing it would make sleep come.

With a huff, I rolled to face Zahir. I probably shouldn't have surprised me to find his brown eyes staring back at me, given all the tossing and turning I'd been doing the last four hours.

"Can't sleep?" he asked quietly.

"Ugh, sorry." I buried my face into the pillow, still caught somewhere between vibrating with pent up energy and misery. The mattress shifted, and I heard the telltale click of the bedside lamp being turned on. "You don't have to stay up with me. You shouldn't have to suffer too."

"I can't sleep either. Not that it would be a burden if I could," he replied, sinking back under the covers and shimmying closer. "The waiting is eating me up. It's been, what, two weeks?"

"Near about," I grumbled. "You don't think Jace would lie about something like this? Send me off on some wild goose chase? Do you?"

He trailed his fingers along my cheek in that soft way he had while his brows scrunched together. "I obviously don't know him well—or at all—but it seems to me that giving you that note was incredibly dangerous for him. Even if it wasn't, he didn't have to."

"Yeah," I sighed. "He didn't have to bring me my bike, either. He could have just turned me in when he found me at the house." Zahir stiffened, and I realized too late that I'd conveniently left out that part when I told him about getting my bike back.

"Vishnu, help me," he muttered as he ran a hand over his face.

"I wouldn't have let them take me," I added in weak defense.

"Are any of your decisions *not* aimed at getting you killed?" he asked, his eyes boring into me. I wriggled beneath his penetrating glower. He kept the stare up another uncomfortable few seconds before letting it go with a sigh. "It's done now. Besides, the present is distracting enough without worrying about the dangers of the past."

"I *am* sorry I didn't tell you about nearly getting caught."

He snorted. "No you're not."

"Am too," I argued. "A little," I added with a playful smirk. All too soon, the grin slid off my face, once again replaced by worry. "Was it enough?"

"It'll have to be. And it's not like anyone has been idle these past weeks. How many times have you told Lee and Daka about the Stormfire Pack now?"

"Too many. I'm dreaming about it. When I can sleep, anyway," I finished with a pout.

"Perhaps what you need is a distraction, something to take your mind off things."

I raised an eyebrow while a smile slowly spread across my face. "I'm liking where this is headed…"

He closed the distance between us and sealed his mouth over mine. When he glided his tongue along my lower lip, I shuddered and happily opened for him. He ran his hand along my bare back, sliding lower and lower with each pass until his fingers dipped below the elastic waist of my sleep pants. I gasped into him as he squeezed my ass and used his hold to pull us against each other.

"You finally gonna let me ride that naga dick?" I teased. While this wasn't the best time to really enjoy that, I also wasn't entirely kidding.

He groaned in the *not* so sexy way, but I could feel his smile. "You're never going to let that go, are you?"

"Don't see why I should. Don't even pretend it wasn't hot as fuck when we got off with your hemi… hyme… penises."

He chuckled. "One is called a hemipenis. The plural is hemipen*ees*," he corrected, emphasizing the distinction.

"I don't care what they're called. I want them." I rolled my hips so our equally straining erections rubbed against each other.

He hissed, and his fingers dug into the globes of my ass. "Okay, fine. *Maybe*. But not tonight," he added, a little out of breath.

"I can work with that." I was debating whether to ask him to grab the oil or just crawl over him and get it myself when a sensation like being doused in warm bath water washed over me.

"Aidan?"

Just like when I'd first shaken Lee's hand, a sense of peace and belonging accompanied the feeling, only this time there was an added current of urgency, of being needed. It was such a stark contrast to whenever Garrett would exercise his Alpha influence and it still threw me.

"Aidan," Zahir said again. "Is something wrong?"

He gradually came back into focus, worry clear on his light brown face. "They're here." Just like that, all thoughts of sexy distractions went up in smoke. I took a deep breath and met his gaze. "It'll be enough," I said, though I wasn't sure who I was trying to convince—him or me.

He nodded and repeated without any trace of the doubt I felt, "It'll be enough."

"Okay, we should get downstairs." We slid out from under the sheets, a heavy sense of foreboding weighing heavily on us.

"Do you need to change?" he asked when it was clear I planned to go down exactly as I was.

I shrugged. "No point in it. Nearly everyone is going to change. And unlike *some* people, werewolves aren't lucky enough to have their clothes shift with them."

He opened his mouth, then closed it and shook his head. "Fair point."

We made our way down the grand staircase to the foyer, where a good chunk of the pack was already gathered, with Lee at the front. A few people in the throng nervously smiled at us as we joined them. Zahir's hand slipped into mine and squeezed when we came to a stop.

"Okay, everyone. This is it," Lee said, his voice carrying easily and silencing any whispered conversations. "The scouts have reported spotting movement in the westernmost woods. It would appear that they plan to flank us."

"But they'll be the ones surprised tonight." A cheer went up as a petite woman with pale skin and the whitest hair I'd ever seen stepped up beside him. I'd thought *I* was weird because of my blond coloring, but it was nothing compared to the near blinding white of Sylvia's coat.

Lee looked fondly at his mate before returning his attention to the increasingly restless gathering. "You know what we're up against. I wish I could promise you that all of us would walk away from this unharmed, but we've fought battles before and the price of freedom is always high."

Several wolves, including Pri and Daka, as well as Sylvia, nodded their heads solemnly. They'd all lost their packs too, though at the hands of fanatic men wearing white coats emblazoned with a fiery staff that bore an uncanny resemblance to the Stormfire patch rather than *weres* with a misguided sense of superiority.

"You all know your places and what to do if your area encounters a concentration," Lee continued. This time almost all heads nodded, including mine and Zahir's. "One more reminder before you head out to change and take your positions. As I'm sure some of you recall, the Order of Light used a gruesome serum designed to inhibit your ability to heal or shift. The wolves coming may well have some with them. And from what I understand, they've made the toxin even nastier." Muted snarls rippled through the crowd. "With that said, be careful out there. Don't go anywhere alone. And send up a signal at first sight of the intruders." Lee's normally relaxed expression turned hard. "None of them leaves here tonight."

I swallowed and shared a look with Zahir. He squeezed my hand again before releasing it, then we were filling out the back of the House along with half of the gathered pack. We'd just made it outside and were about to veer toward the northwest when Ezra jogged up to us.

"I'm glad I caught you," he said, a half second before wrapping me in a quick hug that made my ribs creak in protest. "Thank you again for warning us. Even with everything they've done to you, I can't imagine this is easy."

I released a shaky breath. I hadn't said anything, but it *was* hard. Not everyone in the Stormfire Pack had been awful, and like I'd told Daka, I strongly suspected that, like me, many had no clue what was going on behind the scenes. "Yeah, but this can't keep happening."

"No, it can't." He clasped me on the shoulder, then trotted toward the treeline.

I glanced up at the sky, the freckling of stars the only illumination as we ventured further into the forest. "Should have known they'd attack during a new moon. Fucking assholes," I muttered. In theory, werewolves were at their weakest when the moon was out of sight, though that wasn't saying much.

"No time would have been a good time. They're assholes regardless," Zahir countered.

"You sure you'll be able to see okay?" I asked as we reached our destination roughly a hundred yards into the forest. Lee wanted everyone spread out, but not so far away from each other that we couldn't immediately provide backup.

Zahir sniffed indignantly. "I may not see every color and blade of grass, but my infrared vision will be more than sufficient, furball."

I couldn't help but grin. "Whatever you say, scales." With that, I shook out my shoulders and initiated the change. Everyone else would shift in private before rejoining their assigned partners. It had become abundantly clear that seeing me shift made everyone uncomfortable, including Lee, though I still didn't see what the big deal was. Zahir seemed to be the only one unphased by watching the process.

My legs lengthened, bones snapping in place and muscles banding thickly around my thighs. At the same time, my weight shifted to accommodate the new angles, my ribs cracked outward, expanding my chest and broadening my shoulders. I ignored the excruciating pain as all the bones in my skull broke apart and reformed to better fit a mouthful of deadly sharp teeth. I breathed past the agony that was already subsiding and flexed hands now made of long fingers that ended in wicked claws. I tried not to think about how claws like that could rip through soft scales, but it hovered just at the edge, stubborn as ever.

"Aidan?"

I looked over at Zahir's soft call. "What's up?" I asked just as quietly, moving closer to him. Talking in this half-form wasn't the easiest thing, but it was doable.

"I just..." He wrung his hands, then pinched the bridge of his nose, betraying his anxiety and likely forgetting that I *could* see-see in the dark. Abruptly, he wrapped me in his arms—spotty hair, awkwardly long limbs, and all—and crushed me against him. "Please, no more nearly dying. I meant it when I said I couldn't take it again."

"Got it. Die with conviction," I teased, eager to lighten the mood, if only for a moment. It was too close to my own fears about *his* safety tonight.

"That's not even remotely funny," he grumbled, pushing me to arm's length.

"And yet, you still love me." I'd have smiled, but that *definitely* wasn't happening in this form. It would look more like a predatory leer.

He sighed and reached up to trail the tips of his fingers along my cheek. I leaned into the caress, wishing more than anything that tomorrow was guaranteed and not a hope. "I do. I love you so much. Which is why we're both going to make it through this. There are still so many things I want to do with you."

My heart gave an involuntary stutter. I ached for a future with this man. I wanted to watch him grow into the guru I knew he could be, cheering him on from the sidelines. I wanted to argue about silly things that didn't matter and make up. I wanted to watch the baking show we both loved and amaze him by recreating the desserts. But all of that hinged on the outcome of one night, *this* night.

"And we'll do them," I finally said when I could find my voice and we parted to get into position.

"And Aidan," Zahir said as he transitioned into his naga form, which somehow miraculously blended with the surrounding foliage.

"Yeah?"

"Thank you for not asking me to stay behind. You could have sent me back to Kentucky, and I don't think anyone here would have stopped you."

I frowned. It literally had never crossed my mind. Sure, I wanted him safe, but we were bonded, a team. "We're in this together, Z. Have been since the moment I walked into that bar."

His smile made my heart swell with love and determination. We *would* get to do all the things we dreamed of. I was done letting the Stormfire Pack take everything from me.

Suddenly, a howl split the night. The sharp sound rose above the trees and made my hair stand. "Is that..." Zahir whispered, his speech slightly lisped.

"Someone has eyes on them."

"It came from the west. Should we—"

I held up a hand and strained my ears. We needed more than one call to determine exactly where they were spearheading their assault. And I could have sworn I heard a twig snap. The sound was so small. It could have easily been a raccoon or rabbit out foraging, but then a familiar scent tickled my nose.

"Stay here," I growled as low as I could, then slid deeper into the forest, ignoring Zahir's whispered protest that we were supposed to stay together. I followed the scent of leather and the smoke of a recently snuffed candle, circling around until I was in front of the *were*. Taking a risk, I launched through the brush, stopping just shy of the man that smelled like the promise of Autumn.

"Aidan?" Jace whispered harshly, also in his half-shifted form, as I suspected all the others from Stormfire would be as well. "What the hell are you doing here? You need to leave."

I straightened up to my full height. Though even partially shifted, I was still shorter than him and he had a good fifty pounds on me. Fucker was built like a damn tank. "No, *you* need to leave. Why are you even here? I did what you said. I warned them. This pack won't be the easy mark Garrett expects."

He hesitated, his clawed hands opening and closing as he looked past me. Just in case he decided to make a break for it, I braced myself to stop him. "So... so, did they take you in? This pack?"

"They did," I replied, relaxing just a hair. "They could take you too, but not if they catch you here. No one is getting out alive." Lee hadn't exactly said that, but we all knew.

Jace shook his head. "I won't fit in any better here than I did with the Stormfire Pack."

I dropped the rest of my guard and frowned at him. "What are you saying?"

He took a shaky breath, then met my gaze. "I'm a lone wolf, Aidan. Always have been."

For a hot second, my brain refused to comprehend what I was hearing. Jace couldn't be a lone wolf. He'd been in the pack as long as I'd been, longer. And you couldn't just *fake* pack. "That's not true," I said at last. "It's not possible."

"Not easy, but possible," he countered.

I glanced back to where I'd left Zahir cooling his tail, though I doubted it'd stay that way for long. When I looked back at Jace, the man I'd grown up with, my friend, the guy who'd helped me escape for good, he looked... sad, resigned. "Then this is your chance."

His head shot up to pin me with a confused stare. "What?"

"You heard me. Leave now. Even if somehow the Stormfire Pack manages to walk away from this, they won't go looking for you. They'll assume you died here. So go, and consider us even." Giving him a chance was the least I could do. He'd literally done the same for me. "And maybe you could give me a call sometime? You know, once you get your bearings."

He stared at me for a long second, then finally nodded. "I'd like that. I may not be pack, but you've always been like family to me." Without another word, he spun on his clawed foot and loped back the way he'd come, vanishing into the darkness without so much as a twig snapping to betray him.

Another howl filtered through the trees, followed by two more in quick succession. I didn't bother with being quiet as I rushed back to Zahir. By the time I reached him, there was a chorus of howls, some cutting off abruptly only to be replaced by three more. The Stormfire Pack had made their move.

Chapter 32

Zahir

"Damn it, Aidan," I hissed as loud as I dared while he bolted deeper into the forest—without me. Because apparently, "always stick with someone in the pack and never be alone," *really* meant, "run off into the woods on your own and leave your mate to fend for himself."

I peered through the trees for any hint of where or *why* he'd gone. For the first time, my infrared vision felt woefully inadequate. I'd always found it to be superior as far as night vision went. But being able to see body heat wouldn't do me a damn bit of good if someone was hiding behind a tree—which were fucking *everywhere*—or, better yet, threw something at me.

Several small twigs snapped off to my right. I spun around and stared into the darkness, searching for even the tiniest change in ambient heat. I focused so hard my eyes felt like they might pop out of my head. It wasn't until I was positive that not so much as a field mouse was scurrying about that I finally blinked.

This was ridiculous. I couldn't just stand here, and I wasn't about to endanger the greater plan to pen in the Stormfire pack, which left going after Aidan. "Fucking furball. Vishnu, give me the patience not to strangle my reckless mate." I took a moment to rein in my irritation. If I was going to have any chance at finding him, I needed every ounce of focus I could muster.

Slowly, I slithered in the direction he'd vanished, pausing periodically to taste the air and feel for any vibrations of movement near me. The constant stop-and-go made for glacial progress. At least I could be certain he'd gone this way, not just from the lingering trail of his musk, but an inherent sense of rightness, of getting closer.

I lost track of time and tried not to fixate on how unbelievably lost I was in the unfamiliar woods. All that mattered was finding Aidan. When I did, we'd be having another very serious conversation about his propensity to put himself in situations that could get him killed. A howl split the air. I paused mid-slither over an extensive stretch of exposed roots. I was still trying to determine where the initial howl had come from when another filled the darkness. Then another and another. Each overlapping the next, never relenting, even when some abruptly stopped. That was the signal.

My tongue flicked out to taste the air, my anxiety spiking. Aidan would hear that signal. He'd know that everyone who was able was to converge on the source, effectively surrounding and hopefully overwhelming the Stormfire wolves. But I was torn. Did I follow the plan and turn back, or did I continue to search for Aidan? Could I trust that he'd hear the signal and return? I desperately wanted to believe that he could and would, but the fear of losing him kept me frozen with indecision.

Branches snapping cracked through the forest. I whirled around just as a massive heat signature exploded through the foliage. My heart launched into my throat and my hood reflexively flared as I hissed a threat, fangs fully extended. Then I registered that the creature that had nearly bowled me over was in fact Aidan.

"Where the fuck have you been?" I hissed angrily, my irritation back in full force.

"Come on!" Aidan shouted, barely sparing me a glance as he continued toward the cacophony.

"Fucking furball," I muttered again as I took off after him, hands pressed firmly to my sides and lowering my torso closer to the ground to maximize my speed. In no time at all, I'd slithered up to Aidan, then surpassed him. I briefly caught a hint of his surprise, which only irritated me more. Did he think snakes were slow? I loved the furball, but honestly, the arrogance of werewolves sometimes.

I slithered over roots and divots, swerved around a maze of trunks, the sounds ahead of me eclipsing Aidan's noise. Abruptly, the trees gave way. I soared into the open and absolute chaos. Everywhere I looked, teeth and claws flashed. Fierce snarls and vicious growls buffeted my ears. A fully shifted wolf launched at one of the Stormfire wolves only to be knocked out of the air by the half-turned *were*.

Without thinking, I slithered lightning fast and struck, sinking my fangs deep into the Stormfire wolf's exposed chest while I dug my claws into his misshapen arms to keep them at bay. A glimmer of amusement sparkled in the asshole's eyes, then a heartbeat later, they widened in fear. His breath faltered as I released him, but even in the dark, I could see the venom spreading quickly over his body. By the time Aidan joined me a mere second later, he was dead on the ground without so much as a twitch.

"Fuck," he growled, looking from the corpse to me. Before I could respond, his gaze shifted past my hood.

No sooner did I realize what he was going to do than I suddenly found myself on the ground, a good twenty paces away from where he'd pushed me. I levered myself up only to get bowled over by a different half-shifted *were*. Pure instinct had me digging my claws into whatever meat I could and wrapping my tail around the assailant. I might not be a constrictor, but I was strong, I was fast, and I was fucking *lethal*.

Razor-sharp claws skittered uselessly over my protective scales, searching for a purchase they'd never find. The wolf snapped and snarled, but couldn't pull me off. I tightened my hold on him, winding my tail tighter around his torso and forcing him to carry my full weight. The moment he tilted his head back, likely to howl for aid, my fangs pierced the sensitive skin at his throat. He jerked once, then dropped like a stone.

I quickly uncoiled from the dead body and took stock of the melee. Thanks to fiery arrows dotting the battle, it was all too easy to see the devastation. It was disheartening to discover how many fully shifted wolves lay torn and bleeding on the ground. I counted maybe a dozen half-shifted *weres*, not including Aidan or the two I'd already dispensed, and that was probably being generous. I just prayed that the North Carolina Pack's superior numbers would be enough.

I caught movement out of the corner of my eye. One of the Stormfire wolves had broken free and was now making a beeline straight for me. I braced myself to spring, fangs fully extended, claws at the ready. A half-second too late, I realized he wasn't aiming for me at all. He was barrelling toward Aidan. Who hadn't seen him.

"Aidan!" I shouted as the *were* with murder in his eyes leapt the remaining distance and landed practically on top of him.

Aidan seemed to turn in slow motion, abandoning his latest victory to face the new threat. The second he clocked the attacker, his eyes widened with surprise.

"You're supposed to be dead!" the Stormfire wolf shouted in an eerily familiar voice, fury rolling off of him.

Aidan snarled back. "Maybe next time you should do a better job of it!"

"I'm going to put you in the fucking ground, dog!" Finally, it clicked why I thought I recognized the voice, though I'd only ever heard it once before. This had to be Elliot. And over my dead fucking body was I going to let him harm my mate. *Again*.

I'd scarcely covered half the ground to get to him, when he pulled something off a belt around his waist I hadn't even noticed. Cold horror washed over me as Elliot plunged a fat syringe into Aidan's neck.

"Extra strong," Elliot snarled, getting in Aidan's shocked face before releasing his hold on the syringe and letting Aidan fall back onto the dirt.

"No!" I screamed. In a burst of power, I vaulted the rest of the distance. One second I was airborne, claws extended, ready to rip him apart with my bare hands. The next, I was slamming into a tree that might as well have been a reinforced steel beam. My skull cracked against the wood and bright colored spots popped like fireworks across my vision.

Dragging in a ragged breath, I levered myself up, bracing myself on my arms. The world tilted and kept sliding, making me queasy. A feeling reinforced by a searing pain across my torso. I groaned and closed my eyes against the multitude of pain. A tiny voice whispered it was important to keep them open, but for the life of me, I couldn't hold down a thought long enough to remember *why*.

"Why. Won't. You. Die?!" a voice shouted, causing my inner ear to vibrate painfully.

I forced my eyes open and the reality of what was happening crashed over me in a wave. Elliot looked absolutely furious where he stood heaving. Blood matted his fur nearly all over his body, including, I was pleased to note, from the long rents I'd clawed into his chest. My gaze slid past him to see another half-turned *were* stumbling to their feet. It wasn't until they reached up to yank out the needle stuck in their neck that I realized it was Aidan.

I tried to move toward him, but pain exploded across my head and it took everything I had not to collapse again. Desperate to get to him, to protect him, I sank my claws into the soft earth, determined to crawl on my belly if that's what it took. Even that threatened to make me blackout. I clung to consciousness with a scale cracking grip and pushed on.

Too far away, I watched Aidan toss the needle aside and square off against Elliot. Pure unadulterated hatred shone in his eyes as he growled, "Haven't you heard? Toxins don't work on me anymore."

Something that might have been fear flashed across Elliot's face, but that didn't stop him from flexing elongated fingers tipped with claws and snarling right back. "Like it matters. I'm going to enjoy tearing you apart. Valerie was the one who should have lived, not you!"

Before Aidan could respond, Elliot crashed into him, lowering his shoulder and plowing into Aidan's middle. Instead of going down, Aidan drove his claws into Elliot's back. Elliot howled in pain and shoved Aidan away. The two circled, each dripping blood from indistinguishable wounds.

I tried again to get my body to cooperate, but even crawling was proving to be a near insurmountable task. The world slid into fuzzy darkness. When it cleared again, they were grappling on the ground, each doing their damndest to tear the other's throat out. Aidan somehow got his legs between them and kicked.

Blood blossomed on Aidan's collarbone as he threw Elliot clear, but Aidan didn't let the fresh wounds stop him from getting back on his feet. I watched in amazement as the cuts sealed up before my eyes. Aidan had told me just how advanced their healing could be, but I hadn't really understood. Superior numbers or not, it'd be a miracle if the North Carolina Pack survived this. Except... Except Elliot wasn't healing. He was clutching his middle while his expression flickered between rage and disbelief.

Aidan slowly raised his head, an evil chuckle rolling out of him. "Let's see how you like it." Light glinted off of a narrow bit of metal as he held up another syringe. Empty. He casually tossed it aside and walked toward Elliot like he knew he wouldn't run.

Elliot slashed at him, but Aidan knocked his arm aside like it was nothing. "You can't do this to me! You're nothing! Always have been!" Faster than my eyes could follow, Aidan slipped behind Elliot, wrapping a clawed hand around his throat as he forced him onto his toes. Elliot desperately clawed at Aidan's hand, but despite the streams of red, Aidan didn't relent.

"You never should have touched my mate," Aidan snarled in his ear. Terror flooded Elliot's gaze the instant before Aidan tore out his throat. Elliot's lifeless body fell to the ground, and I belatedly realized most of the other fighting had stopped as well. Somehow, Aidan was the only half-turned *were* still standing.

As he stood panting from exertion, I searched his body in the uneven light to see how injured he was. But between the pickaxe of pain driving through my skull and the fuzzy patches dotting my vision, it was damn near impossible to determine how much of the blood splattered on his body belonged to him.

I watched as if from a distance as Aidan stepped over the body of the werewolf that had made it his life's mission to make Aidan's life a living hell. Aidan didn't so much as glance down at the twisted form as he moved closer. By the time he squatted down in front of me, it was a challenge to remain conscious. I just needed to hang on a little longer.

He sat on the torn earth, subtly shifting closer to his human form, and gently placed my head in his lap. "Z? Talk to me. Are you okay?"

My eyes stung with unshed tears. "You," I croaked and winced at how the sound reverberated in my skull. "You hurt?" I finally pushed out.

He shook his head. "No." He trailed his fingers over his heart where I could just make out the blue undertone. "He can't hurt me anymore. He can't hurt either of us."

"Oh thank fuck," I whispered, then blacked out.

Chapter 33

Aidan

My gaze snagged on the four jagged, silvery lines marking Zahir's right pectoral as he pulled on a fresh shirt. I hated that he'd gotten them during the fight. Hated more that Elliot was the one who gave them to him. But there was no help for the marks now. I'd have to get used to them. Goddess knew I had my own fair share of new scars from that night. Was it really only a week ago?

I forced myself to look away, shaking my head, and focused on changing my own clothes. The House was nice and all, and I appreciated Lee putting us up for as long as he did, but *this* was home. Zahir's small house was perfect in every way and I was beyond relieved that staying at or near the House wasn't a requirement. Not even for new members.

"You sure we don't need to bring anything?" Zahir asked. When I continued to stare at the shirt in my hands instead of answering, he walked over. He gently took the shirt from me and set it aside on the bed. "Talk to me, sweetheart. You've been kind of out of it for a while." Worry brought his dark brows together, crinkling the skin between. "Do you miss the pack? I promise we'll figure something out, even if it means I spend as much time on the road as I do off it."

I shook my head. "No. I'm good on that front. Regular visits and having Ezra nearby will take care of me."

"Is it... the Stormfire Pack?"

I let out a heavy sigh and leaned forward to bury my face against his chest, wrapping my arms around his waist. "Am I doing the right thing? What if... What if the rest of them *do* know?"

Zahir petted my hair with one hand while holding me close with the other. "You didn't."

I snorted and leaned back. "I didn't know a lot of things."

He cupped my face with both hands and looked deeply into my eyes. "And what makes you think it might not be the same for them? Keeping a chunk of the pack oblivious to what was really going on was a form of control. Like so many other things they inflicted on you. On all of you. I think your first instinct was right. Only the members of the pack in the know showed up at the House."

"But what if I'm *wrong*?" I persisted, even though I couldn't imagine Amy, Megan, or even Steph willingly killing a child or even attacking another *were* without serious cause.

"Have more faith in yourself." He chucked me under the chin and smirked. "Isn't that what you're always telling me?"

"Watch it, scales," I growled playfully.

"Make me, furball." He stepped back in that sinuous way he had and the aching need to be naked with this man immediately drowned all my doubts. My phone rang, and I groaned in frustration while Zahir chuckled. He plucked the stupid cock-blocking device from the nightstand and tossed it to me.

"Why do I have one of these again?" I grumbled irritably, which only made him laugh more. When I saw it was Ezra calling, I quickly swiped to answer. "Hey, Ez."

"You two about ready? Some of the others are getting antsy."

I winced inwardly. "Right. Sorry, didn't mean to take so long. Just good to be home, you know?"

"Yeah, I do," he replied wistfully with a hint of something else I couldn't quite place. "Anyway, get your tails in gear. Sylvia wants to make sure there's plenty of daylight to travel back to the House, even if things take longer than we expect."

"We're coming out now." I ended the call and tugged on the discarded shirt, then swivelled to face Zahir. "You ready?"

"Are you?" he countered, quirking an eyebrow.

I put on a wide grin. "Not even a little bit."

We walked outside together then parted ways, me to my Harley, and him to the SUV, though not before he cast an uncertain glance at the bike. I knew he wasn't a fan of separate vehicles, but as much as I longed to get lost on another country ride with him, it made sense for me to approach the rental house on my own first. Well, mostly on my own.

I cranked the engine and knocked back the kickstand in one fluid motion. Zahir nodded at me from the driver's seat of the SUV and we set off. Just past the neighborhood where he lived, we slowed by a vacant lot packed with cars and motorcycles. The lot emptied as the vehicles fell into a procession, with me at the front.

Lee rolled up beside me, and I flashed him a grin. I'd been more than a little surprised to discover he rode, though his ride was an Indian instead of a Harley. He tilted his chin at me in return and I took that as my signal to put things in gear.

The easy ride was exactly what I needed, but when I rolled up to the overly decorative house the Stormfire Pack had been renting, it shot from zero to a thousand. I let out a shaky breath as I pulled up in the front yard and popped the kickstand. The engine was still vibrating when Lee parked beside me. For now, the others—including a grumpy Zahir—would wait further down the road so they wouldn't cause a panic.

"Everything is going to be fine," Lee said, placing a reassuring hand on my shoulder and squeezing.

"Thanks, Alpha."

He rolled his eyes. I'd lost count of how many times he'd told me to call him Lee. Like so many other things I was unlearning though, it would take time. Instead of correcting me—again—he glanced toward the front of the derelict house, where you could clearly see several pairs of eyes peeking curiously through broken blinds and curtains and whatever else we'd found to cover the windows. "Looks like we've got everyone's attention. You go on ahead and I'll wait here until you're ready."

"Yep." I swung my leg over the bike and shook out my nervous energy before making my way to the front door. The closer I got, the more I could make out the surprised murmurs. *What had Garrett told them about me?* I'd made it to the porch and was about to knock, even though everyone *obviously* could see me, when the door opened.

Amy stood in the entryway, arms crossed, scowl on her face. Despite the imposing image she struck filling the frame, wariness colored her scent. She glanced past me toward Lee, then returned her attention to me. "Aidan. You shouldn't be here."

I forced a smile. "I can be anywhere I like."

Her eyes narrowed, and the sharp tang of fear spiked in her scent. "They'll kill you," she hissed. "I don't know how you're not already dead. We... heard what happened." She looked like she was going to say more, but she slowly shook her head, her gaze continuing to slide past me. It took me a moment to realize that she wasn't looking at Lee at all. She was anxious about the rest of the pack showing up.

"He's not coming, Amy. Not of them are."

She jerked and yanked her searching gaze back to me. In the background, all the faces I hadn't seen at the House crowded behind her. "What do you mean?"

I raised my voice so there would be no doubt about what I was about to say. "Garrett is dead and so is everyone who was with him." It was a small lie. Jace wasn't dead, and we'd found neither hide nor hair of the Stormfire Beta, Devin.

Shocked murmurs rippled behind her, and she glanced back. "I don't... I don't understand. He said there were other *weres* in trouble. Did something happen?"

I was already shaking my head before she could finish. "He lied. They weren't going to help anyone. They were attacking another pack. *His* pack," I added, pointing toward Lee where he continued waiting. "They've always been lying and about a lot more than you could imagine."

Megan shoved her way to the front, squishing in beside Amy. "It's true then. He really is gone. We all felt... something. It's been weird. None of us have felt safe enough to go out. Food is running low."

Suddenly, I felt like an asshole for dragging my feet to get here. It never even occurred to me they'd experience the werewolf equivalent of whiplash when Garrett died. "I'm sorry. To all of you," I said, looking past Amy's and Megan's worried faces to all the others. "I should have come sooner." I turned at the sound of gravel crunching and stepped aside to let Lee take center stage. He'd halted a respectful distance from the porch, but that didn't stop the others from eying him warily.

"I'm Liam Heldman—Lee," he added with a small smirk. "I'm the Alpha of the North Carolina Pack. Please, please," he said, holding up his hands in a placating gesture when everyone inside reacted like a kicked anthill. "There's no cause for alarm. It will take time to explain everything, but I wanted to come here today so that you know you're not on your own. I won't force anyone to join the North Carolina Pack who doesn't wish to." His gaze softened, and he dropped his hands. "But I also know how hard it is when your Alpha is taken from you and there's no one else to fill the void."

Amy and Megan shared a look, and I saw the same being passed around behind them. Then, to my amazement, the lot of them rushed forward, all babbling that they wanted to join as they spilled out onto the lawn.

"Easy, there's not a limit. I won't turn anyone away." Despite Lee's reassuring words, they continued to crowd toward him, verging on panic. He let out a heavy sigh. Then closed his eyes and took a deep breath. As he opened them again, he said, "Be calm."

For lack of a better word, energy rippled out from him, washing over everyone. I shuddered when it hit me, though it wasn't unpleasant. The cacophony of voices instantly quieted and everyone stood around with a mildly confused look. Then, one by one, each member of my former pack... smiled. A grin even tugged at my face.

Lee wore a mirroring grin as he shook his head. "Not quite how I expected this to go, but here we are. What would you say to meeting some more of your new pack?"

Right on cue, the vehicles that had been waiting rolled up and parked in front of the house, cluttering the narrow street. Even though Lee's Alpha influence had already instilled a sense of calm, I felt more at ease when I saw Zahir get out and start walking toward us. Also, making their way was a select group of individuals chosen for their ability to empathize with losing an Alpha. Lee felt it was important that anyone who joined knew that they were not alone.

Suddenly, a slim body slammed into me. I let out a grunt and looked down to find Megan squeezing the ever-loving life out of me. "Uh, Meg?"

"Sorry, sorry. I just can't believe you're alive." She pulled back, giving my ribs a break. "How *are* you alive? Even if they didn't outright kill you, you were exiled."

I smiled as Zahir joined us. He wrapped an arm around my shoulders and planted a kiss on the side of my temple. Megan's surprised gaze bounced between the two of us, and my grin broadened. "Funny you should ask that."

"How are you doing, Scaleheart?" Zahir asked, his voice low and intended just for me. Even if everyone nearby *could* hear him.

"Better than I expected. I'm more worried about Lee," I replied. We both looked over to where Lee looked like he was being mobbed by curious werewolves. All wanting an explanation of what had happened. He chuckled, and I returned my attention to Megan. "Megan, this is Zahir. My mate," I finished, practically beaming up at him.

"Uhh, hi?" she said tentatively, reaching out a hand even as her gaze flicked back to me, giant question marks in her eyes.

I laughed outright and the two of them looked at me like I'd lost my damn mind. I didn't care. For the first time I could remember, I felt completely at peace, and above all, *happy*. "I'll explain it all later, but the gist of it is, finding my true mate and cementing the bond staved off any wasting I might have experienced being cut off from a pack."

"That's... good," Megan replied, still seeming out of sorts. "I heard a story once a long time ago about fated mates for werewolves, but that's all I assumed it was—a story."

I slipped an arm around Zahir's waist and tugged him closer. "Oh, they're very real. Caught me totally by surprise—"

Zahir interrupted me with a snort. "You're telling me, fur-ball."

"But I wouldn't trade scales here for anything," I finished.

Megan's face softened into a smile. "I'm really happy for you, Aidan." She swivelled around at a shout from Amy, who was standing close to Lee. "Sounds like I'm needed. Judging by my lady's face, she wants to go over how to retrieve the pups. *That* will take some doing." She took a half step toward them, then paused, looking back at me. "We'll catch up later, yeah?"

"Of course. Now get before Amy comes over here and hauls you off," I said, waving her on. She chuckled and began weaving through the mayhem of bodies.

Zahir squeezed my shoulders again, and I rested my head on his shoulder. "You sure you're doing okay? Things seem to be going well—better than well—but I know this was a lot for you."

"I won't lie. I was scared as hell, but I'm glad I didn't let that stop me. Still, I couldn't have done it without your support. I couldn't have done *any* of it without you." I glanced up at him, my heart so full of love I thought it would burst. "You saved me, Z."

He shook his head and moved to stand in front of me, angling my head up with his knuckle under my chin. "No, sweetheart. *You* saved you. And you saved all of them, too. Somehow, despite everything you've been through, you still have the fiercest heart I've ever had the privilege to witness. I'm honored that I get to spend my life with you and more grateful than words can ever express that you're my mate. I love you, Aidan Moonbow."

I was glad when he leaned forward to press his lips against mine so he couldn't see the overwhelmed tears brimming. "I love you too," I whispered.

Epilogue

Zahir

The afternoon sun warmed my face and legs, where I leaned back in the sand. I kept my face tilted toward the glow until the telltale splashes caught my attention. I opened my eyes and watched with a pleased smile as Aidan splashed his way back to shore from his most recent foray in the Atlantic. The slight chill in the air all but guaranteed we had the beach to ourselves, but that was no deterrent for a hot-blooded werewolf.

The wind plucked at my light jacket, making the fabric rustle. My gaze stayed on Aidan's tan body as he made his way to me, still dripping ocean water. Beautiful as his body was, my focus was riveted on his face, specifically the joy shining there. I'd suspected he'd like the beach, but now I was certain—we both were—that he'd been born on the coast, though maybe not the east coast.

"Are you sure you're not afraid of the waves?" he teased, flopping down beside me in his swim trunks, careful not to kick up sand.

"Ha ha. Just because I don't like the cold doesn't mean I'm afraid of the ocean." In truth, I loved the ocean nearly as much as I loved swimming.

He bumped my shoulder and said with a grin, "I know. I'm really glad you suggested renting the beach house for your parents' visit." He rested his head on my shoulder and gazed out over the waves. "Think we can come back?"

I pressed a kiss to his hair, heedless of the wet strands. "We can come as often as you like. I bet you could even get a group from the pack to come out with you."

"That's a great idea! I didn't even think of that. It would be awesome to run on the beach with the others," he said excitedly, straightening up.

"Speaking of pack..." I began, and he cast me a furtive glance. "Have you thought anymore about Lee's idea of tracking down any remaining members of everyone's birth packs?"

He shrugged, his body uncharacteristically stiff. "It's pretty amazing he's offering at all. I know several of the others want to take him up on it."

"But what about *you*? Do you want to see if they can find anyone from your original pack?" I pressed.

He twisted to face me and considered me before asking, "Have you thought anymore about your mom's suggestion of having a traditional Indian wedding?"

I scowled at him. "That's not the same."

"Doesn't change the fact that you still haven't answered," he countered.

I let out a huff. "I know *she* would love that, and I'm pretty sure Gurudevi would be over the moon."

He snickered at the wolf-ism.

I bumped him. "Shut up. Besides, I wouldn't have figured you'd want a big wedding like that. They can get pretty ostentatious, and there's no way my mother would settle for anything less than the biggest wedding of the century."

He sighed and shook his head. "I didn't ask what your mom wanted, or Gurudevi, or even me. I asked what *you* wanted."

I huffed sullenly and stared at my legs. My mother had been remarkably patient about waiting for our decision, never once dropping hints or pushing. The wedding part was a foregone conclusion, though neither of us had technically asked the other. Did I want a grand show like that to celebrate our love? To celebrate how against every hurdle thrown at us we'd somehow found each other?

"I'll make you a deal," Aidan said, interrupting my thoughts. "I'll tell you exactly what I think about looking for my birth pack and you admit to what you really want wedding wise. No extra explanations or justifications. Just the truth. Whatever it is, we'll make it work together."

"You're lucky you're cute, furball," I grumbled halfheartedly.

"You know you love me. And I'll take that as agreement. For me, I'm terrified to search for my birth pack." I started to offer reassurance, and he held up a hand. "I don't know if I'm more afraid of finding them or *not* finding them. But... but I do think I want to at least try."

I smiled at him and lightly brushed my knuckles along his cheek. "If they're out there, we'll find them."

He grinned back, hope glimmering in his sky-blue eyes. "I know. Now it's your turn. Being completely selfish and not thinking about what anyone else may or may not want, do *you* want a grand traditional Indian wedding?"

I huffed a laugh and surprised myself by immediately responding, "Yeah, I think I do."

He gave me one of those radiant smiles that rivalled the sun and pressed a quick kiss to my lips. "Then it's settled."

"Are you sure?" I asked, doubt creeping in. "I don't want you to do anything that makes you feel uncomfortable."

"I never thought I'd marry or even find someone I wanted to spend my life with. I want what you want. Big, small, all that matters is that you're there." He leaned forward to steal a sweeter kiss. "Does that work for you?" he asked softly, staying close.

I smiled against his lips and answered, "That works." Then I curled a hand behind his neck and brought him closer for a deeper kiss. We kept it slow, a languid glide of tongues, completely unhurried. I was starting to wonder if we had enough time before the meal was ready to slip away when a shout came from back by the house.

"Lunch is ready!" my mother called in her melodic lilt.

Aidan pulled away and surged to his feet with a broad smile, spraying sand everywhere, then ran toward the walk. I spluttered and struggled to dust the sand off of me as I stood and followed him. I caught up just in time to see my mother releasing him from a hug, completely disregarding the sand and salt sticking to him.

"And are you sure you don't mind spicy food, *Jamaai*?" she asked, cupping his cheeks, her expression concerned. I loved seeing her dote on him, using an endearing term for son-in-law even though we weren't even wed yet.

He laughed and kissed her cheek. "Not at all. But next time I expect you to let me help. I can't perfect Zahir's favorite dishes if you don't teach me."

She beamed at him. If she hadn't already adored Aidan before even meeting the wolf, discovering how much he enjoyed cooking and his desire to learn new recipes would have solidified it. "Come. You can clean up and I will tell you some of how I made the meal." She hooked an arm through his and turned to guide them toward the house where my father was waiting at the other end.

"Wait, before we do that." He glanced back at me. I rolled my eyes, but nodded. "Zahir finally admitted he wants a traditional Indian wedding," he said eagerly.

My mother let out a thrilled cry while my father shouted, "It's about time!"

"The bigger the better," Aidan added with a goofy grin as they resumed walking.

"Now hold on..." I began to a chorus of laughter. But who was I kidding? Between the sheer size of the North Carolina Pack and everyone my mother would likely invite, there wasn't a chance our wedding would be anything short of a full-blown spectacle.

And honestly? I was more than okay with that. I loved Aidan more than I knew it was possible to love anyone, and I wanted to share that love with the entire world.

About the Author

Sam Bolanos (she/they) is a genderqueer author and founder of Chaotic Neutral Press LLC. They believe in love, equality, and the Oxford comma. When not playing with her two dogs, who you can follow on Instagram @austendogs, or spending time with her incredible husband, she's probably agonizing over edits or escaping into her latest fantasy.

Welcome to the adventure!

NEWSLETTER: SUBSCRIBE
WEBSITE: BOOKSBYSBOLANOS.COM
READER GROUP: SAM'S SUNBEAMS

Scan for Linktr.ee

9 781956 128550